ALSO BY FREIDA MCFADDEN

THE
TEACHER

FREIDA McFADDEN

Poisoned Pen
PRESS

Published by Poisoned Pen Press, an imprint of Sourcebooks
P.O. Box 4410, Naperville, Illinois 60567-4410
(630) 961-3900
sourcebooks.com

Cataloging-in-Publication Data is on file with the Library of Congress.

Manufactured in the UK by Clays and distributed
by Dorling Kindersley Limited, London
UID 009-342559-Feb/24
10 9 8 7

To my family

PROLOGUE

Digging a grave is hard work.

My whole body hurts. Muscles I didn't even know I had are screaming with pain. Every time I lift the shovel and scoop out a little more dirt, it feels like a knife is digging into a muscle behind my shoulder blade. I thought it was all bone, but clearly, I was wrong. I am acutely aware of every single muscle fiber in my whole body, and all of them hurt. So much.

I pause for a moment, dropping the shovel to give the blisters popping up on my palms a bit of relief. I wipe sweat from my brow with the back of my forearm. Now that the sun is down, the temperature has plunged below freezing, judging by the frost on the ground. But I stopped feeling the cold after the first half hour—I took my coat off almost an hour ago.

The deeper I go, the easier it gets to dig. The first layer of dirt was almost impossible to break through, but then again, I had a partner to help me back then. Now it's just me.

Well, me and *the body*. But it won't be of much help.

I squint down into the blackness of the hole. It looks like an abyss, but it's actually not much deeper than two feet. How deep do I have to go? They always say six feet under, but I assume that's for official graves. Not for unmarked ones in the middle of the woods. But given nobody can discover what is buried here, deeper might be better.

I wonder how deep a body needs to be buried before the animals can't smell it.

I shiver as a gust of wind cools the layer of sweat on my bare skin. With every passing minute, the temperature continues to drop. I've got to get back to work. I'll dig a little bit deeper, just to be safe.

I pick up the shovel once again, and the sore spots in my body all fight to be the center of attention. Right now, my palms are the clear winner—they hurt more than anything. What I wouldn't give for a pair of leather gloves. But all I've got is a pair of big puffy ones that made it hard to grip the shovel. So I've got to make do with my bare hands, blisters and all.

When the hole was shallow, I was able to dig without climbing in. But now the only way I can continue is to be inside the grave. Standing inside a grave feels like bad luck. We all end up in one of these holes eventually, but you also don't have to tempt fate. Sadly, it's unavoidable right now.

As I dig the blade of the shovel into the dry, hard soil once again, my ears perk up. It's quiet here in the woods, except for the wind, but I'm certain I heard something.

Crack!

There it is again... It almost sounds like a branch

snapping in half, although I can't tell if it was coming from behind me or in front of me. I straighten up and squint into the darkness. Is somebody here?

If there is, I am in deep, deep trouble.

"Hello?" I call out, my voice a hoarse whisper.

No answer.

I grip the shovel in my right hand, listening as hard as I can. I hold my breath, quieting the sound of air entering and leaving my lungs.

Crack!

It's another branch, snapping in two. I'm sure of it this time. And not only that, but the sound is closer than last time.

And now I hear leaves crunching.

My stomach clenches. There's no way I can talk my way out of this one. There's no way I can pretend it's all one big misunderstanding. If somebody spots me, it's over. I'm done. Handcuffs snapped on my wrists, a police car with sirens wailing, life in prison without chance of parole—all that jazz.

But then in the moonlight, I catch a glimpse of a squirrel darting out into the clearing. As it scurries past me, another twig snaps under the weight of its small body. As the squirrel disappears into a clearing, the woods descend back into deadly silence.

It wasn't a person after all. It was just a wild animal. The sounds of footsteps were just scampering little paws.

I let out a breath. The immediate danger is gone, but this is not over. Far from it. And I don't have time to take a break. I have to keep digging.

After all, I have to bury this body before the sun comes up.

PART I

CHAPTER 1

THREE MONTHS EARLIER

EVE

People are always telling me how lucky I am.

They tell me that I have a beautiful house, a fulfilling career, and I constantly get compliments on my shoes. But I'm not kidding myself. When people tell me that I'm lucky, they're not talking about my house or my career or even my shoes. They're talking about my husband. They're talking about Nate.

Nate is humming to himself as he brushes his teeth. It took me almost a year of brushing my teeth next to him in the morning before I realized that it's always the same song. "All Shook Up" by Elvis Presley. When I asked him about it, he laughed and told me his mother taught him the song clocks in at exactly two minutes, which is how long you're supposed to brush your teeth for.

I have started to hate that song with every fiber of my being.

The same damn song every single morning for eight years of marriage. I could probably solve the problem if we didn't brush our teeth at the same time each morning, but we always do. We try to maximize our bathroom efficiency in the morning, given that we leave at the same time and are going to the same place.

Nate spits toothpaste in the sink, then rinses his mouth out. I have already finished brushing my teeth, but I linger there. He grabs the mouthwash and gargles the caustic blue liquid.

"I don't know how you stand that stuff," I comment. "Mouthwash tastes like acid to me."

He spits it back into the sink and grins at me. He has perfect teeth. Straight and white, but not so white that you need to look away. "It's *refreshing*. Cleanliness is before godliness, you know."

"It's horrible." I shudder. "Just don't kiss me after gargling with that stuff."

Nate laughs, and I suppose it is funny because he rarely kisses me anyway. One perfunctory peck when we part ways in the morning, one when we greet each other in the evening, and then one before bed. Three kisses per day. Our sex life is equally regimented— the first Saturday of every month. It used to be every Saturday, then every other Saturday, and now for the last two years, we have settled into the current pattern. I'm tempted to program it into our shared iPhone calendar as a recurring appointment.

I pick up the blow-dryer to eliminate the residual dampness from my hair, while Nate runs a hand through his own short strands of brown hair, then picks up a razor to shave his face. As I watch the two of us in the mirror, it's hard to deny the plain fact that Nate is by far the more attractive of the two of us. There's no contest.

My husband is incredibly handsome. If somebody made a movie about his life, they would be tapping all the sexiest stars in Hollywood to fill the role. Short but thick deep brown hair, chiseled features, an adorably lopsided smile, and now that he bought that set of weights to keep in our basement, his chest is turning into solid muscle.

I, on the other hand, am decidedly plain. I've had thirty years to come to terms with it, and I'm absolutely fine with the fact that my muddy brown eyes will never have the playful glimmer that Nate's have, my dull brown hair will never do anything but lie limply on my scalp, and none of my features are quite the right size for my face. I am too skinny—all dangerously sharp angles and no curves to speak of. If someone were to make a movie about my life… Well, there's no point in even talking about it because such a thing would be impossible. People don't make movies about women like me.

When people say I'm lucky, what they really mean is that Nate is way out of my league. But I'm a little younger, so at least there's that.

I leave the bathroom to finish dressing, and Nate follows me to do the same. I select a crisp white blouse, buttoned up to my throat, and I pair it with a tan skirt, because in New England, you've got only three months of skirt weather—four if you're lucky. After sliding into a pair of pantyhose, I slip my feet into a pair of black Jimmy Choo stiletto pumps. It's only after I've got them on my feet that I notice Nate is watching me, his brown tie hanging loose around his neck.

"Eve," he says.

I already know what he's going to say, and I'm hoping he won't say it. "Hmm?"

"Are those new shoes?"

"These?" I don't lift my eyes. "No. These are years old. In fact, I think I wore them on the first day of school last year."

"Oh. Okay…"

He doesn't believe me, but he looks down at his own shoes—a pair of brown leather loafers that really are years old—and doesn't say another word. When he's upset, he never yells. Occasionally, he will scold me for things I should not have done, but he rarely even does that anymore. My husband is admirably even-tempered. And in that way, I suppose I am lucky.

As Nate does the buttons on the cuffs of his shirt, he glances at his watch. "You ready to go? Or do you want to grab breakfast?"

Nate and I both work at Caseham High School, and today is the first day of school. I teach math, and he teaches English. He is probably the most popular teacher in the entire school, especially now that Art Tuttle is gone. My friend and fellow teacher Shelby told me that Nate topped the list that the senior girls made of the five hottest teachers at Caseham High. He won by a landslide.

We rarely carpool to work in the morning. It does seem decadent to leave from the same place and arrive at the same location and yet take two different cars, but he always stays later than me at school, and I don't want to be stuck there. But since today is the first day of school, we are traveling together.

"Let's go," I say. "I'll grab coffee at school."

Nate nods. He never eats breakfast—he says it unsettles his stomach.

My Jimmy Choo pumps clack satisfyingly against the floor as I make my way to the front door of our two-story house. Our house is small—we had to pay for it on two teachers' salaries—but it's new, and in so many ways, it's the house of my dreams. We have three bedrooms, and Nate talks about filling the other two bedrooms with children in the near future, although I'm not sure how we will achieve that on our current schedule of intimacy. I went off birth control a year ago, just to "see what happens," and so far it's been a lot of nothing.

Nate climbs into the driver's seat of his Honda Accord. Whenever we go anywhere together, we always take his car, and he always drives. It's part of our routine. Three kisses per day, sex once a month, and Nate is always the one who drives.

I am so lucky. I have a beautiful house, a fulfilling career, and a husband who is kind and mild mannered and incredibly handsome. And as Nate pulls the car onto the road and starts driving in the direction of the school, all I can think to myself is that I hope a truck blows through a stop sign, plows into the Honda, and kills us both instantly.

CHAPTER 2

ADDIE

I would give anything if it meant I didn't have to get out of this car.

I would cut off all my hair. I would read *War and Peace*. Hell, I would set myself on fire if only I didn't have to walk through the doors of Caseham High. I can't say it enough. *I don't want to go to school.*

"Here we are!" my mother says brightly. And unnecessarily, because I can clearly see we are parked right outside the school. I'm not *that* dumb, in spite of everything that went on last year.

She drove me to school this morning in her gray Mazda, I think because she knew if I took my bike to school like I have for the past two years, there was no chance I would have ended up at the high school. So she took the day off from her nursing job at the local hospital and is babysitting me to make sure that I show up for my first day.

I glance out the passenger side window at the red

four-story brick building that has become such a big part of my life over the last two years. I rub my eyes, exhausted because I woke up at stupid o'clock this morning to get here on time. I remember how excited I was on my first day of freshman year at Caseham High. And I liked high school—I wasn't super popular and my grades were decidedly average, but it wasn't bad at all.

Until it was.

I spent the entire summer babysitting for my neighbors' kids and also campaigning not to go back to school in the fall. There's only one public high school in Caseham, though, and the private schools are way out of our price range. We could have tried to go to school in another town, but it would be too far for me to take my bike, and a school bus wouldn't pick me up. My mother explained this to me with dwindling patience every time I begged her to reconsider.

"Maybe," I say hopefully, "I could be homeschooled?"

"Addie," she sighs, "come on."

"You don't understand." I clutch my backpack to my chest but don't make any move to unbuckle my seat belt. "Everyone is going to hate me."

"They won't hate you. Nobody is even going to remember."

I let out a snort. Has my mother ever *met* a high school student?

"I mean it." Mom kills the engine, even though we're parked in a zone where you're not supposed to leave your car, and someone is probably going to yell at us to move along any minute now. "Teenagers are only interested in themselves. Nobody is going to remember what happened last year. Nobody cares."

She is so wrong. So totally and utterly wrong.

Sure enough, somebody honks at us. First, it's a single honk, then a smattering of honks, then it seems like one person has sat down on their horn accidentally and isn't getting up anytime soon.

"I can pull over somewhere else," Mom offers helplessly as she starts the engine again.

What's the point? If we pull over, she's just going to give me a pep talk. I don't need a pep talk. I need a new school. And if that's not going to happen, this is all a whole lot of pointless.

"Never mind," I mutter.

My mother is calling my name as I leap out of the car, but I don't stop and turn around. My mom is useless. She says all the right stuff, but in the end, she doesn't have to deal with this. She doesn't have to deal with the fallout of what happened last year. Of *what I did*.

As soon as I'm out of the Mazda, I can almost feel everyone's eyes staring at me. There are plenty of girls at the high school who dress for attention, but I was never like that. I always wanted to blend into the crowd. Today I am dressed in a nondescript pair of straight leg jeans and a gray T-shirt paired with an even grayer hoodie. There's a rule at Caseham High that you can't have any lettering on your butt (a rule that outrages many, many girls), but not only is my rear end free of glittery words, I have made sure that I don't have any lettering anywhere. Nothing that would call attention to myself.

Yet every single person is looking at me.

The only positive is that my mother was forced to drive away, so she doesn't get to see the stares and the whispers as I trudge toward the metal front doors, my backpack slung over one shoulder. I freaking *knew* this would happen. *Nobody is going to remember what happened last year.* Yeah, right. What planet does my mother live on?

I already know what they're saying, so I don't stop to listen. I keep my head down and my shoulder slumped as I walk as quickly as I can. I avoid eye contact. But even so, I can hear them murmuring:

That's her. That's Addie Severson. You know what she did, right? She's the one who...

Ugh, this is just too awful. I can't even.

And then I almost make it. I almost reach the school without any incident. The chipping red paint of the front door is within sight, and nobody has said something awful to my face. And then I see *her*.

Her is Kenzie Montgomery. Arguably the most popular girl in our junior class. Unarguably the most beautiful girl in the class. Class president, head cheerleader—you know the type. She is sitting on the steps of the school, wearing a skirt that I am almost one hundred percent sure violates the policy that your skirt or shorts cannot go any higher than the tips of your fingers when your arms are hanging straight at your sides. Other girls have been sent home for such violations, but Kenzie won't be. You can count on it.

She is sitting with her little posse of friends. The girls surrounding her are like a who's who of the most popular kids in school. And there's one addition who would not have been at her side last year, and that's Hudson Jankowski. The new star quarterback.

Kenzie and her friends are nearly blocking the path to the school, but there's a little room to get past them. But then just as I am trying to squeeze through the one-foot open area between Kenzie and the railing of the steps, her eyes meet mine for a split second, and she tosses her backpack there to block me.

Ouch.

She has deliberately left approximately four inches for me to attempt to squeeze through. I could go around the other way, but that would involve walking down all the stairs I just walked up and climbing another set of stairs, which feels a little bit ridiculous considering I'm almost at the top. And it's not like there's a *person* sitting there. It's just a freaking backpack. So while Kenzie is talking to her friends, I attempt to squeeze past her leather bag.

"Excuse me!"

Kenzie's voice shuts me down midstep. She's looking up at me with her big blue eyes fringed with long, dark eyelashes. I first met Kenzie in middle school, when she was in my history class, and I couldn't help but think she was the most perfect-looking human being I had ever seen in real life. Like, I saw pretty girls before, but Kenzie is on a whole other level. She's tall, with a lithe figure and silky long golden-blond hair. Every single feature of hers is more attractive than every single one of mine. Kenzie is living proof that life is not fair.

"Sorry," I mumble. "I was just trying to get through."

Kenzie's long eyelashes flutter. "Do you think you could not step on my backpack?"

Kenzie's friends are watching our interaction and giggling. Kenzie could shift her backpack or take it off the steps altogether so that I could get through. But she's not going to do it, and that is somehow just *so* freaking amusing to all of them. For a second, my eyes make contact with Hudson, who quickly looks down at his dirty sneakers. He's been doing that for the last six months. Avoiding me. Pretending like he didn't used to be my best friend in the entire universe since we were in grade school.

For a second, I fantasize about a universe in which I could take on a girl like Kenzie Montgomery. Where I could step on her stupid backpack with the little pink furry puff hanging off it and spit at her, *What are you going to do about it?*

Nobody *ever* stands up to Kenzie. I could do it. It's not like I have anything to lose.

But instead I mumble an apology and go back down the steps to find another way into the school. Like everyone else, I give in to Kenzie. Because the truth is, as bad as it is now, it could always be worse.

CHAPTER 3

EVE

I didn't even realize how much my head was throbbing until I take my first sip of coffee.

I've got about ten minutes before I have to get to my classroom, and I take that time in the teachers' lounge to sit with my closest friend, Shelby, and decompress. Nate has already gone to his classroom. He took his coffee to go, and then he gave me the first of my three pecks on the cheek.

"So how was your summer?" Shelby asks me, as if we haven't been texting nonstop since the Fourth of July.

"Not bad." I spent most of it teaching summer school. I imagined that when I became a teacher, it would be great to have the summers off, but it hasn't worked out that way. "How about you?"

"Amazing." Shelby sighs as she crosses her legs. She's wearing the same Nine West gray pumps that she wore on the last day of school. I already know that she spent most of the summer on Cape Cod with her tech genius husband and three-year-old son. Her perfectly bronzed skin is a dead giveaway. "I'm so sad to be back. Connor wouldn't stop crying when I dropped him off at pre-school this morning."

"It's good for him," I say, except what do I know?

Shelby takes a long sip from her Styrofoam cup of coffee, leaving behind an imprint of her red lipstick. "Nate looks *good*. Has he been working out all summer or something?"

"Probably." This summer, Nate was teaching a drama program for kids at the high school. He doesn't have a degree in drama, but he's taken classes in college, and moreover, he's a natural. In another life, Nate could have been the next Brad Pitt. But on the days he wasn't work-ing, he went down to the basement to lift weights. I suppose he doesn't want anything to jeopardize his chance to be the hottest teacher at Caseham High for the second year running. "He's very into fitness."

"I wish Justin felt the same," she laughs. "He's only thirty-six, and he's getting a gut already!"

I wonder how many times a day Justin kisses Shelby. If they have sex more than once a month. I wonder if she lies awake next to him in bed at night and wishes she could be married to anyone else or even nobody at all. I wish I could ask her. I've only ever been married to Nate—maybe these feelings are part of every marriage. Maybe it's normal.

"Have you seen Art?" I ask instead.

The smile drops off Shelby's face. "No. He resigned, obviously. And I've heard he hasn't been able to find another teaching job."

Up until the spring, Arthur Tuttle was a math teacher

at Caseham High and also one of the most beloved teachers in the school. When I first started working here fresh out of my master's program, he took me under his wing. But that was the sort of thing Art would do. He was genuinely the nicest person I had ever met, always ready with a comforting word or one of his wife's famous brownies. And every year at the staff Christmas party, Art would dress up as Santa Claus, because even without the red suit, he was a dead ringer.

And now he's ruined.

"I wonder how he and Marsha are doing," I murmur.

"And the kids," she adds. "Two in college now, right?"

I wince, thinking of Art's boys. Part of me wants to try to help him with some money, but he'll never accept it, and anyway, we don't have much to give after our hefty mortgage payments are done. Plus Nate wants to save for the baby we'll never have.

"It's so unfair," I murmur. "He didn't do anything wrong and she…"

Shelby's thin eyebrows shoot up. "We don't entirely know that."

I try to mask my irritation by taking another sip of my coffee. It's not going to help to rant at Shelby, especially this early in the morning. Anyway, this is why Art had to resign. It doesn't matter what happened or didn't happen. It only matters that parents were calling the principal and telling her that they didn't trust *that man* around their children. Art—the nicest person who ever was, who didn't have an evil bone in his body—could no longer be trusted.

"She's in my class, you know," I tell Shelby.

"Oh?"

"Sixth period."

I've only seen her photo in the roster of students, and it was one taken about a year ago for the yearbook. I've never seen her in real life, but she looked painfully ordinary in her photo. Nondescript. Not so different from the way I looked at the same age.

"Be careful." There's a smile playing on Shelby's lips, but at the same time, a look of warning is in her eyes. "That girl is clearly extremely troubled."

She doesn't have to tell me. From the moment I saw the name Adeline Severson on my roster, I had a sinking feeling in the pit of my stomach. In my nearly ten years of teaching, I never once asked to have a student removed from my class, but I almost did it this time.

I have a terrible feeling about this girl.

CHAPTER 4

ADDIE

School is fine until we get to lunch.

I mean, it's not going great or anything. It's not like the most fantastic day of my whole life. But it's fine. A lot of kids socialize during the school day, but it's not like you *have* to talk to other kids. You go into a class-room, you sit your butt down on a chair, and then you listen to the teacher talk for forty minutes. Then you go to your next class.

So it's fine that nobody is talking to me.

But lunch is different. Because everybody is sitting in groups and talking to each other, and if you're not with other kids, then you're some kind of loser who nobody wants to socialize with. And that is me all over today.

Not that I had many friends *before*. For most of my school career, it would be me and Hudson. We would plot to get the same lunch period so we could sit together, because he didn't want to be alone any more than I did. It's funny, because when we were in grade school, Hudson was more of a social pariah than I was. Hudson had a fatal case of the cooties. I was just a quiet kid who had trouble talking to kids I didn't know, but most students actively tormented Hudson. They made his life miserable.

Today, as I walk through the rows of sticky benches clutching my tray containing a hot dog, crinkle-cut french fries, a few packets of ketchup, and a carton of chocolate milk, I literally do not know where I am going to sit. I make eye contact with a few kids who I used to be friendly with, and they quickly look away.

Hudson is here, of course. But he's planted himself at Kenzie's table, his pale hair mussed as he tilts his head toward her, deep in conversation. Hudson is for real Kenzie's latest boy toy. He has officially arrived, and he has not taken me along for the ride. I can't blame him.

I wish he would at least start speaking to me again though.

"Addie! Addie, over here!"

I swivel my head to see who is calling my name. It's Ella Curtis, who I only know because she's the skinniest girl in the junior class by at least ten pounds. Ella and I have barely said a dozen words to each other in the last two years, but now she's sitting at one of the benches, waving vigorously to me. She's not the sort of person I would ordinarily eat with, but I'm deliriously happy to be invited to sit with her. I drop down into the seat across from her, dumping my tray on the table as I manage my first genuine smile of the day.

"Hey," I say. "Thanks."

"No problem." Ella picks up a french fry with one of her skeletal fingers and licks the ketchup off it but doesn't take a bite. "I felt bad for you, just standing there because nobody wants to sit with you."

I don't know what to say to that. She's right, but I feel weird acknowledging it. But I'm glad there are people who are still speaking to me. Maybe my mother is right. Maybe everybody will eventually just forget about it, and it won't be a big deal anymore.

Ella flips her long, stringy brown hair over one shoulder as she looks in the direction of Kenzie's table. I turn my head just in time to see Kenzie resting her blond head on Hudson's shoulder. "Hey, do you think they're dating?" she asks me.

"Dunno," I mumble. I take a bite of my hot dog, which tastes processed, even for a hot dog. It's basically rubber.

"Hudson is so hot." She has finished licking the first french fry and she puts it down. She picks up another fry and starts licking that one. "They make a good couple."

I grunt in response, and I hate to admit that I agree with her. They look good together. Kenzie's golden-blond hair even compliments Hudson's hair color, which is also blond, almost white.

"Didn't you, like, go out with him last year?" she presses me.

I shake my head. "No."

It was never like that between the two of us. Hudson and I became friends in grade school because we both had dads we were ashamed of. His situation was worse though—at least on the outside. My dad is gone now, but in those days, he used to pass out drunk in our living room in a pool of his own vomit, but at least nobody at school saw it. Hudson's dad, on the other hand, was the janitor for our elementary school. He was frequently

24

seen pushing a mop and bucket through the hallways and yelling angry curses at kids in Polish.

The two of us bonded, and even when we got to middle school and Hudson's dad was no longer around to be a constant spectacle, we stayed best friends. Even when we got to high school and Hudson started to be the kind of kid who turned girls' heads and also made a name for himself on the football field, he was loyal to me. Until one day...

Anyway, I don't want to think about it.

Ella is now licking a third french fry. I'm fascinated by this. It's like she's eating ketchup for lunch, and the french fries are merely a vehicle for the real meal. To be fair, I used to do that when my mom made me celery and peanut butter. But what kid wants to eat celery? French fries are french fries though!

"I freaking hate the first day of school," Ella says. "Actually, school in general. It's so lame that we have to come here every day and be forced to learn stupid things that will never be important again."

"I guess." I don't mind the learning part of school. That's not why I didn't want to come here today.

"Like trigonometry." She crinkles her freckled nose. "Like, bro, when will that *ever* be useful in life? Seriously, it's *such* a waste of our time. Who do you have for trig?"

"Mrs. Bennett."

She groans. "She's a total bitch. She gives, like, a ton of homework, and her tests are super hard. That's what I heard anyway."

Great. And math has always been my weakest subject. This year is already off to a fantastic start. "I have *Mr.* Bennett for English."

That gets a giggle out of her. "Okay, that might make up for it. Dude, Mr. Bennett is *hot*. There is a serious hotness discrepancy between those two. Like, how did he end up marrying *her*?"

I don't know what to say to that. I only vaguely know what either of those two teachers look like.

"But maybe he's not your type." Ella winks at me. "Maybe you would prefer somebody who looks more like Mr. Tuttle."

My heart drops into my stomach. This is the last thing I want to talk about. "Not really."

"Seriously." Ella puts down the french fry she was licking and leans across the table, her eyes wide. "What was it like being with Mr. Tuttle? That sounds so gross."

I drop my eyes, avoiding her curious gaze. "Nothing happened with Mr. Tuttle," I mumble. "I never said it did."

"Uh-huh." Her voice is dripping with sarcasm. "So how come he got fired then?"

"I don't know."

A lump forms in my throat. I don't want to talk about this. Instead, I focus on the container of chocolate milk. There's a joke written on the back of the carton. *What does a cloud wear under his raincoat?*

"Oh, come on." She winks at me. "You can admit it. Everyone knows it anyway."

I lift up the carton of milk to see the answer to the riddle. *Thunderwear.*

"He's so *old*," she continues, her sharp voice cutting through the thrum of activity around us. "He's got to be, like, fifty or older. He looks like Santa Claus! I can't believe you did it with him. Seriously, what was that like?"

It hits me now. Ella doesn't want to be my friend. She just wants to hear the gossip about me so she can tell everyone how gross it was that I hooked up with Mr. Tuttle and she got to hear all about it. I knew there was a reason that I never wanted to be friends with Ella.

"Excuse me," I say.

I stand up from the table, grabbing my lunch tray. I've barely eaten any of my food, but I'm not that hungry anyway. And I'm not going to sit here while Ella pumps me for information about something *that never happened*.

I toss the contents of my tray into the garbage, leaving Ella at the table. She doesn't even try to get me to stay. I hear her giggling to herself as I walk away.

On my way out of the cafeteria, I pass Kenzie's table. She's deep in conversation with her friends, but I realize Hudson has been watching the entire interaction. His pale blue eyes meet mine for a split second, and then he looks away like he always does these days. He has officially decided we will never speak again. Maybe if that hadn't happened, none of this crap would've gone down with Mr. Tuttle. Maybe I wouldn't be the school pariah.

In any case, I storm out of the cafeteria and sit in the library at a table all by myself, waiting quietly for sixth period to begin.

CHAPTER 5

EVE

My husband is with another woman.

We are both in the staff cafeteria but at different tables, like always. When I first started working here, we used to eat together every day, but Nate made a joke about how we would get sick of each other spending so much time together, and I took the hint. So today I am sitting with Shelby and half listening while she talks more about her wonderful summer on Cape Cod. Meanwhile, Nate is two tables over, sitting with Ed Rice, the physical education teacher, and a new teacher who must have started today.

The new teacher is clearly straight out of college. Her face has that fresh look that eight years teaching high school math has flushed out of me. She's pretty in a young and perky sort of way. If she put on a pair of jeans and a T-shirt, she could easily pass for one of the students, but instead she's wearing a pink blouse and brown skirt, paired with brown loafer heels that I saw at Target last week for twenty-five dollars.

I nudge Shelby, who is midsentence, gushing about some restaurant that served the best stuffed shrimp she's ever had. "Who is that?"

Shelby looks across the cafeteria at the young woman cozying up to my husband. "I think her name is Hailey. She's the new...um, French teacher?"

French teacher. It's almost too cliché.

Shelby's eyes narrow at me. "You're not worried, are you? Come on. Nate is a good guy."

I want to believe that. I want to believe that the late nights last year were all just because he was sticking around to grade papers or supervise extracurricular activities. I want to believe that our regimented one night of sex per month is all just because he has a low sex drive.

"Yes," I finally say. "I'm sure you're right."

And now Hailey, the pretty French teacher, has a hand on his forearm. I want to scratch her eyes out. The only saving grace is that Ed Rice, who is chronically single, seems to actively be putting the moves on Hailey. But it's clear who Hailey's choice would be between the two men. Ed is twenty years her senior and balding.

Fortunately, the bell for the next period rings before I can do anything I would regret.

Usually, Nate and I dash out of the cafeteria to go in our separate directions after lunch is over. But this time, I stride purposefully in his direction, my heels clicking loudly against the floor. I grab him by the arm, in the same place where Hailey was touching him moments earlier.

"Hey," I say. "How's your first day going?"

Nate blinks at me, surprised that I've spoken to him

on school grounds. But he quickly smiles. "Swimmingly. How about you, my darling?"

"Good so far."

"Fantastic."

Nate raises an eyebrow, clearly wondering why I approached him. I'm not sure if Hailey is watching us, but just in case she is, I reach out and grab his brown tie, tugging him close to me. If I were a cat, I would have peed on him, but since I'm a human, I plant a kiss on his lips that is markedly steamier than our usual three kisses per day.

He seems surprised, and as always, he's the one who breaks away from the kiss first. And after he does, he brushes at his lower lip with his index finger. "Well then," he says. "That was a nice send-off."

He's smiling, but I've been married to him long enough to know when it's not a real smile. But Hailey doesn't know.

My classroom is on the third floor, and I make it there with two minutes to spare before the next bell rings. The new students are filtering into the classroom, sitting wherever they want. I'll have to reorganize them. I've learned from prior experience that if I don't separate teenagers from their friends, I'll never be able to keep their attention.

But before I can get into the classroom, a girl steps in front of me. I recognize her as Jasmine Owens, who was in my class all of last year. I gave her an A-plus both semesters. She's paired a nice blouse with her blue jeans for the first day of school, and she's traded her usual sneakers for a pair of closed-toed sandals with flowers decorating the toes.

"Mrs. Bennett," she says. "I'm so sorry to bother you, but I was just hoping to catch you before your class started."

"What's wrong, Jasmine?"

She flashes me a nervous smile. "I'm trying to get my college applications sorted out, and I was hoping you could write me a letter of recommendation." Before I can answer, she adds, "You've been my favorite teacher, like, *ever*. I'm planning to get a degree in education, and I want to be a math teacher—like you."

My cheeks flush with pleasure, and some of the anger I was feeling back in the cafeteria drains out of me. Jasmine was an amazing student, so I'm not surprised she's already working on her college applications. And it feels good to hear that I made a difference in a student's life. There are days when I feel like I'm just teaching kids a subject that they hate and—let's face it—will almost certainly never use again. It's hard to make an argument for sines and cosines being useful in day-to-day life.

"Absolutely," I tell her. "Please send me an email, and we'll work out the details. And let me know if there's anything else I can do to help you."

Now Jasmine's cheeks have turned pink as well. "Thank you, Mrs. Bennett. I really appreciate it."

I get a much-needed boost from that interaction, and it keeps me going even when the students whine about having to be sorted into different seats. Nate lets them sit wherever the hell they want, but to be fair, when they are in his class, they are all mesmerized by his magnetic charm. I don't have that particular gift, but I do believe I am a good teacher.

By the time I get to the end of the alphabet, I had

nearly forgotten about the one name on my roster that I had been dreading ever since I got the list a few weeks ago. "Adeline Severson," I call out.

A girl of average height steps forward to claim the next empty seat in line. Adeline Severson is absolutely the least remarkable girl I have ever seen. She could easily blend into any crowd. Her hair is the color of a brown paper bag, and her facial features are all symmetrical but unremarkable. She could be pretty if she tried to be, but she's not trying—at all. I watch as she slides into her desk and respectfully folds her hands in front of her. If her name weren't Adeline Severson, I would never think this girl was capable of giving me a moment of trouble.

"Addie," she tells me.

I raise my eyebrows.

She chews on her thumbnail. "That's what I like to be called. Addie."

I make a note of it, even though I am well aware that people call her Addie. That's what Art called her when he told me about her. *I was just being nice to Addie. The poor girl lost her father only a few months ago, Eve. I had no idea…*

I didn't want her in my class. Art is the best person I've ever had the honor of knowing. A dedicated teacher who truly cared about every single one of his students. If he weren't that way, he would never have gotten into trouble in the first place. And now, because of this girl, his life is ruined.

But if I had really thought about it, I would have known that it doesn't make a difference at all if Addie Severson is in my class. The thing I really need to worry about?

Addie is in my husband's class too.

CHAPTER 6

ADDIE

The first day of school usually isn't so bad. I mean, in terms of work. Mostly, teachers are just telling you what the year is going to be like. Whether they're going to give weekend assignments or not. If they're going to give us a bunch of small tests over the semester or one ginormous test at the end.

And then at the end of the day, you don't have that much homework. Maybe just a couple of easy assignments, like *Write five hundred words to tell me a little bit about yourself*. The kind of assignments that I can finish on the living room sofa while watching television and stuffing cheese doodles in my mouth.

English is my final period class. It's also my best subject. Don't laugh, but my dream job is to become a poet, even though I know that is not a real job that most people could get in this century, and I'll probably end up being a nurse like my mom. My teacher this year is Mr. Bennett, who everybody loves. Mostly, a lot of girls love him because they think he's super good-looking, but I don't usually care about stuff like that, despite what Ella was implying.

Unlike Mrs. Bennett, who marched us all into assigned seats based on our last names, Mr. Bennett's classroom is a free-for-all. Most of the kids are trying to sit near their friends, but since I apparently don't have any, I take a seat near the window in the second row. I like sitting near the window in English class. It inspires me.

A second after the bell rings, something jolts my chair. It takes me a second to realize somebody just kicked one of the legs of my chair. I look up to find Kenzie and one of her minions, Bella, standing over me.

"This is my seat," Kenzie informs me.

I blink at her. "Oh. But…it's the first day and nobody was sitting here, so…"

Kenzie's vivid blue eyes rimmed with dark mascara bore into me. "This is where I *always* sit."

What? This is the first day of school, and we literally *just got here*. How could this be where she always sits?

"Oh," I say again. "But—"

"Are you deaf?" Bella snaps at me. "Kenzie said this is her seat. Get up."

I glance around the room. Most of the best seats are taken, although the one that's next to me is still empty since nobody is willing to sit next to me anymore. Presumably, that's where Bella would sit if Kenzie takes this seat.

Given everything already going on with me, the last thing I want is to make an enemy out of Kenzie Montgomery. So I gather up my bag and trudge over to one of the remaining empty seats. It's right in the front row, practically sitting in Mr. Bennett's lap. Great.

Mr. Bennett is behind his desk, looking down at the roster. There's a book on his desk, and I take a peek at the spine—it's a book of poetry from Edgar Allan Poe, who is for sure my favorite poet in the whole world. It's pretty much the only thing the entire day that has lifted my spirits.

After the bell rings for class to begin, Mr. Bennett lifts his eyes from the roster. His face crinkles in a smile, and as the corners of his lips turn up, I get a little jolt. I had seen Mr. Bennett a bunch of times before in the hallway, but until that second, watching him smile from about two feet away, I never realized how stupidly handsome he truly is. I can't even say why exactly, but there's something in the ruggedness of his features and the twinkle in his eye.

There are worse things than having to be up in the first row during English class.

Of course, he's super old. He's in his mid- or even late thirties. And married, of course, to a woman who gave us homework *on the very first day of school*. (So wrong...) But I can't say he isn't hot. This class is *not* going to be torture.

Mr. Tuttle wasn't handsome. Nobody ever would have called him hot. He was even older than Mr. Bennett, and he had a big belly that hung over his belt. But it was never about that with him.

"Hello there." Mr. Bennett rises from his seat and walks around to the front of his desk, where he takes a seat perched on top. "Welcome to eleventh grade English. If you are not supposed to be in eleventh grade English, then I would suggest you make a quick exit before anyone notices."

Nobody leaves. I have a feeling even if a student found themselves in the wrong place, they might stick around.

"Excellent." He drums his fingertips on his right thigh. "Let's get down to business then. This year, we are going to have an emphasis on poetry. You're going to read so many poems this year, you're going to be rhyming in your sleep."

Mr. Bennett rubs a hand over his right knee, and I can't help but notice that the fabric of his pants is slightly worn over his kneecap. I wonder how much money he makes as a teacher. None of his clothes are new or expensive.

Then again, Mrs. Bennett was wearing a pair of shoes that look like they cost a fortune. Not that I know much about shoes, but my mom has a pair like that, and she won't let me wear them because she says they're too expensive and I'll ruin them. She's probably right.

"Now," he says, "I want to go around the room, and you tell me your favorite poem. And only tell me your favorite poem if you actually have one. I don't want you to make one up just to impress me, because *I will know*."

A few hands shoot up, because honestly, it's clear everybody is eager to impress Mr. Bennett. Especially the *girls* in the class. And when he smiles at them, they each giggle in turn.

After about a dozen students in the class name their favorite poems, dropping big names like Angelou or Dickinson or Silverstein, Mr. Bennett turns his attention to me, even though I didn't raise my hand. I haven't raised my hand once today—this year, I'm working on being invisible. "Adeline?" he says.

I hate it when people call me by my full name in

general, because it reminds me of being in trouble. "Addie," I correct him.

"Addie." He nods. "How about you? What's your favorite poem?"

"'Annabel Lee,'" I say without hesitation. I know it's contained in the book of poems on his desk, but that's not why I said it. I have always loved that poem. It's beautiful, haunting, and romantic all at once. I can recite every word of it from memory.

"Ah, another lover of the great Poe!" He looks genuinely pleased. "My personal favorite is 'The Raven,' but 'Annabel Lee' contains some of his most haunting verses." He grins at me, and the fine lines around his eyes crinkle. "'And so, all the night-tide, I lie down by the side of my darling—my darling—my life and my bride, in her sepulchre there by the sea, in her tomb by the sounding sea.'"

A chill goes through me, just like in the poem.

He rests his brown eyes squarely on my face, like I am the only person in the room. "Do you know what it's about, Addie?"

"It's about a girl he loved when he was young," I say. "A childhood sweetheart who died. I read that nobody knows exactly who inspired him to write the poem."

"We'll discuss this poem in greater detail this year," he says. "As well as Poe's love of the letter L. Annabel *Lee. Lenore.* Eu*lalie.*" He winks at me. "Ade*line.*"

At this moment, I don't care if everyone in the school hates me. I don't care if nobody is willing to sit with me in the cafeteria. I don't care that I have a stupid amount of math homework for the first day of class. Because my English teacher loves Poe as much as I do.

And he winked at me.

CHAPTER 7

EVE

As always, Nate stayed late at school today. He is one of the supervisors of the school newspaper, in addition to that poetry magazine they put out twice a year, so he's always got something going on. I technically supervise the chess team, but I was informed that I am not required to stay for the meetings, so I generally don't. The last thing I want to do when the school day is over and my head is throbbing is watch a bunch of teenagers push rooks and knights around a board.

Since we carpooled this morning, I ask Shelby to drive me home. When she drops me off at my front door, it's only 3:30. Usually this would be the time when I would dig into a two-inch stack of homework papers, but since it's the first day, I find myself at a loss for what to do. It's too early in the day for my nightly overflowing glass of wine.

I climb into my Kia, not entirely sure where I'm going even as I am driving down Washington Street.

Every town in Massachusetts has a Washington Street and a Liberty Street and often a Massachusetts Street. Whoever named the streets in the state was not very creative.

I keep driving until I reach the mall at the west border of Caseham, where the lot is overflowing with cars. There are a number of teenagers there, enjoying their last free afternoon before the piles of homework set in. Watching all the kids filtering in through the front doors gives me pause. Whenever I run into my students outside school, they seem absolutely mortified to see me. I should shrug it off, but something about their humiliation reflects back on me.

I sit for a moment in the car, my hands gripping the steering wheel. I wonder what Nate is doing right now—he wouldn't be stressed by the idea of running into his students at the mall. He's probably talking to the new editor in chief of the school newspaper, a bright young boy named Bryce Evans. I had Bryce in my class last year, and he was another A-plus student. Never missed a homework assignment. That kid has Ivy League written all over him.

I count to ten, then I count from ten backward. After I do this three times, my shoulders relax.

I climb out of my car, clutching my light-blue purse, which is so large that Nate always teases me that it will make my spine crooked. However, my purse is mostly empty today, so I suppose my spine is safe.

As soon as I walk through the sliding doors for the entrance, the smell of cinnamon sugar from the pretzel stand smacks me in the face. I'd love to get a big cup of pretzel bites, and if I were a high school student, I would do just that. But my metabolism isn't what it used to be, so I hold my breath as I walk by the pretzel stand and also by the Godiva chocolates. Yes, I'd love a chocolate-covered strawberry, but it isn't in the stars for today.

I keep walking until I reach a store called Footsies.

For a moment, I simply linger outside. The store has a display of Christian Louboutin pumps and boots gracing the window, including a pair of black patent leather heels, although the heel itself is gold. I look down at my Jimmy Choos, which I purchased new two weeks ago despite what I told Nate. He'll find out when he sees the credit card bill.

I love high heels. I've always been a bit on the short side at five two, and I hate being shorter than my students. A pair of three-inch heels gives me a boost that improves my confidence. I prefer when I don't have to tilt my head quite so much to look up at my husband, who is five ten.

And for the most part, aside from these shoes, I've been well behaved. I've got shoes in shopping carts on practically every online site, but the point is I haven't purchased any of those items. I put the shoes in the shopping cart, and I never check out. So why shouldn't I treat myself every once in a while?

Footsies is an upscale store but relatively large, and there's only one girl manning the shop, sitting at a counter in the back by the cash register, scrolling through her phone. Despite how many teenagers are crowding the mall, there are only a handful of customers here. This store doesn't sell Doc Martens or sneakers most teenagers would buy. These are shoes for "old people," like me.

The girl at the counter doesn't make any attempt

to help me, so I browse on my own. The Christian Louboutin pumps are set up in a display inside the store, and when I check inside the shoes, I discover they are in my size—a seven.

I remove them from the display and find a bench on the side to try them on. I slip off the shoes I've been wearing all day, and I slide my stocking feet into the brand-new pumps. I feel very much like Cinderella when they fit me perfectly. They don't cut into my heel or pinch my toes. I could wear these shoes all day.

Actually, it would be quite a sensible purchase.

And why not? I worked all summer. I deserve a treat. I don't know why, but I get a little rush every time I purchase a pair of shoes. I don't even know what part is my favorite. I love the excitement as I'm bringing them to the counter and then as the clerk is ringing them up and the anticipation that they will soon belong to me. Or setting them up inside my closet, neatly lined up next to all my other shoes. And of course, the first time I get to wear them outside the house. I may be plain, especially compared to my husband, but shoes like this make me feel glamorous. Like I might actually be attractive enough to be married to the gorgeous Nathaniel Bennett.

Except then I turn over one of the pumps and see the price tag. Oh. Oh wow. Nate will *not* approve of this.

The dopamine rush vanishes. As much as I want them, these shoes will never be mine. Even if I didn't have to face my husband when the credit card bill arrives, I could never justify spending this much on a pair of shoes. I stare down at my feet, a wave of sadness coming over me. I want these shoes.

So much.

I glance up at the clerk, still sitting at the counter. There's an elderly woman who is purchasing some shoes, so her attention is occupied. The woman is shuffling around inside her purse, searching for her wallet. She's probably going to try to pay with a check or something. They're not going to be done anytime soon.

And my giant purse is gapingly empty.

Before I can stop myself, I slide the pair of Christian Louboutin pumps inside my sky-blue purse. They fit perfectly, like they were meant to be there. When I zip up my purse, you can't tell they are even inside. And most shoes don't have anything that will alarm when they are taken out of the store. They don't have a security tag.

I start to stand up, but my legs wobble and I fall back down. Am I really going to do this? Am I really going to *steal* these shoes? I've never done anything like this before.

Well, not in a long time.

I won't get caught. The clerk has barely glanced up at me while I've been here, and now that the elderly woman is done paying for her shoes, she's gone back to her phone. I can walk right out of here, and she'll never know. I haven't seen any cameras.

Am I really going to do this?

I guess I am.

I stand up more successfully this time, my legs trembling but still maintaining me upright. With a shaking hand, I tuck a strand of my limp, muddy-brown hair behind one ear. The elderly woman is shuffling in the direction of the door, clutching the plastic bag with her own shoebox in her gnarled right hand. I follow her, also heading toward the exit. When I glance behind me, the clerk is looking back down at her phone again. She's never going to notice me leaving with these shoes. I'm going to get away with this, and Nate won't be able to complain about the credit card bill.

And just as I am congratulating myself, the alarm blasts through the store.

CHAPTER 8

ADDIE

I go home immediately after school because that's what my mother told me to do.

I grab a ride on the school bus because I don't have my bike, and it's just a bit too far to walk, especially with my heavy backpack. Most of the kids on the school bus are younger, because a lot of the juniors and seniors drive to school. I turned sixteen over the summer, and I got my learner's permit, but my mom made the executive decision that I wasn't ready for driving lessons, no matter how much I begged. I did manage to convince her to take me out in our car a few times in a parking lot though. Better than nothing.

Hudson has a car now. He turned sixteen almost ten months ago, back when we were still speaking. He couldn't wait to get his learner's permit and pass the driving exam so that he could get a limited license. As usual, he included me in his plans. *I'll swing by and give you a ride to school every morning, Addie.*

The car he bought looks like he scraped it together from pieces at the junkyard, and I'm sure he paid for it himself with money from his summer or after-school jobs. But his new girlfriend Kenzie didn't seem to have any qualms about climbing into it.

When I get to the front door, my mother yanks it open before I can even dig my key out of my backpack. She was obviously watching the front of the house, waiting for me to return. She is wearing a pair of gray yoga pants, and her graying hair has come partially unraveled from her ponytail.

"How was school?" she asks me before I can even manage to step into the house.

"Great," I say. "It was the best day of school ever."

"Don't be a smart aleck."

I dump my backpack on the floor by the front door, even though I should probably bring it up to my room since I have homework. Both Mr. Bennett and Mrs. Bennett managed to assign homework today. But at least I'm looking forward to the English assignment. He wants us to write about our summer, but in poem form.

Mom wrings her hands together, hovering over me even though she knows I hate it when she does that. "Did you make any friends?"

I groan. "No."

"What about Hudson?"

I just shake my head.

"I don't understand what happened between the two of you." She tugs at her yoga pants, which look too tight. "He's such a nice boy. You used to be inseparable."

"I don't know."

"Do you want me to call his mother?"

I groan again. I definitely do *not* want her calling Mrs. Jankowski, who at least speaks slightly better English than her husband but is no less strange. Besides, I know exactly why Hudson isn't speaking to me. And my mom can never, ever find out.

"It's fine," I say. "He's busy all the time with football anyway."

Thankfully, she lets it go, which is a major achievement. A few years ago, my mom and I had an easy relationship, whereas my dad was a loose cannon—always angry when he'd been drinking and ready to explode over the tiniest thing. And now my dad is gone, and my mom has turned into this hovering worried mother. But at least I don't think she's drinking like he did.

No, I know she's not. She would never.

Mom arches an eyebrow. "Was Mr. Tuttle there?"

"No." I drop my eyes. "He got… I mean, he was fired or quit or something. But he's gone."

"Oh."

I can tell my mother is relieved. Like a lot of people, she never quite believed me when I told her nothing happened between me and my math teacher. Maybe because my story kept changing just enough to make people wonder.

She looks like she wants to ask me about it again, and if she does, I swear to God, I'm going to start screaming. I don't want to talk about it again. I told her the truth. I told the principal the truth. And I told the police everything there was to tell.

Well, not everything.

I mean, I'm not a complete idiot.

CHAPTER 9

EVE

The alarm is going off in the shoe store. It's blaring throughout the entire store, and it's hard to believe that everyone in the mall can't hear it.

Oh God, I never should've taken those shoes. What was I thinking? I already have enough shoes. I just bought a pair only two weeks ago. I got greedy. But I just wanted them so badly...

What is *wrong* with me? I'm *sick*. Nate is right—I have a problem.

There's a security guard jogging toward the store. I don't know what the policy is on prosecution of shoplifters, but this is not good. I don't know how it will look for my job if I have a shoplifting charge against me. I could get *fired*.

What is Nate going to say about all this? He's going to be so disappointed in me. I can't even face him after all this.

I clutch my purse to my chest, the blood rushing in

my ears. The clerk is also hurrying toward the exit, and it only vaguely registers that she pushes past me without giving me a second look.

That's when something occurs to me. I have not yet gone through the exit. The only one who went through is the old woman who just bought a pair of shoes.

"I'm so sorry!" the clerk cries. "I totally forgot to take off the security strip on your shoes!" She flashes the security guard an apologetic look. "This was my bad. She paid for those shoes."

The clerk leads the nonplussed elderly woman back to the cash register to disarm the security strip, while I stand in the corner of the store, trembling down to my core. I hadn't realized there was a security strip in the shoes. If I had gone through the exit first, the alarm would have gone off, and the security guard would have found the stolen shoes in my purse.

I dodged a major bullet.

While the clerk is busy, I pull the shoes out of my purse and slip them back into place. I can't believe I almost did that. I almost screwed up my entire life over a stupid pair of shoes. How could I have done something so risky?

It takes all my focus to drive home without getting killed. My whole body feels like it's buzzing, and not in a good way. I should never have attempted something so stupid. Just goes to show that I haven't changed at all over the years. Sometimes I try to kid myself that I'm an adult now, but how can I be an adult when I still feel fifteen half the time?

When I get home, I'm relieved to find Nate's car is in the driveway. I don't have to sit at home and wonder when he'll be back for a change. And when I get inside the house, I smell tomato sauce wafting from the kitchen. He's even gotten dinner started.

I hang my purse on the coat rack like I always do and wander into the kitchen. Nate is standing in front of the stove, the sleeves of his blue dress shirt rolled up as he stirs the contents of a pot on the stove. I imagine an alternate reality where I had to tell Nate I was arrested for shoplifting. Thank God I didn't go through with it.

Nate notices my presence in the kitchen, and he looks up with a smile for me. He is so incredibly handsome when he smiles. Even after all this time, I still think so. Who wouldn't?

"I got dinner started," he tells me. "I hope you don't mind."

"Of course not," I say. "I'm glad you did. You're so thoughtful." I smile back at him, although I recognize my own smile doesn't have as much impact as his does. "I have the best husband ever."

He laughs and turns his attention back to his pot of tomato sauce. "I'm pleased you think so."

Something stirs inside me. Maybe it's all the adrenaline from almost getting caught stealing those expensive shoes, but suddenly, I want Nate. I want him right now, even though it's not the first Saturday of the month.

I come up behind my husband, sliding my arms around his firm chest. I lower my lips onto the back of his neck. "Nate…"

He laughs again. "Eve, what are you doing? I'm trying to cook us a feast here."

"I've been thinking about you all day." My hands

move south, even as his body stiffens. "Maybe you can take a break from cooking dinner…"

Gently, he disentangles himself from my embrace. I get a distinct jab of déjà vu. "Darling, I'm starving. Let's have dinner first, okay?"

"Okay." I don't attempt to wrap my arms around him again, but I stay close, my hand on his shoulder. "After dinner then?"

"Right after devouring a big plate of ziti? That hardly sounds sexy."

Of course. Yet another excuse. I'm not even surprised at this point.

He leans in to kiss the tip of my nose. "Later tonight. I promise."

"You promise?"

His laugh sounds hollow this time. "My God, you're making it sound like I don't want to make love to my own wife! It's just been a long day, and I want to have some dinner and relax with a book, you know?"

And that will be his excuse later, when I reach for him tonight in bed. *It's been a long day and I'm tired. Tomorrow, okay, Eve?* Perhaps there will even be a headache involved. There's a point when it becomes humiliating to even ask, and he knows that. He's counting on it.

CHAPTER 10

ADDIE

In all my years of taking gym in high school and middle school, I've worked up a sweat maybe five times.

The only time I get sweaty is when they make us do laps. But anytime we're playing some sort of sport, I manage to avoid any type of major physical exertion. It's my greatest skill. What can I say? I'm not much of an athlete.

Today we were playing volleyball, which is a great sport if you just want to sit around and not do much. Like, I'm sure if I were making any attempt whatsoever to connect with the ball, I'd get sweaty. But it's pretty easy to stand in the corner and pretend you're trying to hit the ball when you're really not.

Unfortunately, our gym teacher, Mrs. Cavanaugh, makes us have a shower after gym, whether we got sweaty or not. And that, by far, is my least favorite part of gym.

If I looked like Kenzie Montgomery, who incidentally

is in my gym class, I might not mind public showering. But unfortunately, I look like me, so my goal for post-gym showering is to get in and out as quickly as possible. If I could get in and out of the shower without having to get wet, that would be ideal.

Unfortunately, the second I strip off my gym clothes by the lockers, a burst of giggles comes from behind me. I quickly grab my towel and wrap it around myself, but the giggles continue. I whip my head around to find Kenzie and one of her buddies staring at me.

It's been about two weeks since school started. Unfortunately, my social life has not improved one bit. Everybody is still avoiding me like the plague, except apparently to laugh at me while I am in the locker room.

Kenzie and her friend won't stop giggling as they stare at me. I don't know what is so hilarious. I mean, yes, my towel is being held up by practically nonexistent boobs. But I'm not sure that's *laugh out loud* funny.

"Addie," Kenzie says. "You know, there are these things called *razors*…"

Well, at least now I know what she's laughing at. I look down at my legs sticking out from under the towel, and admittedly, they are pretty hairy. As soon as September hit, the temperature dropped precipitously in western Massachusetts, and because I haven't had the opportunity to wear shorts (I wore leggings today in gym), I haven't bothered to shave. I may not shave the entire winter. Why should I? It's not like I have a boyfriend who is going to be looking at my legs.

But apparently, I need to shave for Kenzie.

I try to ignore her as I stomp off in the direction of the showers. As usual, I barely even get wet before I jump back out and wrap my towel back around my body and my hairy legs. The only thing keeping me going these days is my English class with Mr. Bennett. And the fact that it's the last period of the day makes me look forward to it all the more.

I think Mr. Bennett likes me too. In trig class, Mrs. Bennett seems perpetually disappointed in me (which is fair enough, since I don't understand a lot of what's going on in the class), but Mr. Bennett responds to all my answers with enthusiastic nods. Even Mr. Tuttle wasn't as encouraging as he is.

And anyway, this is a completely different situation. I'm not going to think about Mr. Tuttle anymore.

When I get to English class, Mr. Bennett is sitting at his desk like he always is. He's wearing a light blue shirt, paired with a darker blue tie. Not all my teachers wear ties, but I like it that Mr. Bennett wears one. It suits him. As the students start filtering into the room, he looks up and flashes a smile. He is the sort of teacher who genuinely enjoys what he does. Sometimes my teachers act like they wish they were anywhere but school.

Not that I can't relate to that feeling. But somehow knowing that he wants to be here makes *me* want to be here.

Once the students are seated, Mr. Bennett comes around the side of his desk and sits on it, like he always does. And he places his hands on his knees, like he always does. He has large knuckles. I've noticed that about him.

"I graded the poems you wrote," he tells us. "I'll return them after class, but I want to say, in general, it was a good effort. And I want to reiterate the fact that poems do not necessarily need to rhyme. But..." His eyes rest on Austin Vargas in the third row. "For the record, 'barf' does not rhyme with 'fart,' okay?"

There is a smattering of laughter. I'm not surprised that Austin would make a poem involving potty humor. Frankly, I would expect it from a lot of my classmates. It annoys me that there are people not taking this class seriously. I don't intend to be one of them.

At the end of the lesson, Mr. Bennett walks down the aisles and hands out our poems with comments at the top. My stomach is filled with butterflies, waiting to see what he thought of what I wrote. It was a very personal poem, and I spent hours on it, even though it's only a page long. I hope he can see how much effort I put into it.

Except when Mr. Bennett reaches my desk, he finds the paper on which I wrote my poem, places it in front of me face down, and taps his index finger against it.

I stare down at the page, confused. He's been handing out all the poems face up, and mine alone was placed face down. Was that a mistake?

Slowly, I pick up the paper and turn it over. Right away, I recognize his handwriting at the top of the page in red ink. *See me after class.*

That's not good.

Why does he want to see me after class? Does he think that I *copied* the poem? I didn't copy it. I would never. I extracted it from my very *soul*.

But for whatever reason, he found my poem troubling. He wants to talk to me "after class." And I'm not sure I want to hear what he has to say.

CHAPTER 11

EVE

I am at the grocery store after school, poking at avocados in the produce department, when I spot him.

Art Tuttle.

He's wearing a turtleneck, which strikes me as oddly casual. Nate always wears a dress shirt and tie to school, and although Art wasn't nearly as formal, he did always wear a nice shirt. The turtleneck seems out of place. Plus it's a little too tight for his Santa Claus belly. And even stranger, he's got on a pair of open-toed sandals, which he is of course wearing with a pair of white gym socks. He has a plastic bag filled with oranges gripped in his right hand, which also strikes me as odd because I don't know if I've ever seen him eat an orange in all the time I've known him. And we have shared many, many lunches together and even a few dinners.

"Eve." He manages a smile that doesn't show his teeth, which is strange because Art used to have the toothiest smile I'd ever seen. "Hello. How are you doing?"

"I'm fine." I smile, although it feels crooked on my face, like I've forgotten how to smile. "How are *you* doing, Art?"

I promised myself if I ran into Art, I wouldn't say it that way. With a tilt of my head, like he's somebody I'm visiting in a mental hospital. Like I feel sorry for him.

Except I *do* feel sorry for him.

The whole mess started at the middle of the second semester of last year. It all started with that *girl*—Addie Severson. I don't know the entire story, but all of a sudden, everyone was whispering that Art Tuttle was hooking up with one of the sophomores. The first time I heard that rumor, it was like being punched in the gut. Art was like a father figure to me, especially since my own father and I barely speak. I had heard stories of other teachers behaving inappropriately with other female students, but I didn't expect it from Art. Never him.

But the evidence was pretty damn suspicious. Addie had been struggling in math class, which doesn't surprise me based on what I've seen so far from her, and he spent several hours of his own free time tutoring her to help her with the material, free of charge. He invited the girl over to his house for dinner on more than one occasion. And he drove her home multiple times.

Add that to the fact that Addie was a troubled girl. The daughter of an abusive alcoholic who finally drank himself to death during the fall semester. Everyone felt that she was an obvious target for a predatory teacher.

And then…

Well, something else happened.

Addie never technically accused Art of anything. But when all was said and done, his reputation was completely destroyed. He couldn't work at Caseham High anymore. He'll be lucky if he can work *anywhere*.

"I've been better," Art tells me. He coughs into his palm, and it's a rattling cough, like something's stuck in his lungs. "I miss the school."

"We miss you too." I abandon my quest for the perfect avocado to redirect my attention to Art. "It's so unfair what happened to you. Did you have to resign?"

He lets out a wheeze. "Come on, Eve. You know I did. Nobody looked at me the same way after that happened. I couldn't have stayed even if the parents weren't kicking up a fuss."

He's right, of course. But that doesn't make it less unfair. "Have you found anything else?"

"No bites yet." He sighs and rubs at his short, gray hair. "I've got a bunch of applications out, but the situation isn't great. If I can find something, I may have to move because it's not going to be in western Massachusetts. I'll be lucky if it's in New England."

I want to ask him if he's okay with money, but I don't want to embarrass him. I have a feeling the answer is no. How can he be okay if he's out of work and has two boys in college?

"And how is Marsha?" I ask.

"Good," he says.

His wife, Marsha, works for some kind of nonprofit, which means she isn't making nearly enough money to support them. As far as I know, she believed him that nothing went on between him and Addie, but I wonder what sort of impact something like this might have had on his marriage. They were such a good couple, but these kinds of accusations are enough to rattle the most solid of marriages.

"She's in my class," I blurt out.

Art's eyebrows shoot up. "What?"

I wince. I didn't mean to bring her up, but it's hard not to address the elephant in the room. The girl who ruined his life.

"Addie Severson," I say. "She's in one of my trig classes this year."

"Ah," he says.

I study his round face, trying to read his expression. Is he curious about how she's doing? Does he want to ask about her, but he's afraid it will look strange if he does? As the thoughts swirl around my head, something hits me:

Like everyone else in the world, I'm still not entirely sure Art Tuttle is innocent.

I know he's good-hearted and not a dirty old man. But there's something about the whole situation that just doesn't sit right with me. After all, how could he be so stupid? How could he have that girl alone with him in his classroom every day after school and not realize how it would look?

"She seems nice," I finally say. "Not one of the stronger students."

Art's bushy white eyebrows knit together. "No, she's not."

We stand there for a moment, him with his oranges and turtleneck and socks with sandals, and me with my shopping cart, which needs one or two decent avocados. We never had trouble talking to each other before, but the awkwardness is almost suffocating. I want to invite him and his wife to our house for dinner, but I can't quite make myself extend the invitation.

In any case, I can understand why he felt that he had to resign.

"Anyway," I say, "it was good seeing you, Art."

"You too, Eve." He nods at the avocados. "The trick is that when you push your finger into the skin, you get a little bit of give with gentle pressure but not too much."

"Thanks." Even now, he's still trying to teach me. "And...good luck. With everything."

I turn away, returning to the mountain of avocados. I pick one off the pile that is brown and feels like it has a slight give under my fingertips. Just as I'm about to test it, fingers close around my upper arm. It takes me a second to realize that Art is still behind me and has grabbed me. His chubby fingers bite into my bare skin, and all I can think is if we weren't in the middle of a grocery store, I would scream.

"Eve, wait," his voice hisses in my ear. "You need to listen to me. Right now."

CHAPTER 12

ADDIE

See me after class.

Has anything good ever started with those four words? I'm going to say no. It has not.

Thankfully, this is the last period of the day and it's almost over, so I only have to freak out for about ten minutes until the bell rings. Everybody else slips out of their chairs and filters out of the room, but I stay glued to my seat. And so does Mr. Bennett.

I hazard a quick look in his direction. Does he look disappointed in me? I can't even tell. "See me after class" is really bad, but there are worse things. During that whole mess with Mr. Tuttle, they didn't wait until after class. The principal pulled me right out of biology and asked me what was going on.

"Addie?"

I got so lost in my thoughts that I didn't even realize that all the other students were gone, and now Mr. Bennett and I are the only ones left. He is looking at me with raised eyebrows, like maybe he thinks something is wrong with me. I manage to flash him a weak smile.

"Sorry. Just spaced out for a moment." I rise unsteadily from my seat and approach the desk, clutching my poem. "So, um, what's wrong?"

"Wrong?" he says. Now that I'm closer to Mr. Bennett, I can see tiny dark seeds of what would become a beard if he didn't shave every day. "Nothing's wrong. Just the opposite."

I glance down at the writing in red on my poem. "What do you mean?"

"I mean," he says, "your poem is amazing."

Your poem is amazing. Those four words are *so* much better than "see me after class." For the first time since this stupid school year began, I feel a little jolt of happiness. "Really?"

"Oh yes." He tugs it out of my hand. "The imagery is incredible. 'His fists a volcano, spouting lava from her lips with each blow.' Addie, I was so moved. It's a lyrical masterpiece."

"Thank you." I drop my eyes, trying not to think of my inspiration: all the nights when my dad stumbled home drunk and angry. "I appreciate that."

"And I think you should publish it."

I jerk my head up. "What?"

"I mean it." A smile curls his lips. "This is really good, and you need to share it with the world. You know I'm the staff supervisor for the school's poetry magazine, right?"

I know about the poetry magazine, *Reflections.* I always wanted to join, but I was scared they would think my poems were dumb. After all, what do I know about writing poetry? All I've ever done is scribble them in a marble notebook in my bedroom. But for the first time, somebody who actually knows what he's talking about is telling me that I might have talent.

"Maybe...if you think so," I say carefully.

He bobs his head vigorously. "I do. I think you would enjoy working on the magazine. And it would help you make some friends."

Oh my God. Does Mr. Bennett know about my problem making friends this year? That is mortifying beyond words. But then again, of course he would know. Everybody knows about the scandal with me and Mr. Tuttle. It was stupid to think he might not know.

"I just mean," he adds quickly when he sees my expression, "you would meet other students like you, with similar interests."

Mr. Bennett is kind—pretty much the only person to be kind to me this year, including the teachers. He's trying not to make me feel like a loser, which I appreciate, even though I am a loser. I'm sure he never had problems like this when he was in high school. I mean, look at the guy. I bet he had a posse of girls following him around, hanging on his every word.

Then it hits me. Maybe he doesn't like my poem after all. Maybe he's just saying all this nice stuff because he feels sorry for me. Maybe when some kids who actually have talent read my poetry, they'll laugh at me.

"I'm not sure if this is a great idea," I finally say.

He frowns. "Really? I think you would truly enjoy it."

"I..." I look down at the poem in my hands, the one he claims he loved. "I'm not sure."

"Come to a meeting." Mr. Bennett's eyes hold

mine. I love the dark brown color—like a chocolate bar. "You're not under any obligation to ever return. But I believe you will."

And somehow I find myself agreeing, although a nagging voice in the back of my head won't stop telling me it's a bad idea.

CHAPTER 13

EVE

When I turn around this time, Art is very close to me. So close that I can make out red spiderwebs in the whites of his eyes. So close that I can detect a hint of whiskey on his breath. It hits me now that what happened to him has destroyed him in more than one way.

"Eve." His voice sounds slightly choked. "I need to tell you something."

"Art," I murmur. I'm not sure I want to know what he has to say.

"Listen," he says, "you need to be careful around Addie Severson."

My mouth feels dry as I look into his bloodshot eyes. "Art, do you need a ride home?"

"No, that's not what I'm trying to say!" His jaw clenches in frustration. "Look, I kept my mouth shut for her sake, but that girl is not well. There's...there's stuff you don't know."

"Art...."

"You need to hear this, Eve." A muscle twitches under his right eye. I've never seen him quite like this, although if he's been drinking, that does sort of explain it. "You're like me, and you try to help students who need it. But you have to be very careful around her. She's... Addie is a troubled girl."

"I will," I say in a small voice.

Art finally lets go of my arm, and his whole body seems to deflate. He drops his eyes, and his shoulders sag. I reach out and put my own hand on his shoulder.

"Let me give you a ride home, okay?" I say. I'm sure he came with his car, but I don't think he's in any position to be driving right now.

"Okay," he says in a small, defeated voice.

I abandon my quest for the perfect avocado, and I lead Art back to the parking lot. I drive him to his house, where thankfully his wife is home. I explain the situation to her, trying not to use the word "drunk" although it's hard. The worst part is that Marsha doesn't seem to be the slightest bit surprised. It's obvious that since the whole mess went down with Addie Severson, their lives have taken a downhill turn.

Addie is a troubled girl.

I have no doubt that Art must harbor a serious grudge against Addie. But at the same time, nobody is going to accuse *me* of having an affair with her. She's in my class, so I'm going to teach her like I do every other student. Nothing more.

CHAPTER 14

ADDIE

So today—two days after Mr. Bennett first invited me and I've been floating around on a cloud—I'll be going to the first meeting of *Reflections*, the poetry magazine. It's almost enough to make everything okay.

Almost.

But despite how much I'm looking forward to the meeting, it doesn't entirely take the sting out of the fact that I have eaten lunch alone every day since the school year started. If I join a table of students who I already know, they glance at me and make a concerted effort to ignore me, like I don't exist. So it's less painful to find an empty table.

When my mother asks me how things are going at school, I pretend like things are getting better. Like I'm starting to make some friends, even though it's a blatant lie. Everyone loved Mr. Tuttle so much, and the general feeling is that whatever happened between the two of us, it's my fault and also super gross. So everyone is still avoiding me. Probably forever.

It's just as well I'm sitting alone at lunch today, because it gives me a chance to try to figure out what the hell is going on in math class. I've got the trig textbook out in front of me, and I'm reading it, but it might as well be in Greek for all it helps me. Actually, some of it really is in Greek. Like that circle symbol with a line through it, whatever *that* is.

Without Mr. Tuttle tutoring me, I am in serious danger of failing this semester. Even a few weeks into the term, it's starting to feel hopeless. And it's pretty clear that Mrs. Bennett is not going to go above and beyond the way he did.

Just as I'm trying to understand why graphing a particular equation creates this weird squiggly line, something jolts my arm. I look up, and none other than Kenzie Montgomery is standing over me, holding her tray stacked with food. There is zero chance that Kenzie wants to join me for lunch, so I already know this is going to be something bad.

"Hey," Kenzie says. "One person can't take up a whole empty table. You need to move."

I look down at my tray of food. I've only taken about five bites of my burger, and more than half of it is still left. "But I—"

"Get *up*." Now it's Kenzie's minion, Bella. Well, one of her minions. She's got several behind her—a mini army. "You're taking up a whole table for yourself. That's so selfish, Addie."

"But, um…" I glance over at the empty table. "You can just sit in the empty seats."

"Yes, but we have private stuff to discuss." Kenzie

67

drops her tray on the table, pushing mine out of the way. "So you need to move."

I open my mouth, although I'm not entirely sure what to say. But before I can think of anything, Kenzie grabs my tray from the table while Bella snatches my textbook. I stare at them in shock.

"Hey!" I cry.

"Where do you want to sit?" Kenzie asks me. She picked up my tray so roughly that my chocolate milk toppled over and is now spilling all over the tray, soaking the napkins with brown liquid. "Decide, or else we'll just dump your stuff in the garbage."

My heart is pounding. I should stand up to her somehow, but how can I? What am I supposed to do? Fight her in the middle of the cafeteria? Insult her? I can't think of any insult I could pay Kenzie Montgomery that would be true. She's literally perfect.

"Hey." A voice from the back of Kenzie's posse is achingly familiar. Hudson Jankowski pushes his way to the front of the group. "What's going on?"

Kenzie makes a face. "Addie is taking up this entire table, and she won't move."

Hudson looks down at the table, and his pale blue eyes skim over my face. It's like he doesn't even recognize me anymore, but I feel a glimmer of hope when he says, "Why does she need to move?"

Kenzie snorts. "Do *you* want to sit with her?"

I remain at the table, waiting for Hudson to stick up for me. *Addie is my best friend, and I would be happy to sit next to her. She was my only friend when nobody else would go near me.* But instead, he says, "Come on, Kenzie. There's another table right over there."

"This one is right near the snack machines," Kenzie whines. "And why should *we* have to move? She's here all by herself."

I can't listen to this argument anymore. Hudson may be sticking up for me a little bit, but not the way I want him to. He's decided we're not friends anymore, and that hurts more than anything.

So I get up from the table and snatch my math book out of Bella's hands. "Fine," I say. "Take the table."

Kenzie lifts an eyebrow. "Don't you want your tray?"

I want to tell her that I've lost my appetite, but I'm pretty sure if I say anything, I'm going to start crying. And we all know that's the worst thing you can do. So I march out of the cafeteria with my head held high. I almost think that I maybe hear Hudson calling out my name, but I must be hallucinating, because I doubt he would do that.

CHAPTER 15

ADDIE

As I'm hurrying to the meeting of the poetry magazine, I run into Kenzie and Hudson.

Actually, I don't run into them so much as I see them. Hudson has football practice, and Kenzie probably has a cheerleader practice, but they're taking a few minutes together before they head out, hidden in one of the quiet nooks on the fourth floor, behind a set of lockers.

They do look good together, both of them with their matching perfect blond hair. If anything ever happened between me and Hudson, we would not have looked nearly as well matched. Not that anything ever did. There was a time when... Well, let me just say that I wrote a few bad poems about Hudson Jankowski. We spent so much time together, and he was my best friend in the whole world, yet he was the one I fantasized about when I was alone in my bedroom.

And now he's with Kenzie. They're not kissing, but they're standing very, very close together, talking softly.

The weird thing is, we used to make fun of Kenzie and her minions. *They're required to make a shrine to her in their bedrooms*, Hudson joked. *And give her twenty percent of all their earnings.*

She is *really pretty though*, I pointed out to him once. And Hudson made barfing sounds. Of course, he was only thirteen then. As he stares into her eyes now, he doesn't look like he's going to start making barfing sounds any time soon.

Ugh, they're about to start kissing. I can't even watch.

I look down at the two backpacks that were abandoned against the wall. Hudson's is the cheap, black one. Kenzie's is trimmed with leather, with lots of buttons and ornaments hanging off it. There's one key chain that has the name *Kenzie* on it in diamond lettering. I wonder if it was custom-made. I also happen to notice that the key chain has a couple of keys hanging off it. Her house key.

I hazard a look back up at Kenzie and Hudson. They're still talking, completely absorbed in each other. I never thought I'd see the day when Hudson became one of her minions—worse, her *boyfriend*. Quietly, I slide the key chain off the zipper of her backpack and slip it into my pocket.

As I walk away, I expect to hear Kenzie yelling after me. She already hates me, and this would be the final straw if she saw me take her keys. And what if she tells the principal? Why would I take this kind of risk and get in trouble again?

Except she doesn't catch me. I make it all the way down to the stairwell, and by the time I get to the third floor, I realize that I'm home free.

The key chain is still in my pocket when I reach the

meeting for the poetry magazine. I'm surprised how few students have shown up. I would have guessed, based on how popular Mr. Bennett is, that the room would be packed. But then again, he also works on the school newspaper. Maybe that's enough of an opportunity for the girls to flirt with him. Anyway, I'm glad there aren't too many kids here. It's less intimidating this way.

When I step into the room, Mr. Bennett is talking to another student, but he lifts his eyes, and that great smile stretches across his face. He excuses himself from the conversation with the other student and jogs over to speak to me.

"Addie!" he says. "I'm so elated you could make it!"

I'm so overcome by his enthusiasm, I can only manage to nod.

"Well, come on in," he says, because I'm still lingering in the doorway. "You can see we don't have a lot of people, but everyone who attends is extremely dedicated. And I'd like you to meet our editor-in-chief."

He leads me to a girl who I recognize from the senior class. I'm pretty sure her name is Mary. She has jet-black hair cropped close to her head on the bottom and shaggy on the top, falling into her eyes. She's wearing a hoodie sweatshirt zipped up to her neck, and she's got a spiral notebook open in front of her, with a page covered in angry black scrawl and half-finished drawings of skeletons. She scowls when she sees me.

"Hi, Mary," I say, hoping she'll be impressed that I know her name.

The girl does *not* look pleased. "It's *Lotus*. Not Mary. Do I look like a Mary to you?"

That feels like a rhetorical question, but even so, I

shake my head no. I'm still pretty sure her real name is Mary, but I'll call her Lotus if she wants me to.

"Lotus, I'd like you to show Addie the ropes here," Mr. Bennett tells her. "Also, Addie has a phenomenal poem she submitted in my class." He winks at me. "I feel like it might be first-page material."

It was probably the wrong thing to say in terms of endearing me to this hostile girl, but at the same time, the praise makes my knees wobble. I've always been a mediocre student, and this might be the first time in my life that I have ever felt like maybe I'm good at something.

I can just imagine telling my mom that I want to be a poet. She would have a stroke.

I drop down into the desk next to Lotus/Mary. She doesn't seem thrilled, but she reluctantly turns to look at me. "So let's see this poem," she says.

I dig around in my backpack and pull out the two-inch binder that contains most of my papers from school. I've always been organized, and I love dividing my work with color-coded tabs. I flip to the English section and immediately locate the poem about my father, which I don't mention is the best of dozens of angry poems I've written about him over the years.

I hand it over to Lotus, who scans the page with narrowed eyes. She's wearing black eye makeup that reminds me of Cleopatra. When she finishes, she comments, "This is really dark."

I'm not sure if it's a compliment or not. "I know."

"Is this, like, real?"

I nod slowly.

Lotus lets out a low breath. "Okay, well, it's pretty good. Maybe needs a little work. Mr. Bennett will help

73

with that. He gives good suggestions. And, you know, I can help too. Like, you have sort of a color theme going here with the blood coming out of her face, but you could push it even more. More colors, you know?"

I nod vigorously. "Yes, totally."

She gives me a long look. "Aren't you the one who hooked up with Mr. Tuttle?"

I flinch. "No."

"Yeah, you are. Addie Severson, right?"

"Right, but…" I nibble on the tip of my thumbnail. "Nothing happened. It was all a misunderstanding."

"Okay, then how come he got fired?"

I get a jab of guilt in my chest. It's all my fault, but there was nothing I could do about it. There was nothing I could say to make it right again. "I don't know."

"He's pretty gross." She starts scribbling listlessly in her spiral notebook. She has drawn a pair of crossbones, and she outlines them again and again. "I don't know how you could do that with *him*. Like, *anyone* would be better."

"Right. I didn't."

She shrugs like she doesn't believe me. For a moment, I thought maybe Lotus could be a friend, but I'm not sure anymore. My reputation is too tainted, which is why I was so desperate to change schools. Maybe it's not too late. Maybe I could swap to a different school in the spring.

But then I look up, and Mr. Bennett is across the room. I catch his eye, and he gives me an enthusiastic thumbs-up. I imagine telling him that I'm leaving Caseham High, and I imagine his disappointment.

But really, what gives me the confidence to stay is the set of Kenzie's keys in my pocket.

CHAPTER 16

EVE

When Nate gets home from work tonight, he's in a good mood.

He's whistling when he walks in the door, and even though it's not one of our three designated kiss times, he strides over to where I'm sitting on the sofa and lays one on my cheek. But I know from prior experience not to get too excited.

"Good day?" I ask him.

"Phenomenal." He hesitates, then adds, "The poetry magazine met today. A lot of raw talent there. There's one girl whose work is a bit reminiscent of Carol Ann Duffy."

Whoever that is. Nate has always fancied himself a poet. He published a book of poetry several years ago, which his parents bought as well as about five friends, and I'm fairly sure that's it. Maybe it was different in Shakespeare's time, but there's no money these days in being a poet.

Still, it was romantic when we were first together. He used to write poems for me. *About* me. And then he would recite them for me, in some utterly romantic location like while drifting along the lake in a rowboat. It made me feel like I was a goddess—the sort of woman worthy of poetry being composed about her.

I saved a few of them. I keep them in a shoebox in the back of my closet. I used to reread them all the time, but I haven't in years. It makes me depressed to look at them now. Nate hasn't written a poem about me in a long time. I'm beginning to think he never will again.

"So what do you want for dinner?" he asks me. "I can make some pasta."

I look down at the stack of papers on my lap. I have graded more than half of them. I don't check every single answer on the homework, unless I have concerns about the student. For example, I checked Addie Severson's homework. She's batting about 50 percent, which does not bode well for the first exam. She needs that feedback ASAP.

"Actually," I say, "I'm going out to dinner tonight with Shelby."

The lie rolls right off my tongue.

Nate nods, unconcerned. He likes it when I go out for the evening, and when I come home, he'll ask how dinner was, and when I tell him fine, he won't ask any follow-up questions. He certainly would never call Shelby to confirm that I am with her, which is a good thing, because she does not know we are supposed to be together.

"Do you have any plans for tonight?" I ask him.

He shrugs. "Nothing too exciting. Although…I'm feeling inspired. Maybe I can get some writing done."

"I'll stay out of your hair then. I don't want to bother you if you're trying to write."

"You're never a bother, my darling."

My husband says all the right things.

An hour later, I have completed grading all the papers, and I head out the door. Even though it's only September, the weather has gotten a bit nippy, so I grab a jacket, and I slide my feet into my Manolo boots, which have three-inch heels. My philosophy is if your shoes don't make you at least three inches taller, it's hardly even worth it. You might as well wear socks.

I hesitate by the front door, wondering if I should say goodbye to Nate. But he's locked himself up in the bedroom, and if he's deep in concentration, I don't want to disturb him. He won't be upset if I leave without saying goodbye.

It's a twenty-minute drive in my Kia to Simon's Shoes. I know the way without using my GPS, and I navigate the streets while a dance radio station plays in my car, the seats vibrating with the bass. I can't tell entirely if it's the music or my heart that is thudding. Maybe a little of both.

The sun has started to dip in the sky by the time I make it to the shoe store. I pull into the parking lot, which serves both the shoe store and the pizza parlor next door. As I step out of the car, the smell of greasy tomato sauce and melting cheese assaults my nostrils, and my stomach growls. I haven't eaten dinner yet. Maybe I'll stop for pizza later.

I hover outside the door to Simon's Shoes and look down at the sign with the store hours. On Tuesday, they close at 7:00 p.m. My wrist watch reports that the time is 6:50.

Just in time.

I push open the door and nearly knock into a middle-aged woman holding far too many shoeboxes. She must have at least four. Four new pairs of shoes. I can't help but feel a stab of jealousy. When I smile at her, she flashes an apologetic look and says, "I think they're closing in a few minutes."

"It's okay," I say. "I'll be quick."

The store is practically empty—there's only one remaining customer at the cash register. I make a beeline for the designer shoes, and because I'm so familiar with the store, I quickly find the shoes in my size. They have a pair of Christian Louboutin pumps that look a lot like the ones I almost got nailed for at the mall, although these are less expensive.

Maybe I should buy them. I deserve a treat—I haven't bought one new pair of shoes since the ones I wore to the first day of school. Maybe I could put them on a different credit card to throw Nate off the mark.

I could try them on at least. There's no harm in that.

"Those would look great on you."

The voice belongs to a man wearing a pair of dark brown Rockports. I glance up at the salesman standing over me, looking appreciatively at the shoes I'm holding.

He nods in the direction of the storeroom. "Is that your size, or do you need another pair?"

"These should fit…"

He gently pries them out of my hands. "May I?"

Obediently, I settle down on the wooden bench supplied for trying on shoes. Before I can do it myself, the salesman lowers the zippers of my boots and slides them off my feet. He has muscular forearms and strong-looking hands, and his fingers linger just a moment longer than necessary on the arch of my foot. Then he picks up one of the pumps and slides it into place.

"Cinderella." He smiles up at me with a lopsided grin. He has a slightly chipped incisor on the right, but his teeth are white and otherwise well cared for. "A perfect fit. You have to get them."

"Hmm," I say. "I bet you say that to every customer."

"Absolutely not."

I look over his shoulder. As opposed to when I walked in, the store is now dim. The sign on the entrance has been turned around to state that the establishment is closed. Presumably, that means he has locked the doors with us inside.

His right hand lowers to my knee, then creeps up my thigh. "So what do you say?"

"I think…" My breath catches in my throat. "I may need some convincing."

That's when he grabs me.

And lowers his lips onto mine.

CHAPTER 17

EVE

God, he is such a good kisser. He makes me melt. I used to think Nate was a good kisser, but I was wrong. This man is far better.

"Eve," he murmurs. "I wasn't sure you were coming."

"And miss out on this? Never."

A smile lingers on Jay's lips as his eyes fill with desire. I haven't seen my husband look at me that way in a long time, and I have to admit, it's a rush. Enough of a rush to keep me coming back here every single week for the last three months. And I don't even feel guilty about it.

Well, a *tiny* bit guilty. But I wouldn't do it if my own husband didn't act like he was scared of touching me.

Jay glances behind him at the open street where anyone could see us kissing. He holds out a hand to help me to my feet. I kick off my one remaining pump and follow him to the storeroom.

We make love among the piles of shoes. It's a small space, but somehow that makes it even hotter. Although on one occasion, I did roll onto the heel of a stiletto, and it nearly broke my skin. Jay was apologetic about that. He always tries to be gentle, but after a week apart, we are practically ripping each other's clothing off.

It lasts about as long as sex in the storeroom of a shoe store could possibly last. Weirdly enough, when it's over, I don't want those shoes quite as much anymore. The two of us lie on the cold, hard floor for a minute, catching our breath. Jay is gasping for air like he just ran a marathon, and when he rolls his head over to look at me, his skin is glowing and shiny with sweat.

"This is the best part of my week." He grabs me to kiss me again. "It was all I could think about the whole day. I wasn't sure you would come."

I sit up on the floor and grab my bra, which is hanging off a shoebox on the second shelf. I don't want to tell him that it's the best part of my week too. Not just that, but if we didn't have these sessions together, I would throw myself off the top of the school building.

It started about four months ago. It was innocent enough at first. I was at Simon's to buy a pair of shoes. Somehow, I keep thinking the right pair of shoes will fix everything. Like if I walked into our house in the perfect pair of pumps, suddenly Nate would find me attractive again.

I had it down to two pairs of shoes: a pair of strappy Stuart Weitzman sandals and a pair of Cole Haan black leather pumps. I could only afford to buy one of them, and I kept looking between the two pairs, trying to make up my mind. I sat there for over an hour, unable to decide which of the two shoes might make Nate love me again. Finally, the salesman approached me.

There was something familiar about him, although I couldn't quite place it at first. Of course, he was the sort of person any woman would notice. As handsome as Nate, but in a different way. Broad and strong, whereas Nate is thinner and lankier. He stood over me and said in a heartbreakingly gentle voice, *We're closing in a few minutes. Can I ring you up?*

It was all too much for me. I burst into tears.

Jay closed the store, and we talked for the next two hours. I didn't tell him everything, but I told him enough. He told me he didn't understand how it was possible that my husband didn't find me attractive. I assumed he was just being nice—until he kissed me.

There is something ironic about the fact that I have fallen head over heels for a shoe salesman.

Jay's phone starts ringing, and he reaches to retrieve it from the pocket of his khaki slacks, now crumpled on the storeroom floor. He sucks in a breath when he sees the name on the screen. He glances at me before taking the call. Even though the phone is close to his ear, I can hear the female voice on the other line, but I can't make out what she's saying.

"I'm sorry," Jay mumbles into the phone. "I got stuck at work again doing inventory."

He doesn't want me to hear him lying to another woman, but it's unavoidable. I turn my head at least to give him some semblance of privacy.

"I'll be home in about half an hour." He rubs at his messy hair. "The traffic should be light so... yeah, don't worry about dinner. I'll just grab some pizza next door."

If Jay and I are both getting pizza, I'll have to go into the restaurant after he does. He's paranoid like that. He doesn't want his lies to be found out. And the truth is, neither do I.

"Yeah," he says into the phone. "I will. Yeah...sure. I'll do it when I get home." He hesitates, glancing over at me. "Love you too." When he hangs up, his neck is bright red. "Shit, I'm sorry about that, Eve."

"Don't be," I said, even though that call is a bitter reminder of yet another reason why we can never be together.

Some of the post-sex euphoria dissipates in the wake of that phone call. It's funny that in all the months Jay and I have been sneaking around, I've never once been interrupted by a call or even a text message from Nate. He seems glad to have me out of the house.

Jay chews on the lower corner of his lip. "Next week?"

"Absolutely." It's the best part of my week—I would never miss it.

As the two of us get dressed among the boxes of shoes in every single size, I can't help but think about how much this means to me. It's not just the best part of my week—it's *everything* to me. There isn't a day that goes by when I don't wish Jay and I could run off together.

But in my heart, I know this will all end horribly.

CHAPTER 18

ADDIE

As today's meeting of *Reflections* is coming to a close, Mr. Bennett crooks a finger at me. "Addie, can I talk to you for a minute?"

I've been going to meetings of the poetry magazine for a few weeks now, and I'm finally starting to feel like I'm part of something. Lotus sometimes waits for me after the meeting is over, and we walk to our bikes together, although I still am not sure if she likes me or not. Sometimes I think she despises me and would murder me in my sleep if she had the option, but other times she seems to be happily tolerating me. In any case, I wave to her to go on without me, although I can see in her eyes she's curious about what he wants to discuss with me. Lotus absolutely idolizes Mr. Bennett.

I hang back in the classroom while Mr. Bennett shuffles through some papers on his desk. He waits until everyone is gone before he lowers the papers and smiles up at me. "Addie," he says. "Guess what?"

I love the way Mr. Bennett's eyes crinkle when he smiles. In the month I have been in his class, I have noticed he has two kinds of smiles. There's one he uses in class when he's trying to encourage students, but it's not as genuine. When his eyes crinkle, that's when I can tell he's actually happy.

"Good news?" I ask.

"So there's a statewide poetry competition." He rubs his palms together. "And every year, I have the opportunity to submit one poem from all my classes. And this year, I want to submit your poem."

My mouth falls open. Mr. Bennett teaches multiple English classes, and on top of that, he's got all the kids from the magazine to choose from. Lotus, for example, is an incredibly talented poet. All her poems are better than any one of mine. Has he *lost his mind*? Does he think that I'm Lotus somehow? "Mine?" I finally squeak.

He beams at me. "Yes! I want to submit 'He Was There.' I think it's brilliant. One of the most moving things I've ever read."

That's the piece about my father. I'm having a serious choked-up moment. I've learned to get used to his praise, but not this much praise. It might be *too* much, like I might explode from the amount of approval I'm receiving right now. Like when a starving person suddenly gets a bunch of food and then they die from it.

"Are you sure?" I say.

"Addie." He folds his arms across his chest. At some point after the last bell rang, he undid the cuffs of his sleeves and rolled the sleeves of his dress shirt up to his forearms—now I can see the dark hairs on his arm. None of the boys in my class have that much hair on their arms. Hudson just had a little, and it's pale blond like the hair on his head. "Addie, you have to believe in yourself a little bit. Because I sure do."

"Yeah," I mumble.

"Your poem is amazing." His brown eyes hold my gaze. "*You* are amazing, okay? You are a master of this craft, even at sixteen."

If anyone else said it to me, I would think they were being patronizing. But somehow, when Mr. Bennett tells me I'm amazing, I actually feel that way. Like maybe there is something out there that I'm good at, even though being a poet would be a stupid and ridiculous career for me and I really should become a nurse like my mother says I should.

"I'm not amazing at math," I blurt out.

I feel dumb for having said that, but for some reason, it makes Mr. Bennett laugh. He throws his head back and gives a great big belly laugh. I can make out a tiny silver filling in one of his back teeth. "Is my wife giving you a hard time?"

I lift one shoulder. "It's not her fault I suck at math."

"I know how she is. She's strict, isn't she?"

I press my lips together, reluctant to say anything negative about his wife. But the truth is, while Mr. Bennett is one of the most popular teachers in the school, only the best math students are fans of Mrs. Bennett. She is really strict, and she doesn't have much patience for kids who don't get the material right away.

But the worst thing people say about her is they don't get why Mr. Bennett married her. He's the hottest and most beloved teacher in the school. Mrs. Bennett is pretty, I guess, although not on the same level as her husband. And she's definitely *not* beloved. In fact, she's actually kind of a...

Well, she's a bitch. There, I said it.

"My wife is very concrete," he says. "She's only interested in logic and reasoning. She isn't a dreamer, like we are. For her, words only serve a utilitarian purpose."

"It's fine," I reassure him. "I just need to study." And also pray for a miracle.

"If she's ever too hard on you," he says, "let me know. Seriously."

I will seriously never let him know.

"I completely understand," he adds. "I was also terrible in math when I was in high school. And biology."

"Really?" He has zeroed in on my two least favorite subjects.

He grins at me and his eyes crinkle in that way I have come to love. "Oh yes. I refused to dissect a frog because I thought it was wrong. The teacher was going to fail me, so I had to do an extra credit project just to scrape by!"

I didn't think it was possible to like Mr. Bennett any more than I already do, but there it is.

"Anyway..." He looks down at his watch and seems surprised by the time. "I apologize—I didn't realize it was so late. Sorry to keep you. Do you need a ride home?"

I'm so shocked by his offer, I almost drop my backpack. Is he for real offering me a ride home? Doesn't he know what happened to Mr. Tuttle? There is no way I'm taking a ride from another teacher who actually makes an effort to care about me. I'm not letting anything like that ever happen again.

"That's okay," I say quickly. "I have my bike."

"Are you sure? It's no trouble."

"Positive."

He shrugs. "Okay. Well, I'll see you tomorrow then."

He seems so unconcerned, it almost makes me wonder if I overreacted somehow. After all, a ride is just a ride. Other kids *do* occasionally get rides from teachers, and the teachers don't end up fired and disgraced. Maybe I made too much of the whole thing.

It seems too late to change my mind though, so I grab my backpack and head out of the room—and almost run smack into Lotus. She's leaning against the wall, her bag propped up against her Doc Martens, a slightly manic expression on her face.

"Hey," I say. "I told you not to wait for me."

She rubs her nose with the back of her hand. "Bro, what was *that* about?"

"Oh." I have to suppress a smile. "There's some state-wide contest he wants to enter one of my poems into. So, you know."

"Wait." She sucks in a breath. "The Massachusetts Poetry Contest?"

"Maybe?"

Lotus swears under her breath. "That's bullshit, you know?"

I *don't* know. "What do you mean?"

"I mean…" She grits her teeth. Lotus has a lot of small, sharp-looking teeth. "That poetry contest is a big deal, and he only gets to submit one poem from the whole school."

"Yes…"

"And, like, you're just a beginner." Her heavily mascaraed eyelashes flutter. "I mean, you're good for a

88

beginner, but there are at least three other kids at the magazine who are better than you. And I am a senior, and he has *never* picked one of my poems."

I don't know what to say. "It wasn't like it was my decision."

"Yes, but it was a *bad* decision." Her eyes narrow at me. "You should tell him it's a bad decision. He shouldn't pick you just because you're the teacher's pet."

I already suggested to Mr. Bennett that there might be better poems out there, but he insisted. "What do you want me to do, Lotus?"

"I want you to go back in that room and tell him that he should pick somebody else's poem to submit."

I don't know what is more shocking: the fact that Mr. Bennett told me he was choosing my poem in the first place or what Lotus has just asked me to do.

"I'm not doing that," I say.

She folds her arms across her flat chest. "So you want our school to lose?"

"I don't want us to lose, but Mr. Bennett picked my poem for a reason. He must think it's capable of winning."

She sneers at me. "Oh, you really think that's why he picked your poem?"

My mouth falls open. "Yes..."

"I mean, it's not enough you got Mr. Tuttle fired, now you have to go after Mr. Bennett?"

My face burns. I had thought maybe Lotus and I were friends, but I was sorely mistaken. "I have to go home," I mumble. "I'll see you next week. *Mary*."

As I walk away from Lotus, clutching the straps of my backpack, my thoughts won't stop racing. I hate that she called me out on all my darkest fears. Mr. Bennett had a lot of poems to choose from. Why did he choose mine? Objectively, I don't think my poem was the best one. There were so many other amazing choices—including the ones Lotus wrote.

So why me?

Is it possible she could be right? Is it possible that Mr. Bennett had some sort of ulterior motive in picking an inferior poem to enter in the contest? Was this nothing more than favoritism on his part? Or something even more than favoritism?

The worst part of all though is the shiver of excitement that goes through me at the possibility that Lotus could be right.

CHAPTER 19

EVE

Today is my birthday.

I'm turning thirty, which feels like a milestone of sorts, although my life hasn't changed much in the last eight years or so, since I started teaching at Caseham High. It feels like time has moved so quickly. In the blink of an eye, it was my first day as a teacher, and now I'm coming up on nearly a decade.

My twenties are over. In another blink of an eye, I'll be forty and my thirties will be gone too. Then one day, I'll be lying on this bed, ninety years old, and wondering where my whole life went.

I stare into the closet, trying to decide what footwear I want to wear for my birthday. I'll be working, so I can't wear sandals—not that I would in the middle of October. I scan the rows of shoes that line the bottom of the closet; then I hesitate. Nate is still in the bathroom, shaving—he'll be there for at least a few more minutes.

I take the opportunity to reach for the large suitcase

stuffed into the side of the closet. I heave it out, and with one more quick glance at the bathroom door, I undo the zipper. I let out a sigh when I look down at the contents.

There are dozens of shoes in that luggage.

Nate doesn't know about this particular stash. He thinks the number of shoes I have at the bottom of the closet is bad enough. He's already monitoring the credit card bill for shoe purchases and has hinted that he thinks I have a problem. If he knew about this luggage, he might have me committed.

Which means I don't have much time.

I get out my favorite pair of Louis Vuitton pumps. Well, I only have one pair of Louis Vuittons, because they cost a small fortune. They're made from black patent calf leather with sleek lines and a stiletto heel. Nate never would have approved of me buying them, so I saved up the cash until I had enough. I keep them hidden away and only wear them on special occasions.

I quickly slide the pumps onto my feet, and then I stuff the luggage back into the closet just as Nate emerges from the bathroom with his face clean-shaven. He's got a white towel cinched around his waist, and even though he is not quite as muscular as Jay, he is incredibly hand-some. Despite everything, I am still intensely attracted to my husband.

The only problem is he doesn't seem to feel the same way.

I'm wearing only a bra and pantyhose, and I take the opportunity to walk over to him in my Louis Vuitton pumps. With those shoes adding inches to my height and him in his bare feet, I am much closer to his height. I tilt my face up to his, and he pecks me on the lips.

I run a finger down his chest. "How about a little birthday present?"

He stiffens. "*Now?*"

"Sure. Just a quickie."

"Eve." He rolls his eyes. "You can't possibly be serious."

Right. Why would I be stupid enough to think my husband would want to have sex with me on my birthday?

As always when he rejects me, I get that pang of shame in my chest. At least there's a man out there who wants me. Maybe it's not me—it's him. Maybe he's asexual. Isn't that a thing?

Of course, he sure didn't act asexual when we were first dating. He couldn't get enough of me back then.

Nate notices the look on my face and quickly adds, "I just took a shower, and we have to be at school soon. Anyway, I'm taking you out to dinner tonight."

He hasn't mentioned any sort of present, and I'm beginning to think there isn't one. A few years ago, Nate said something about how presents didn't make sense when we're sharing the same money. Sure enough, he has not bought me a present in the last three years. I suppose dinner is my present.

"We're going to have a great time tonight." He places his hands on my shoulders and grants me a second kiss, pressing his lips firmly against mine but not making any attempt to slip me some tongue. "Wherever you want to go."

"Great," I say, and I think I do a good job of not saying it sarcastically.

As Nate gets dressed, my phone lets out a buzz, signifying a text message. I snatch it off the table, noting that I have a message on Snapflash. I downloaded that app about four months ago—I heard about the kids at school using it, because it has the feature of text messages and images disappearing exactly sixty seconds after you open them. It's a perfect way for kids to communicate without their parents discovering what they are up to.

It's also a great way to communicate with the attractive shoe salesman who I've been seeing for the last several months.

I hold my breath as I open the app. I told Jay not to message me unless it was important, but I can't help but smile at the message from him:

Jay: Happy birthday! Wish we could spend it together.

I stare at the message for the sixty seconds until it disappears from the screen. My first smile since I woke up this morning spreads across my face. Even though it's dangerous for him to message me, it's always the best part of my day. I write back:

Me: So do I.

I stare at the screen for another few seconds, and sure enough, another message appears:

Jay: I've got something for you.

"Eve?"

I nearly drop my phone. Nate is dressed and looking at me curiously. I suppose that's fair enough, considering I'm still just wearing a bra and pantyhose. "Yes?" I say.

94

"We have to get going." He taps his watch. "You're going to be late."

I grab a dress out of my closet and throw it on as quickly as I can while Nate casts pointed looks at his watch. By the time I grab my phone again, the message from Jay has vanished. And there is nothing more on the screen.

CHAPTER 20

ADDIE

For once, I have worked up a sweat in gym class.

I've been running laps, which is my least favorite thing to do. We spent the entire class running, with the requirement of doing fifty laps. I'm almost entirely sure that Kenzie did half of that, but when she told Mrs. Cavanaugh she was done, the teacher just waved her to the bleachers to sit down. But when I tried to tell Mrs. Cavanaugh I was done after forty-eight laps, she shook her head at me and told me to keep running.

So today, I'm grateful to take a shower after class is over. I can't believe I still have three periods left before I can go home. Except the worst part is that I can't even just veg out on my sofa for the rest of the evening. Mom has the day off, and she said when I get home, she wants us to visit the cemetery and see my dad. *It's been two months since we've been there*, she reminded me. As if he's lying in that grave, looking at the calendar on his watch, and wondering why it's been so long since we came by.

Whatever. After I turn eighteen, I'm never visiting that grave ever again.

I shower quickly. I've been trying to shave my legs more frequently so the girls won't have a reason to make fun of me, but at the same time, it seems kind of dumb to shave just for gym class. Especially since they make fun of me whether my legs are baby smooth or not. Today, unfortunately, my legs are on the hairier side, so I try to be as quick as possible.

I trudge back to my locker, to retrieve my jeans and oversize sweatshirt. Except when I get there, the lock is hanging open.

I rip the locker open, my stomach sinking. Right away, I see my backpack is still there, so that's good. And my gym shorts, underwear, and sweaty T-shirt are still lying on top of the backpack. But that's it. The clothes I came to school with are gone.

That's when I noticed Kenzie and her friends at the other end of the hallway, watching me and giggling to each other.

I square my shoulders and turn to look at them. "Can you please give me back my clothes?"

Kenzie blinks her big blue eyes at me. She's already dressed and ready to take off to our next class. "What's wrong? You've got clothes in there. Wasn't that what you were wearing all day?"

I grit my teeth. "No, it wasn't. Look, I need my clothing back, okay?"

"I have an idea," she says. "Why don't you write a *poem* about it? Isn't that what you're good at?" She taps one of her manicured fingers against her chin. "Woe is me, my clothes were let free, and now everyone will see my hairy knee."

Kenzie's friends burst out laughing and then head for the exit. For a moment, I am seized with the almost irrepressible urge to run after Kenzie, grab a handful of her blond hair, and rip it right out of her skull. I bet she'd stop laughing if I did that. And bonus: I'd probably be expelled.

Honestly, the only thing that keeps me from doing it is thinking about how disappointed Mr. Bennett would be.

I look back at my locker, weighing my options. I really, really don't want to put on my sweaty gym clothes again. But what am I supposed to do? Go to class wearing a terry cloth towel? All the other students have already gone to their next class, and in a second, the next group will be filtering in.

I decide to do a lap around the locker room, figuring that Kenzie likely would not have thrown my clothing away. I check every single aisle, but I don't see any sign of my jeans or sweatshirt. It isn't until I get to the showers that I spot a little ball of clothing in the corner. I dart into the shower, and sure enough, it's my outfit from this morning. Except now absolutely soaked from the shower.

Well, my options have just gotten a little more limited.

The next group of students are coming into the locker room. There's no way I can put on my sopping wet clothes, so I have no choice but to put my gym shorts and sweaty T-shirt back on. The T-shirt smells terrible, but what can I do?

And the worst part of all? I've got Mrs. Bennett's math class next.

The hallways are empty as I trudge up to the third floor for math class. The sweat on my T-shirt is not quite dry, and it feels uncomfortable on my skin. Also, I didn't know what to do with my sopping wet jeans and sweat-shirt, so I stuffed them into my backpack, and now it weighs, like, a thousand pounds.

I can see from outside the door that Mrs. Bennett is already in the middle of her lesson. She's writing on the blackboard, and she turns to address the class. Ugh, this is going to be awful. I almost consider skipping, but she told us in no uncertain terms at the beginning of the semester that an unexcused absence would drop our grade by ten points (which would make my grade minus ten points). So I open the door to the classroom, sweaty T-shirt and gym shorts and all.

Mrs. Bennett swivels her head to look at me. She does *not* look happy. I mean, she never looks happy, but even less than usual right now. She folds her hands across her chest and glares at me. She doesn't seem impressed by my gym clothes and hairy legs.

"Nice of you to join us, Addie," she snips at me.

"Sorry," I mumble. I drop into my seat as quietly as I possibly can.

I expect Mrs. Bennett to go back to teaching the class, but instead, she is still staring at me with her hands across her chest. I don't know what she wants from me. Yes, I'm late, but there's nothing I can do about it now, unless she wants me to somehow turn back time? Does she want me to start flying around the earth backward until I can go back to ten minutes earlier and be on time for her class? Is that what she expects from me?

"Your homework, Addie," she says impatiently.

Oh.

I fish around in my bag until I find my homework

assignment on a piece of loose-leaf paper. But as I pull it out, I realize I have made a dire mistake. The paper was not in my binder, because I was working on it during lunch, and because I put my soaking wet clothes in the bag, the water has completely obliterated all the writing. It's totally illegible, but I have no choice but to hand it over.

"Really, Addie?" Mrs. Bennett says as she looks down at my soggy homework assignment.

"It got wet," I say lamely.

"I can see that." She balls it up in her hand and tosses it into the trash. "Well, since I can't possibly grade this, why don't you give me another copy tomorrow?"

It takes all my self-restraint not to groan out loud. It was enough torture doing the assignment the first time. Now I have to do it *again*? This time on top of tonight's impossible homework as well? But what can I do? I can't afford to get an incomplete on the homework. I need every point I can get. "Yes, ma'am," I say.

Mrs. Bennett shoots me a look, and then she goes back to teaching the lesson. I would say that she hates me more than anyone else, but truthfully, she doesn't seem fond of *any* of the students. She just seems like a miserable person. Honestly, I feel sorry for Mr. Bennett sometimes.

CHAPTER 21

EVE

So far, my birthday has not been particularly wonderful. My husband outright refused my advances this morning, one of my stockings got a rip in it, and Addie Severson just referred to me as "ma'am." The only good part of the day was that text message from Jay. And the present he has assured me I will receive.

During my free period, I return a phone call from my parents. It's been ages since we talked. If I had to guess, I'd say we haven't had a phone call since Father's Day. We have become the sort of family that contacts each other on major holidays, and that's it. So I'd imagine the next time I talk to them after this will be on Christmas.

I can't remember the last time I've seen them. Three years, I think.

"Eve," Mom says when she picks up the phone. From the echo, it sounds like she is on speakerphone. "Dad and I are calling to wish you happy birthday."

"Thank you," I say stiffly.

"Hello, Evie," my father speaks up. "Happy birthday, honey."

"Thank you."

We are so awkward and polite around each other. I never would have thought we would be like this. I was always close to my family when I was younger.

"Are you doing anything special tonight?" my mother asks.

"Nate is taking me out to dinner."

"How is Nate doing?" When my mother asks the question, I imagine her crinkling her face in disgust.

"He's fine."

"Any...news?"

My mother wants to know if I'm pregnant. It's not clear whether she wants me to be pregnant or not. She'd like to have grandchildren, but with the way our relationship has been, who knows if she would ever see them? And I'm sure that she doesn't like the idea of me having children with Nate.

"No news," I say.

"Oh." She lets out a sigh. She's relieved. "Well, I'm glad you're doing well. Do you think you might come out to New Jersey for Christmas?"

"Maybe." We have visited Nate's family for the last two Christmases. Technically, it should be my parents' turn, but I'm not excited to see them and have them judge me. "I'll let you know."

The silence hangs between us. There are so many things left unsaid between me and my parents. But the biggest one of all is the thing that I am most reluctant to say:

You were right. I should never have married him.

CHAPTER 22

ADDIE

Oh my God, if I have to spend another minute in these stupid gym clothes, I'm going to throw myself out a window.

They aren't sweaty anymore at least. But now that they have dried, they feel kind of crusty. And also, I smell. Even though I showered, my clothes smell bad, and people are scrunching up their noses at me. It wasn't bad enough that I was the girl who slept with Mr. Tuttle. Now I'm the smelly girl who slept with Mr. Tuttle.

And my wet clothes are totally ruining my backpack and everything inside. Before I go to my last period, I make an effort to try to wring them out in the bathroom sink. It doesn't work, and I get water all over my T-shirt. I end up stuffing the clothes back in my bag, then racing to get to class before I'm late yet again.

I arrive at Mr. Bennett's classroom seconds after the bell rings. He's just getting up from his desk to close the door to the classroom when I appear in the doorway.

His brown eyes rake over me, and when they widen in shock, my mortification is complete. Mr. Bennett, my favorite teacher in the whole world, has now seen me in my smelly, dirty gym clothes with my legs unshaven.

As awful as it was when Mrs. Bennett yelled at me in math class, this is way worse. I'm dying a little bit inside.

"Addie?" His brows bunch together. "Are you okay?"

"Fine," I gulp. I just want to slide into my seat and disappear for the rest of class. Only forty minutes left and this stupid day will be over.

Mr. Bennett rubs his chin, as if considering whether to accept my answer. Finally, he walks over to his desk, scribbles something on a piece of paper, and hands it to me.

"Go home early," he murmurs, low enough that the buzzing students behind us can't hear him. "Here's a note in case they give you any trouble."

"What?" I blurt out.

"You look like you're having a rough time," he acknowledges. "So I'm giving you permission to skip this class. There won't be any homework tonight. Just relax."

"But..." I can't quite wrap my head around this one, but at the same time, I don't want to stand here and argue with him. I *do* want to go home. I'm dirty and sweaty and my temples are starting to throb. "Okay. Um, thank you."

He winks at me. "No problem."

Every time Mr. Bennett winks at me, my heart flutters a little bit. It makes me feel all the worse that he is looking at me in my disgusting gym clothes.

In any case, I take the scribbled permission slip that he wrote and slide it into my pocket, but I won't need it. I take off early, hopping onto my bike and peddling as fast as I can to get home so I can change.

Except I don't quite make it home.

I know where Kenzie Montgomery lives. There's a directory of all the students' addresses, and after I "borrowed" her house keys, I looked up her address. It's right on the way back to my own house, and I took the time to check out the location. There's no harm in looking.

And today I decide to take another look.

CHAPTER 23

ADDIE

Of course, Kenzie's house is much larger than mine. It's practically a mansion.

I'm pretty sure two or maybe even three of my houses could fit into Kenzie's. Even her lawn looks prettier than ours—green and lush, even though everyone else's grass seems to be wilting as the fall goes on. Does she have fake grass on her lawn? Is that a thing?

I hover by the walkway of her house, still on my bicycle. The windows of her house are dark. Her parents both have some high-powered jobs, like lawyers or CEOs—I've heard her bragging that they are never home as she plans parties that only her exclusive guest list of friends are allowed to attend. Only the school's elite have been inside Kenzie's house. Hudson and I used to make fun of those parties. Now he's probably, like, the guest of honor.

I pull off my backpack. I fish around in the small pocket until I pull out the house keys I've been carrying around since I swiped them from her bag. What I'm contemplating is risky. Kenzie's parents might not be home, but that doesn't mean they don't have some sort of elaborate alarm system. Or perhaps a pit bull will leap out at me the second I cross the threshold. That sounds like the kind of luck I usually have.

No. It's not worth it. My life won't be better if I get mauled by a pit bull.

Instead, I continue on my way home. When I get there, my mom is sitting on the sofa, reading. She loves to read, which was something that drove my father wild. *You like spending time with your books more than you like spending time with me.* I don't think it was true, but if it was, could anyone blame her?

"Addie." She looks up when she sees me, and she sticks a bookmark inside her book. I always dog-ear pages, but she hates doing that. She treats her books so delicately. "You're home early. Are you ready to go visit your dad?"

Somehow I almost forgot her plan to drive out to the cemetery today to visit that asshole's grave. This day just keeps getting worse and worse. Especially when my mother stands up from the sofa, looks me up and down, and says, "Did you seriously dress like that today at school?"

"Yep," I say, because I just don't want to tell her the story about what happened to me. It was embarrassing enough to live it, I don't want to share it with anyone else—even my mom.

She rolls her eyes. "You can't dress like that at the cemetery. Why don't you go change your clothes?"

I dump my backpack on the floor. "No. I'm not changing."

"Well, you're not going like that."

"Fine, then I won't go."

"Adeline!" she exclaims. "That's a terrible thing to say!"

"I mean it." I tug at the hem of my sweaty gym T-shirt. "He was always drunk, and he hit you. He doesn't deserve for us to visit him."

My father was terrible. For most of my childhood, he was drunk. Even though people made fun of Hudson for his dad, I would've taken his embarrassing father over mine in a heartbeat, Polish curses and all. My dad never even held down a job—even as a school janitor. Every time somebody gave him a chance, he would show up drunk for work and get fired. My mom supported us through my whole childhood.

I was at Hudson's house studying when I got the call from my mother that they found my father at the bottom of the stairs, not breathing. And I didn't even feel the slightest bit sad.

"Addie," she says quietly, the lines under her face deepening, "he was still your father."

I don't budge from my spot in the living room. I'm not going to change. Not for him. If she forces me, maybe I'll go, but once I turn eighteen, that will be the last time ever.

"Fine." Mom's shoulders sag. "We don't have to go."

I'm shocked. My mother is super stubborn, and I thought for sure we were going to be arguing about this for the next hour. I can't believe she just let it go like that. "Really?"

"Really. But please get changed. You smell terrible."

"Okay..."

She offers a smile. "And let's go out to dinner tonight. We could both use a night out."

I can't disagree with that sentiment.

CHAPTER 24

EVE

For my birthday dinner, I put on my Louis Vuitton pumps and a red dress that clings to my body. I may not be the curviest woman in the world, but I've kept in good shape, and this dress accentuates my figure—Jay would appreciate it very much. But when I march into the living room, where Nate is watching television, he barely looks at me.

"Ready to go?" he asks. He hasn't changed out of the dress shirt and slacks he wore to work, but in his defense, he always looks incredibly handsome.

"I'm ready." I grab my purse from where I left it on the table next to the front door. "I thought we could go to Maggiano's tonight."

Nate looks at me like I just suggested we dash off to Italy to have dinner tonight. "Maggiano's? That's kind of far away, isn't it? And pricey."

"It's my birthday," I start to point out, but I don't feel like arguing. And the truth is, I'm not excited to be sitting in a car with him for the next forty-five minutes either. "Fine. Do you want to go to Piazza?"

Piazza is a popular Italian restaurant about ten minutes away from here. It's cheap and fast. Not exactly the kind of place I dream about going to on a special occasion, but I have a feeling nothing about this night is going to be anything special. May as well make the picture complete.

"Sure," he says.

As always, Nate drives. He turns up the classical music station to a high enough volume that we don't need to speak to each other. When we first got married, I thought about what future birthdays would be like with this man. He was so affectionate, I used to think that even at thirty or forty or even eighty, we wouldn't be able to keep our hands off each other. I never imagined we would be driving to a birthday dinner at a cheap Italian restaurant, struggling to find something to say.

"We have some good talent this year on the poetry magazine," he says.

"Oh, that's great," I say, even though I literally could not possibly care less.

"Those raw emotions are so intense. Only a teenager could write something so utterly compelling."

I nod. "All those hormones. I can't even remember what it was like to feel everything so strongly. But I know I did."

My husband is quiet then, lost in thought. He always seems like he's a million miles away these days. We have the same job, so it seems like it should be easy to come up with something to say to each other, yet we can't. We have become strangers to each other.

Maybe this is my fault. Maybe I need to try harder

to connect with him. When we were first together, we used to sit in the park together, curled up under a tree, and he would read poetry to me. If he suggested such a thing now, I would roll my eyes at him. I liked the poems he wrote for me, because they came from his heart, but I never enjoyed poetry in general. It all seemed so silly—especially the ones that don't even rhyme. I mean, I'm a math teacher. I would sooner sit in the park with him and solve quadratic equations.

Maybe I should suggest it now. Maybe this weekend, we can go to the park and share some poetry. And maybe I need to cool things down with Jay. As much as that tryst has meant to me, if I have any interest in saving my marriage, hooking up with another man is not the best way to go about it.

I've decided—tomorrow, on the second day of my fourth decade of life, I'm going to make things right. I'm going to spend more time with Nate, and I'm going to tell Jay that it's over.

When we get to Piazza, Nate pulls into a spot at the end of the parking lot, as far as he can get from the restaurant. He does that all the time. There are plenty of parking spots right next to the door, and yet he parks half a mile away.

"Can you park a little closer?" I say.

He throws the car into park and frowns at me. "What are you talking about? I'm already parked."

"Right, but there are other spots that are closer."

"You really want me to take my car out of the spot and then move to a different spot, like, ten feet away?"

"It's not ten feet. And you're not wearing four-inch heels."

His eyes flicker down to my Louis Vuitton pumps. "Well, who told you to wear those anyway?" He narrows his eyes. "Are those new? They look expensive."

"I've had them for ages. I wore them for my birthday last year." I can't help but think to myself that *Jay* would recognize these shoes.

"Yeah, right," he mutters under his breath.

Nate climbs out of the car, and I hurry after him, although it's hard to keep up in these shoes. They are absolutely gorgeous, but nobody is going to argue that they're comfortable. "What is that supposed to mean?"

He doesn't slow down to give me a chance to keep up. "I mean, we'll see how new they are when we get the credit card bill, won't we?"

I want to tell him how unfair that is, but the truth is, the credit card will have a few surprises on it for him. I hate that he is the one who always pays it. It's this habit we got into years ago. When we got married, all our money was pooled together. I can't do anything or buy anything without him knowing about it.

Me telling him that I want my own credit card and my own bank account might not be a step in the right direction for our marriage. Then again, he doesn't seem to care about these things as much as he used to. When I would go out without him, he used to ask me so many questions about where I was going and what I would be doing, and now it's like he doesn't care at all. He's just glad I'm out of the house.

Nate at least holds the door open for me when we get to the restaurant. I've already decided I'm going to get the most decadent dessert on the menu. I deserve one treat today, considering the only present I've received the entire day from my birthday is a key chain from Shelby that she got in Cape Cod.

"Table for two," Nate tells the hostess. She's a busty blond in her twenties, and I'm glad to see at the very least he isn't staring at her breasts.

"It's my birthday," I blurt out.

I don't know why I said that. Nate looks slightly mortified, but I've only got a few hours left of this day, and I just want somebody to acknowledge that it's special for me. But it's not that gratifying when the hostess flashes me a quick smile, says happy birthday, and then leads us to the same crappy table we were going to get anyway. She doesn't take us to some special birthday table covered with streamers, not that I was expecting anything like that.

Just as we are settling into our seats, Nate stiffens. He's looking at something across the dining area, his brown eyes widening.

"What's wrong?" I ask him. "What are you looking at?"

"What? Nothing."

He was definitely looking at something, although he doesn't want to tell me. Did he see one of the employees come out of the bathroom without washing his hands? Did he spot a pair of shoes that I purchased without his consent?

"It's one of my students," he finally says. "Addie Severson. She must be eating with her mother."

Now it's my turn to go as rigid as a board. "I didn't realize Addie was in your class."

"Yes. Last period."

I don't know why the idea of Addie being in Nate's class makes me uneasy. I can't help but think of Art

Tuttle's warning when we were at the supermarket. *That girl is not well.*

"She's really talented," he says. "She could be a great poet someday."

"That's not a very practical career."

Nate's face falls. He looks hurt by my comment, but what does he expect? Being a poet is *not* a practical career aspiration.

"I just think it's something she might enjoy," he says. "She has a lyrical mind. And her favorite poet is also Poe, although she's partial to 'Annabel Lee.'"

One thing I do know about my husband is that his favorite poet is Edgar Allan Poe, and he loves "The Raven." If I were making a list of five important facts about Nathaniel Bennett, that would top the list.

It occurs to me that we haven't even ordered dinner yet, and I'm already looking forward to being done with this meal.

"Listen," I say, "you should be careful around Addie. You saw what happened with Art Tuttle. He was just trying to be nice to her, and look what happened."

Nate's eyes darken. "If you think Art Tuttle isn't a creep, then you're blind."

I feel a flash of irritation at his comment. Art is *not* a creep. When I started working at the school, he was the first person to help me. And he never did or said anything inappropriate. He was just a good friend to me. I knew he was tutoring Addie and even saw them getting in his car together after school, but I truly never thought anything of it. Nobody did.

That all changed when a neighbor saw Addie skulking around the back of Art's house and called the police.

It doesn't look good for a middle-aged teacher when your fifteen-year-old student is found outside your house late at night..

But in the end, nobody could prove any wrongdoing on his part. As silly as it sounds, the only thing Art was guilty of was "caring too much." He knew Addie didn't have money for tutoring, so he was trying to help her through math class on his own. He gave her a ride home a few times because it was raining or snowing and he didn't want her to have to bike home in inclement weather. And the dinners were about as innocent as it could get— he invited both Addie and her mother to dine with him and his wife.

As for Addie being found outside his house, that was one Art couldn't quite explain. When he and I talked about it, he hung his head. *I was trying to be nice to her because she lost her father recently, and I think she just got too attached. She became fixated on me.*

I didn't doubt him. It's exactly the sort of thing that could happen to a troubled teenage girl.

"I'm just saying," I murmur to Nate, "the girl is troubled. She recently lost her father, and she will cling on to anyone who gets too close to her."

"So basically, we should keep her isolated?"

"That's not what I'm saying at all!"

I am forced to pause my rant while our waitress interrupts to bring us our water glasses. She is young and attractive, like all the waitresses here. She spends what feels like half an hour telling us about the specials, and every time Nate asks a question, she lays her hand on his shoulder. I have to say, I'm getting sick of women hitting on my husband right in front of my face.

"I'm just saying," I continue after the waitress has finally left us alone again, "the girl needs friends her own age—not a teacher who is pushing forty. Just be careful."

"Noted," Nate says through his teeth.

But I can see on his face that his mood has soured. I don't know what he's so upset about though. I'm just trying my best to protect him from ending up like Art Tuttle.

CHAPTER 25

ADDIE

After Mr. Bennett comes into Piazza, it's basically all I can think about.

Like, there could be a Lil Nas X concert happening in the corner of the room, and I would not even notice. That's how distracted I am. And my mom is getting annoyed, because she keeps trying to talk to me, and I keep saying "What?"

"Addie!" she snaps at me.

"What?" I say again.

She lets out a long sigh. "You've hardly eaten any of your food."

I look down at the plate in front of me. I got a tomato and pesto flatbread, although it's not very good. Usually, though, I would have scarfed it down by now. Instead, I have eaten only a teeny tiny slice of it.

"I'm not hungry," I finally say.

Mr. Bennett ordered some sort of ravioli. I can't tell what it is from here, and it's not like I could go over there and ask. I'm curious what it is though. Is it plain cheese ravioli, or is it the one with mushrooms? Does Mr. Bennett like mushrooms? Or does he think that it's weird that people eat fungus, the same way I do?

I'm trying not to call attention to the fact that I've been staring at him through the entire meal ever since he walked in. But it's hard not to. I mean, he's handsome enough that I'm sure I'm not the only person looking at him in this place. The waitress is definitely flirting—at one point, she had her hand on his shoulder, and I thought he looked annoyed, but I wasn't sure. I was glad that he wasn't charmed by the boobalicious waitress.

The other thing I can't help but notice is he's not having much fun with Mrs. Bennett. She's not my favorite person, if only because math is my weakest subject and she doesn't make it easy, but I assumed he likes her. I mean, he's *married* to her. Plus, she looks irritatingly pretty tonight, with smoky makeup lining her big eyes and a red dress that emphasizes her cute, trim figure. So I would think he must like her, but they have been sitting together for at least twenty minutes now, and they have barely said two words to one another.

If Mr. Bennett and I were having dinner together, we would have a lot to talk about. I would bring a book of poetry—maybe Poe—and I would just love to hear his thoughts on each of them. Even though that's what we do in class every day, I would never get sick of it. Not in a million billion years.

Doesn't Mrs. Bennett realize how incredible her husband is? When all my clothes got soaked today and she made me sit through her lesson and even repeat my homework, it was like she didn't care. Or worse, she thought I *deserved* to suffer. He was the only one who noticed how uncomfortable I was and sent me home. She doesn't appreciate being married to someone who is so kind and considerate, because she's the opposite.

"Well, if that's all you're going to eat," Mom says, "I may as well get the check."

I don't want to leave the restaurant. While I'm sitting here, it's almost like I'm having dinner with Mr. Bennett, even though that's kind of dumb because he is across the entire dining room and he doesn't even know that I'm here. We are about as far from having dinner together as possible, yet I still don't want to leave.

"Wait," I say. "Let me go to the bathroom first, then I'll eat some more."

My mother looks skeptical, but what is she supposed to say—I can't use the bathroom? So I follow the signs to the hidden hallway that contains the bathroom. Naturally, there's a line for the single women's bathroom, but that's fine because it will just make it take longer. Especially since I don't actually need to go at all.

"Addie?" a familiar voice startles me while I'm scrolling on my phone.

I'm totally surprised to see Mr. Bennett standing behind me. I guess he needed the bathroom too. I *knew* we were on the same wavelength.

"Hey," I say awkwardly. Since our last encounter, I have showered and am wearing a clean pair of blue jeans. I even put on a nice pink dress shirt that my mom says complements my skin tone, although I am skeptical.

"I saw you in the restaurant," he says. "That's your mother, right?"

A little thrill goes through me at the idea that Mr. Bennett noticed me, even in the crowded dining room. "Uh-huh."

I wonder if it's okay to be talking to him in this isolated area. If someone saw us here together, they might get the wrong idea. The last thing I want would be for Mr. Bennett to end up like Mr. Tuttle.

He cocks his head to the side. "Are you okay? You looked like you were having a pretty bad day earlier."

That is a massive understatement, but honestly, I don't want to complain about Kenzie and her friends right now. I don't want him to think of me as some loser who is getting bullied by the popular kids. "Sort of."

"What happened?"

"It wasn't a big deal." I try to laugh, to show how not upset I am about what happened, even though it's phony. "Some kids in gym threw my clothes in the shower, so everything got soaked."

Mr. Bennett winces. "Jesus, that's awful. Who did that to you?"

I shake my head. "I don't know."

"You can tell me." When I don't say anything, he raises his eyebrow. "I can keep it between us."

I really can't tell him, even though I like the idea of me and Mr. Bennett sharing a secret. No matter what he says, he's still a teacher, and he might talk to Kenzie if I tell him about it. And if I rat her out, she's going to be worse. The last thing I want is for Kenzie to hate me more. I'm better off taking her abuse.

"I don't know," I repeat.

His brown eyes hold mine for a moment, and a little thrill goes through me. I'm not sure why though. Maybe it just feels nice to have a teacher on my side again. Or *anyone* on my side again. After the whole thing with Mr. Tuttle, it feels like everyone hates me.

"I'll tell you what," he says. "The rest of the class has another homework assignment today, analyzing a poem we talked about in class. But I have special homework that I want you to do tonight."

If Mrs. Bennett—or really any other teacher—said that to me, I would have been horrified. But right now, I'm intrigued. "Okay…"

"I want you to write an angry letter to the person who took your clothes," he says. I start to protest, but then he adds, "Not a poem, but a letter. You don't have to use their name, but I want you to get out that anger. Let your anger out on the page for me. Tell me what you want to do to this person."

"What I want to do?"

He bobs his head. "Exactly. Write a revenge letter. Tell me what you would do if you had five minutes alone with this person and nobody would ever know."

He has no idea I've got Kenzie's house keys in my backpack. I imagine what would have happened if I had snuck into her bedroom and waited for her in the closet. I might have actually had five minutes alone with her. And let me tell you, those five minutes would have involved some serious payback.

A smile twitches at my lips. "Okay."

I can already imagine what I'm going to write:

You have everything in the world. And you are in a relationship with the greatest guy I've ever known. But you don't deserve any of that. What you deserve is to get your eyes scratched out. No, that's too good for you.

121

"Anyway," he says, "it looks like you're having a nice meal with your mother."

"Yeah." I rub at the back of my elbow. "And you know, I hope you're having a nice night with Mrs. Bennett."

For a moment, his eyes cloud over. "It's her birthday."

I'm not sure what that means exactly. "Oh."

"So yeah." He lifts his shoulders. "It's fine. The food here is good."

Oh boy. I was *right*.

Mr. Bennett isn't having a good time with his wife. My impression of her in class is more accurate than I thought. She is not someone who goes home and then immediately becomes this super nice person who is totally different from the way she is at work. She's a legit awful person. Mr. Bennett doesn't like being married to her any more than I like having her as a teacher.

That's why instead of using the empty men's room and hurrying back to his table to be with her, he has been standing out in the hallway talking to me for the last five minutes.

At that moment, the person who was in front of me leaves the ladies' room, and now it's my turn. But I would much rather stand out here and talk to Mr. Bennett. Maybe I can let the person behind me skip ahead.

But before I can propose the idea, Mr. Bennett smiles at me. "I don't want to keep you, Addie. I'll see you in class tomorrow. And don't forget that letter."

I feel a twinge of regret as Mr. Bennett disappears into the men's room. It occurs to me that as angry as I am at Kenzie, I'm even angrier at Mrs. Bennett for making him so unhappy.

CHAPTER 26

EVE

Nate seemed even more distracted than usual during the meal and then subsequently on the drive home. And as soon as we walk in through the door to the garage, he lets out an exaggerated yawn.

"Oh, man," he says. "I'm beat, Eve."

His attempts to get out of sex are becoming more and more uncreative. Next, he will be telling me he has a migraine. "It's fine," I say. "Go to bed—you're off the hook."

He raises his eyebrows. "Off the hook?"

"I just mean we don't need to have sex tonight."

Nate looks taken aback. "If you want to have sex..."

The last thing I want is to get into a big, emotional argument with my husband on my birthday. So I just shake my head. "I'm tired too. I'll meet you upstairs."

And that's what I will do on my first day of being thirty years old. I will turn in for the night at a record 9:30 in the evening.

While Nate heads upstairs, I hear a buzzing sound from inside my purse. When I retrieve my phone from my purse, I see a new message on Snapflash. There's only one man who messages me on Snapflash, and at the beginning of the night, I had vowed to end things with that man.

Jay: I left a present for you at the door.

I smile down at the message for the sixty seconds until it disappears. I look up the stairwell to make sure Nate has disappeared into the bedroom. Then I creep over to our front door and crack it open.

There's a shoebox at our door.

I snatch the shoebox off the front porch before anyone can see it. Jay must've slipped over to drop it off while we were at dinner, because the box definitely wasn't here when we left.

I pull the lid off the box, and I can't help but let out a gasp.

It's a pair of Sam Edelman sling pumps in a glossy red color. I had been admiring them a couple of weeks ago in the store, and I was disappointed when the last pair disappeared, because they were just barely within my price range.

And now I realize where the pumps disappeared to. Even though money is tight for him, Jay used his minimal funds to buy me a birthday present he knew I would love.

Another message pops up on my phone:

Jay: Did you get it?

Me: I love them. Thank you so much.
Jay: I knew you would.

My eyes tear up. Life is so incredibly unfair. I am stuck in what I am increasingly realizing is a loveless marriage, and meanwhile, I have no chance of being with the man who I really love.

I'm about to try on my new pair of shoes when I hear a noise outside the door. My heart leaps. I don't even care if the neighbors see—I want more than anything for Jay to be standing outside my door.

I yank open the front door, ready to greet him with a big sloppy kiss. Except when I look out the front door, there's nobody there. Aside from the porch lights, everything is dark.

"Hello?" I call out.

No answer.

More quietly this time, I say, "Jay?"

There's no reply.

That's so strange. I was sure I heard a noise that sounded like it was coming from right outside the door. I'm shocked that there isn't somebody standing there. But it seems like I must have imagined it.

After all, there isn't anyone out there.

CHAPTER 27

ADDIE

When I get to my locker at the end of the day, the lock has been cut.

I stare at it for a moment, my eyes bugging out. The lock is still hanging exactly where it was the last time I came to my locker, but the metal bar has been sliced by a lock cutter. I've heard the staff will sometimes do it if they think there are drugs in your locker, but I don't know why anyone would think that about me.

But then when I open my locker, I know exactly who did this.

My locker is completely filled with shaving cream.

I gasp at the sheer quantity of shaving cream filling the locker. There are probably books and papers in there, and also my coat, but right now, it basically looks like a locker of shaving cream. If there's anything I want in my locker, I'm going to have to stick my hands in and sift through what looks like three gallons' worth of foam.

Several students have witnessed this spectacle, and

based on the number of giggles, it's apparently hilarious. I don't have to guess why this was done to me. Kenzie has made enough snide comments in gym about shaving my legs, even though I've been diligently running a razor over my legs twice a week.

"Oh wow." Before I even turn around, I know who the voice behind me belongs to. "I bet all that shaving cream will come in handy. Someone did you a huge favor."

I blink the tears from my eyes before I turn around to look at Kenzie. She and Bella are watching me at my locker, drawing closer than any other student dares to get. How long have they been standing here and waiting for me to witness this disaster? I should feel sorry for them that their lives are so small, but I don't. I mostly just feel sorry for myself.

Why is Kenzie doing this to me? Is she jealous because she thinks Hudson likes me better than her? That's clearly not the case. He's dating *her*. If he has any lingering feelings for me, even as a friend, that would be a big surprise to me. He won't even *speak* to me.

A crowd has gathered around me now. Everyone is watching to see what I'll do next. Really, they're watching and feeling glad that they aren't the ones with a locker filled with shaving cream. Nobody wants to be on Kenzie Montgomery's bad side. Yet here I am, and I don't even know what I did to get here.

"Excuse me!" an adult voice rings out from the periphery of the crowd. Oh, thank God. "Will you please let me through right now?"

My momentary relief that there would finally be an adult who could help me deal with the situation vanishes when I see who has pushed her way through the crowd.

It's Mrs. Bennett—the worst possible person. And when she sees the contents of my locker, she looks decidedly pissed. Then again, I've never seen her *not* look pissed, so it's hard to tell the difference.

"Addie!" she says sharply. "What is going on here?"

Kenzie hasn't budged. You might think she has a lot of nerve, but really, she knows I'm not going to rat her out. That would be social suicide, especially if I did it in front of everyone else. If I have any chance of coming back from something like this, it will vanish if I tell on her now. And anyway, she'll just deny it, and everyone will believe her instead of me.

Besides, I've got her house keys. I can get my revenge.

Mrs. Bennett folds her arms across her chest, waiting for my answer. "Addie…"

"I don't know," I finally say. "I guess someone put shaving cream in my locker."

"Who?" she presses me.

I shrug.

She tilts her head. "Really? You don't have any idea whatsoever who might have broken into your locker and filled it with shaving cream?"

I shake my head slowly.

Mrs. Bennett looks around at the crowd of kids who have become an audience to my humiliation. "All of you. Go home." Her beady eyes zero back in on me—a stark contrast from her husband's kind brown eyes. "And *you*. Clean this up, Addie."

Seriously, what is her problem? She is so *harsh*. And she is married to a freaking poet—the nicest teacher in the whole school. Why is she like this? Why is she always so mean?

But at least she gets the kids to stop gawking at me, so that's something. Although Kenzie and her friends linger at the end of the row of lockers, still watching. I can hear their giggles as I contemplate my situation. Like, what am I supposed to do now that my locker is filled with shaving cream? I don't even know how to begin to clean all this up. Not to mention the fact that my books are wrecked.

I guess I could scoop it up. I wish I could just take a hose to the entire thing. And also, I don't have anything to clean it up with. If I were home, it would be easier, but what am I supposed to do to clean up a bunch of shaving cream in the middle of the hallway at my high school?

"What are you waiting for?" Kenzie calls out. "Do you need us to get you a razor?"

Bella laughs at that. "Don't give her a razor. She would probably slit her wrists!"

Kenzie says something to Bella, and I can't quite make it out, but it kind of sounds like she said "So what?"

Every time I think I've experienced the worst day yet, there is a new winner.

Just to make my humiliation complete, Hudson appears to join their little group. He's wearing his football uniform, but it's not yet caked in dirt, which means he's heading over to practice. I'm sure he wanted to see the look on my face as I experienced the locker of shaving cream. Hell, for all I know, he's the one who cut the lock. I doubt Kenzie did that herself.

"What's going on?" he says, his pale blue eyes looking right at me for a change.

Kenzie snickers. "Addie is having some *issues*. Anyway, we better get to practice."

Hudson is staring in my direction, a frown on his face. Through most of elementary school, he got bullied pretty badly. I remember once on the playground, after a morning of rain, the ground was all muddy, and some kids pushed him so that he fell face down in the mud. He didn't fight back though. He just took it, like he always did. I was the one who helped him up and took him to the bathroom to get cleaned up after.

To my surprise, instead of joining Kenzie, Hudson walks over to where I'm standing in front of my shaving cream–filled locker. For a moment, I get the urge to throw my arms around his padded shoulders for the hug he would have given me before our whole friendship fell apart. "Addie? What's going on?"

"Nothing," I mumble. "I just need to get this cleaned up."

His eyes rake over the gallons of shaving cream in my locker. "Jesus."

"Yeah."

He glances back to where Kenzie and her friends are standing, then looks back at me. "Let me help you get it cleaned up."

These are literally the most words Hudson has said to me in months. He means well, but he has to realize that he can't help me clean up my locker. Kenzie won't allow it.

Sure enough, Kenzie's voice calls out, "Hudson! We have to get to practice!"

"You should go," I tell him. "Your girlfriend is going to be mad at you."

His eyes darken. "She's not my boss. I'm going to help you."

"Hudson!" She doesn't come closer to us, but her sharp voice fills the hallway. "We're going to be late if you don't come right now!"

"Screw her," he mumbles under his breath. "Come on. We can get this done quickly."

I look over at Kenzie, who seems nothing short of furious. She broke into my locker and vandalized it, and I haven't even done anything to her to deserve it. I can't imagine what hell she'll bring down on me for hijacking her boyfriend.

"Listen," I say, "you've got practice. You should go."

"No," he says firmly. "I'm going to help you. I want to."

"Except you're making it worse."

He jerks his head back. He was trying to be a good guy and help an old friend, but he has to realize I'm right. Kenzie is getting angrier by the second, and if I let him help me, there will be retribution. As painful as it will be to clean this up by myself, it's better this way.

"Addie..." he says.

"Really. Go to practice. You've done enough."

Hudson doesn't look happy about it, but he obligingly turns around to join Kenzie. Although before he disappears down the hallway, he turns around to look at me one last time. And he looks so sad.

That surprises me. I mean, Hudson is now one of the most popular kids in school. His life is infinitely better than it was when it was just us two losers hanging out together. But for a moment, I wonder if he misses when it was just the two of us. I wonder if he misses me as much as I miss him.

But we're never going to be able to be friends again.

Things will never be the way they used to be between the two of us.

Not since Hudson helped me kill my father.

CHAPTER 28

ADDIE

I end up grabbing a lot of paper towels.

The best thing would be if I could figure out how to get a hose and spray down the entire locker. I grabbed most of my books from the bottom of the locker, and I formed a little stack on the floor. For the most part, they seem to have survived the shaving cream, so there's that.

It would've been easier if Hudson were helping me. Of course it would be. It almost killed me to have to send him away, especially since he was extending the first olive branch since it all went down nearly a year ago.

I will never forget that day. The best and worst day of my life.

As I clean out the shaving cream from my locker, I close my eyes and remember the evening my father stumbled home drunk for the zillionth time. It wasn't even that late, but of course, it didn't matter. My dad could be drunk at two in the afternoon.

Hudson was at my house studying. We often studied

together, although now he had football practice and on top of that a part-time job, but whenever he could, he came by. Hudson's strongest subject was math and weakest was English, the reverse from me, so we tried to help each other.

He looked alarmed when we heard my father yelling downstairs. I remember telling him, *Just ignore it. He'll probably pass out soon.*

But that wasn't what happened.

My father bounded up the stairs of our house, yelling and screaming. And when he found Hudson in my room with the door closed, he was livid. Despite the fact that he knew we were friends, we were clearly studying, and Hudson had been coming around since we were little kids, he started yelling about how I was a slut and Hudson was taking advantage of his daughter. And he just wouldn't *stop*.

It was Hudson who finally stood up to him. He had been working out for football for nearly a year and a half, and he had grown over the summer and was now taller than my father. He stood over him and said in a low growl, *You can't talk to Addie like that.*

Anyone with common sense would have backed down at that point, but not a guy who had recently downed a bottle of whiskey. Hudson was only making him angrier.

The two of them kept shouting at each other in the hallway. It was my father who shoved Hudson first, right in his chest. I don't know what Hudson would have done next. I don't know if he had it in him to punch my father in the face, even though his hand was already balling into a fist.

As it turned out, though, I was the one who shoved my father back.

I didn't even realize how close we were to the stairwell. I was as surprised as anyone when he stumbled hard backward and then went tumbling down the stairs. Hudson and I both flinched when we heard the sickening thump at the bottom of the stairs. We raced down the steps and found my father lying in a crumpled pile, his neck twisted at an unnatural angle.

Hudson was freaking out. I saw him endure years of bullying and never shed a tear, but this was the first time he looked like he might cry. *He's dead, Addie! We killed him!*

I wasn't absolutely sure he was dead, but I wasn't going to get close enough to him to find out. And I wasn't going to take the heat for giving him exactly what he deserved.

We have to get out of here, I told Hudson.

He stared at me, blinking his watery eyes. *What are you talking about? We have to call the police. Or...or an ambulance...*

You want to go to jail?

I had to drag Hudson out the back door. We took the shortcut from my house to his back door, and ten minutes later, we were safely locked in his bedroom. I tried my best to stay calm, but Hudson continued freaking out. *This is wrong*, he kept saying. *We have to tell someone what happened. We have to call the police, Addie.*

Of course, only an hour later, my mom came home from her shift at the hospital and found my father lying dead at the bottom of the stairs. There was no evidence of foul play, and his blood alcohol level made it clear that he had lost his balance at the top of the stairs and taken a tragic fall. And as far as anyone knew, Hudson and I were together in his room studying the whole evening. So nobody ever found out about our roles in his death.

But Hudson never forgave me.

We got away with it, but the next day at school, Hudson would barely look at me. I kept trying to talk to him, and he just kept saying, *I can't, I can't.* Somehow I didn't realize quite how shaken he was. I didn't realize it was the sort of thing he would never be able to get past.

Without Hudson, I was a disaster in math the next semester. And without his friendship, I was even more of a disaster. The only other person I had to talk to was my mother, and she was also in mourning. I had nobody. So when Mr. Tuttle was nice to me, what was I supposed to do? Turn him down?

He was just trying to be nice. Even though no one would believe me, he never did anything inappropriate. If I had a father like him, maybe I wouldn't be so messed up. It kills me that his whole life got screwed up because of me.

It takes me over an hour, but I finally get my locker mostly cleaned out. My books are sort of damp, but I'll just have to let them dry out overnight. There's nothing more I can do.

Just as I'm making one last trip to the bathroom for paper towels, I look out one of the windows in the hallway—it's pouring, of course. I did remember seeing on the forecast that it was going to rain later, but I figured I would be able to beat the weather. Now I'm going to have to bike home while buckets of water are being dumped on my head.

I do one final wipe down of my locker, and just as I'm finishing, none other than Mr. Bennett comes down the hallway. I blink my eyes in surprise at the sight of him. He's here late a lot, though, because he's the staff supervisor for the school newspaper.

"Hello, Addie," he says. He looks into my locker, which still has a tiny bit of shaving cream clinging to the corners I couldn't quite reach. "What are you doing?"

My instinct is telling me I should lie, but instead I blurt out, "Someone sprayed shaving cream all over my locker."

He flinches. "Ouch. Who was it?"

I just shake my head. He raises his eyebrows, but there's no way I'm telling him.

"Fine." He glances into my locker. "Need any help cleaning it up?"

Mr. Bennett's reaction is such a stark contrast from the way his wife snapped at me earlier. "Actually, maybe you can reach some of the shaving cream in that corner over there."

"You got it."

Mr. Bennett winds up helping me clean out the rest of the shaving cream, and we devise a way to put the books back in the locker to optimize them drying out. It all kind of feels like a geometry problem I don't know how to do, but it will be fine. I've done the best I can anyway.

"Thanks," I tell Mr. Bennett as we get my locker closed. I have to remove the broken lock, and I replace it with the one from my gym locker. "That would have been tricky."

"No problem." He arches an eyebrow. "You need a ride home?"

I wince. Mr. Tuttle drove me home a few times, which was one of the examples of "inappropriate behavior" that the principal cited. "No, thanks."

"It's pouring though," he points out. "And you don't have a car, do you?"

I snort. "I don't even have a driver's license. Just a stupid permit."

"Well then. Maybe you shouldn't turn down a perfectly good ride."

I don't know what to say. Obviously, I would rather get a ride in Mr. Bennett's nice, dry car than have to attempt to ride my bike home or, worse, walk it home in the rain. My mom is still at her shift at the hospital, so there's no chance of her picking me up for at least another couple of hours.

"I don't want to get you in trouble," I finally say.

He nods soberly. "I appreciate that. But honestly, it will be fine. I've driven other students home, and I haven't lost my job yet."

When he says it like that, it doesn't sound like such a big deal. It's just a ride from one human being to another. Just because he's my teacher, he can't give me a ride home? That seems ridiculous.

"Okay," I finally say.

This is not a big deal. Nothing bad will happen.

CHAPTER 29

ADDIE

Mr. Bennett is parked close to the back entrance of the school, but he still produces an umbrella, and I huddle close to him to keep from getting wet. But not too close, obviously.

His car turns out to be a gray Honda Accord. It's weird because I expected something flashier, like a bright red convertible or something, which is weird because it's not like Mr. Bennett is flashy. But this car just seems so much like an *adult* car, even though Mr. Bennett seems like one of the kids.

Also, the inside smells like him. I don't know what exactly the smell is, maybe a cologne or aftershave or something, but I have noticed that he has a nice smell. I can't smell it when he's at his desk, but when he comes around the side of his desk and I am in my seat in the first row, I get a whiff of it.

"Sorry it's messy," he tells me as he clears a few papers off the passenger's seat. It's not that messy, though, especially compared to my mother's car. In all the time I have been getting into her car, I have never seen it without fast-food french fries on the floor.

I slide into the passenger seat and buckle my seat belt. When Mr. Bennett gets into the driver's seat, that feels even more weird. It doesn't feel like we are teacher and student anymore but more like two friends going home together. The only person I ever ride like this in the car with is my mother, and she is much older than Mr. Bennett. Like by at least ten years, maybe more.

And he's not like any other adults I know. I rode in the car with Mr. Tuttle, but he was old, like my father or even kind of like my grandfather or something. But Mr. Bennett isn't like that. He is really handsome—more handsome than basically all the boys in our class—and it's hard not to notice that.

Of course, if we were friends, I wouldn't call him Mr. Bennett. His first name is Nathaniel. Nathaniel Bennett. It makes me think of Nathaniel Hawthorne, who wrote *The Scarlet Letter*, which I had to read in last year's English class. There's something poetic about the name Nathaniel.

Nathaniel and Adeline. We sound like a couple from hundreds of years ago.

I've heard other teachers refer to him as Nate. If we were friends, that's probably what I would call him. But since we're not actually friends, I will still be calling him Mr. Bennett.

"Thank you again," I tell him as he starts the engine.

"No problem." He pulls out of his parking spot, the wiper blades furiously swishing back and forth.

"Couldn't let you walk home in this mess. And I'm not in any rush. Eve is going out with a friend tonight."

I sit beside him as he navigates onto the road. I told him my address, and he seems to know how to get there without his GPS. So I sit there, playing with a loose thread on the seam of my jeans. I'm trying to think of something to say conversation wise, but everything in my head just seems so completely lame. I mean, I'm sixteen years old. I don't think there's anything interesting I can say to him. Usually, when we talk, it's about poetry, but that conversation seems out of place here.

"So," he finally says, "is the person who put shaving cream in your locker the same one who ruined your clothes?"

I hesitate for a moment before nodding. I submitted my letter to Kenzie in lieu of an assignment, although to be honest, some of the angry thoughts were aimed at Mrs. Bennett as well. Mr. Bennett never graded it or returned it to me, but when I handed it in, he said to me, *I bet it felt good to write that.*

It really did.

But not as good as it would feel to *do* all those things.

"I'm sorry that's been happening to you," he says. "You don't deserve to be treated that way. Nobody does. And you should know, there's nothing wrong with standing up for yourself."

"It's kind of hard to stand up for myself when the other person has their own posse."

I brace myself, waiting for some sort of motivational lecture like I get from every adult, but instead Mr. Bennett just nods. "I'm not gonna lie. Sometimes high school sucks."

"I'm sure it didn't suck for you."

"Hmm. I don't think you realize what it was like to be a sixteen-year-old boy who enjoyed writing poetry."

Despite everything, I have to laugh. It's hard to imagine Mr. Bennett being sixteen years old like me. But there are times he seems very young. I can almost imagine him being a teenager, sitting under that tree outside the school, writing poems.

"What was the first poem you ever wrote?" I ask him.

My face burns slightly, wondering if I asked him a stupid question, but he doesn't act like he thinks it's stupid. He purses his lips like he's thinking about the answer. I give myself permission to look at him, and I notice a little healing cut on his chin from when he must've been shaving this morning. A lot of the boys in my class don't shave yet, and they just have scattered strands of this gross scraggly hair on their chins.

"I wrote a poem when I was six," he says. "For my mom, for Mother's Day. She hung it up on the refrigerator, and it was there for years, so I still remember it. Let me think. *I love my mom, and I know why. She makes me food so I don't die.*"

"That's, like, the cutest thing ever," I squeal.

"I know. I was adorable." He grins at me. "How about you?"

"I don't think I wrote anything quite that cute. Anyway, I didn't become a serious poet until I was in high school." Now my face feels like it's on fire. "I didn't mean to say I'm a poet or anything. I'm not. I just mean that I didn't start writing poetry seriously until then. Sort of serious."

"You are a poet though." The smile drops off his

face. "Don't say you're not, because you absolutely are. More than a lot of adults who claim to be."

I squeeze my hands between my knees. Sometimes adults say things that are patronizing, but this doesn't sound like that. He sounds like he truly means it.

I almost feel sad when my house comes into view. I feel like I could talk to Mr. Bennett in the car for the next hour or two. Usually when I'm in the car with my mom, I turn on the radio because talking can get awkward, but I don't feel the urge to do that at all with Mr. Bennett.

"Thanks for the ride," I say as he pulls up to my curb.

"It was my pleasure."

He throws the car into park, and for a split second, it almost feels like the two of us are on a date and he's dropping me off at home at the end of the evening. It's so preposterous, but at the same time, it feels that way. And for a moment, I almost feel like I'm supposed to lean in for a good-night kiss.

But that's ridiculous.

"Thank you again." I grab my bag off the floor and open the door to the car. "Really."

"Any time, Addie."

As I dart from the Honda to my front door, trying to avoid the raindrops splashing down on me, I find myself smiling like an idiot.

CHAPTER 30

EVE

N ow these are a perfect fit."

Jay is kneeling beside me, in a back row of Simon's Shoes, having placed a pair of Calvin Klein green pumps on my feet. We do this sometimes after our session in the storeroom, if *she* hasn't called him to come home. We go out to the main part of the store, and he helps me try on shoes. There are already half a dozen boxes on the floor beside me.

"I can't afford these," I remind him, although they do admittedly look gorgeous.

"I wish I could buy them for you." His eyes meet mine. "I wish I could buy all these shoes for you."

"And I wish I didn't have to go home to *him*."

I blurted that out without thinking, but as the words leave my mouth, I realize how true they are. On my birthday, I was considering recommitting to my marriage, but now I realize that Nate and I can never crawl back to each other. The abyss between us widens every day.

"Why not leave him?" Jay says.

I snort as I kick off the pumps. I like them *too* much, and it's frustrating. "And then what? We run off together?"

Even though I say it sarcastically, the truth is that I dream of a happy ending for me and Jay. It will never happen—we both have too many entanglements—but if only we could. In the end, though, I couldn't do it to Nate. I couldn't humiliate him that way.

Sometimes I think he would barely miss me though. He came home tonight, dripping wet, and he told me he had taken a walk in the rain to inspire himself. Then he went up to his office on the second floor, and he closed the door. I knocked to tell him I was leaving, but he barely acknowledged me.

As if on cue, Jay's phone starts ringing. This time while he is talking, I can hear a baby crying in the background. I rest my chin on my hands, trying to push away the stabbing guilt in my chest. No matter what happens with Nate, I need to end things with Jay. Sooner rather than later.

"You have to go," I acknowledge as soon as Jay ends the call.

"She wants me home." He sighs. "The baby is… Anyway. Next week?"

While he is still crouched beside me, I reach out and run my fingers along an old jagged scar just below his hairline. He told me he got it when he was a child, trying to worm his way under a fence. One of these weeks, it will be the last time for the two of us. But I hope that won't be this week or next week.

It will be soon though.

"Yes," I say. "I'll see you next week."

Jay looks down at the shoeboxes scattered at my feet. "I better put all these away. I don't want to get in trouble."

All the boxes came from the storeroom, so we each grab a bunch of them to carry back there. Almost like Pavlov's dogs, I start to get turned on the second we get close to the storeroom. It doesn't matter that we've already gone at it twice tonight. I still want him. And by the look on his face when he glances over at me, he feels the same way.

"Next week…" He says it as much to himself as he does to me. "I already can't wait."

We leave the store together. He locks up, and then as always, he walks me to my car first, parked in the tiny lot. I always get a bit anxious when Jay and I are out in public together, but usually it's only briefly as we're walking to our cars. But today I get this uneasy feeling, like somebody is watching us.

When I get near to my Kia, Jay grabs my arm and leans in to kiss me again. Then he heads off to his own car, back to his home with the crying baby. I climb into my Kia and return to my husband who doesn't love me.

CHAPTER 31

ADDIE

I have a math midterm today and I am so screwed.

I don't understand any of the material. Under the best of circumstances, I usually struggle. When he was still speaking to me, before I made him cover up my father's (accidental) murder, Hudson used to sit with me and patiently explain the material to me. And then later on, Mr. Tuttle did the same. However, it seems like I have systematically isolated everyone who used to offer me free help.

I should ask my mom for a tutor. Mrs. Bennett is not going to slow down her pace for me. But I've been hesitant to ask for a tutor, because money has been tight. Mom has been picking up extra shifts at the hospital, and I overheard her having a scary conversation with the bank about our mortgage payments. So the last thing I want to do is ask her to blow more money on me because I'm too stupid to understand trigonometry.

And even if I get a tutor, that's not going to help me

right now, as Mrs. Bennett is passing back copies of the midterm exam. Nothing can help me now.

I check out the first question, hoping that the test is miraculously much easier than expected. Maybe I'm more prepared than I think. Hey, crazier things have happened.

A swimmer has to retrieve an object 15 feet away from the wall of the swimming pool. If the angle of depression of the object from the pool platform is 30°, find the vertical distance they have to swim in order to retrieve the object.

This isn't hard. I can do this.

Focus, Addie!

As I'm staring down at the test paper in front of me, I can't help but notice that I have a perfect view of Kyle Lewis's test paper. He's sitting just in front of me and to my left, but because he is left-handed, I've got a great view of his paper. And Kyle always gets straight A's in math.

Of course, that would be *cheating*. There's no two ways about it—looking at the test paper of another student would be seriously wrong, and while I have done a lot of bad things in my life, I always thought of myself as the sort of person who would never do that.

Except if I don't, I am definitely going to fail this midterm.

Damn it.

Okay, what if I just look at the answer for a few of the questions? I don't need to copy all of them, just enough to get a passing grade. I mean, it's not like trigonometry is something that will be useful to me in the future. It's not like I'm missing out on some extremely important life skill. Poetry is probably more useful than trigonometry, and that's saying a lot.

Before I can stop myself, I find myself copying down Kyle's answers. Thankfully, they are multiple choice questions, and showing work is not required, although I try to scrawl down a few things because I don't want it to look like… Well, I don't want it to look like I copied the answers off the guy sitting in front of me.

After Mrs. Bennett calls time, I pass my paper up to the front with the rest of the class. Even though most of my answers are correct for a change, I have a sick feeling in the pit of my stomach.

I cheated. I've never done anything like that before.

Maybe deep down, I'm just as bad as my father.

But I need to look on the bright side. I was looking at a failing grade on that exam, and while I didn't copy all of Kyle's answers, because that would've been super suspicious, I'm pretty sure I got enough right to score a B.

As I pack up my belongings, a shadow falls over me. I raise my head, and Kenzie is looking down on me. She sits two seats behind me on the left, and I'd managed to nearly forget she was there, except for the fact that she always manages to kick my backpack when she walks by me. But now she isn't walking by me. She is standing directly over me.

"So, Addie," she says, "did you get a good look at Kyle's paper?"

All the blood drains out of my face. "What?"

"Dude, you were *so* obvious." She rolls her eyes. "I'm sure even Mrs. Bennett saw you staring at his paper. But in case she didn't…"

I realize what she is getting at. Kenzie saw me looking at Kyle's test paper, and she's going to tell on me. If I did something like that to her, I would be tormented for it. But Kenzie can get away with anything.

"Please don't do this." I hate to beg her, but I can't have another scandal at the school. I *can't*. "I wasn't… I mean, maybe just one or two answers, that's it."

She shrugs. "I know what I saw, Addie."

Kenzie strides out of the classroom, going much faster than me with her long, slender legs. She really is just physically so obnoxiously perfect. I can't even blame Hudson for liking her. Even though I hate her.

"Kenzie…" I am huffing and puffing to keep up with her as she walks down the hall, in the opposite direction of my next class. I'm probably going to end up being late, but I need to prioritize. "Please don't talk to Mrs. Bennett. Please. I'll do anything you want."

Kenzie comes to an abrupt halt. She turns to look at me, her blue eyes flashing. "Anything?"

"Yes! Anything."

"Fine." She taps a finger against her teeth. Her nails are painted ice blue. "When we get to English class today, I want you to get down on your hands and knees and lick the floor."

My mouth falls open. "Lick the *floor*?"

She nods. "For sixty seconds."

I don't even know what to say. If it were some other class… Well, I'm not sure I would do it, because, like, gross. But I definitely am not going to lick the floor in front of Mr. Bennett. God, what would he think of me?

"I'm not doing that," I say.

"In that case…" Her eyes twinkle. "I guess Mrs. Bennett and I are going to have a little talk."

"Please, Kenzie," I whimper. "I made a terrible mistake. I've never done anything like that before. I'm *not* a bad person."

"That," Kenzie says, "is debatable."

With those words, she turns away from me, practically smacking me in the face with her long blond hair. Why does Kenzie hate me so much? I never did anything to her. And it doesn't seem like she would do this because of Mr. Tuttle. It must have something to do with Hudson.

Is it possible Hudson told her our secret?

If that's true, I have even worse problems than Mrs. Bennett finding out that I cheated on the trigonometry midterm.

CHAPTER 32

ADDIE

While I am sitting in Mr. Bennett's English class (*not* licking the floor, even though Kenzie keeps shooting me pointed looks), a student enters the room with a folded piece of paper in her hand, interrupting Mr. Bennett right in the middle of discussing a Robert Frost poem. When he raises his eyebrows, the student says, "I have a note for Adeline Severson."

Mr. Bennett takes the note. He opens it up and reads the contents, and his lips turn down. For a moment, his brown eyes meet mine. "Thank you," he says to the student. "I'll make sure she gets it."

I've never wished for superpowers before, but right now, I would give anything for X-ray vision to let me see what is on that piece of paper. But Mr. Bennett puts it down on his desk, and he goes right back to discussing Robert Frost. As if I could concentrate on how nothing gold can stay right now.

Sure enough, as soon as the bell rings, Mr. Bennett

cocks his finger at me. I trudge over to his desk, and he holds out the note to me. I can't stop my hands from shaking slightly as I read the contents:

Adeline,

Please come to my classroom immediately after your last period.

Eve Bennett

Oh no. I can't believe Kenzie told her so quickly.

"What's that all about?" Mr. Bennett asks me, although his voice is gentle. There's a tiny crease between his eyebrows.

"I have no idea," I lie.

Mr. Bennett doesn't look like he believes me, but he doesn't push me further. "If you have any problems, you know you can tell me, right?"

His offer is so nice, I almost burst into tears. But the worst part is that if he knew what I did—that I copied off another student—he would be so disappointed in me. I wouldn't want to get his help for that reason alone. Then again, Mrs. Bennett is his wife. There's no confidentiality here, and if she thinks I did something wrong, she'll tell him all about it. She'll tell *everyone*.

"I'm fine," I say. It's another lie, but whatever.

Mr. Bennett's eyes are on my back as I walk out of the room. I try to tell myself that this could be about something else. The ominous note does not necessarily mean that Mrs. Bennett knows I was copying Kyle's paper. Maybe she just wants to help me with some tutoring suggestions. But then why would she ask to see me "immediately" and have another student send me a note?

When I get to Mrs. Bennett's classroom, she is sitting at her desk and appears to be grading some of the midterm exams. She's gripping her red pen, and her brow is furrowed in concentration. As I watch her, I genuinely can't figure out what Mr. Bennett could possibly see in her. She's attractive enough, but she's got a frown permanently burned into her face. How can he stand it?

"Mrs. Bennett?" I knock gently on the door to her classroom, even though it's already open. "Do you want to see me?"

"Yes." Her lips are a straight line across her face, almost like they have vanished into her mouth. "Have a seat, Adeline."

The fact that she's calling me by my full name is making me nervous. My mother does that too when she thinks I have been behaving badly. But I do what she says, sliding into the desk directly in front of hers.

"So." Mrs. Bennett focuses her attention on me. Her eyes are too small and look beady. "Is there anything you would like to tell me?"

I stare at her. I don't say a word. Whatever Kenzie told her, there's no proof.

When it's obvious I'm not going to confirm or deny anything, she pulls two test papers out from under the pile on her desk and throws them down in front of her. "You copied Kyle's test paper. You are right behind him, you were looking at his paper, and you copied his answers."

I open my mouth to say something, but it feels like

there's something stuck in my throat, and nothing comes out. I can't believe this is happening. I've never cheated in my whole life, and the one time I did it, I get caught, like, an hour later. I have the worst luck.

To be fair, I didn't get caught for killing my dad.

"Well?" Her eyebrows shoot up. "Do you have anything to say for yourself?"

There are still no words coming. What am I supposed to say? I did cheat. I don't want to lie on top of what I've already done. "I'm so sorry," I finally squeak out.

Mrs. Bennett looks completely unmoved. That's no surprise. She reminds me of the wicked witch in one of those Disney movies. All she needs is a cape. "Cheating is an extremely serious matter. Tomorrow morning, I'm going to be discussing this with the principal."

Principal Higgins already does not like me. She used to like me. Well, for the first year and a half I went to Caseham High, she didn't even know who I was, which is probably the best possible situation. The first time I went in to talk to her, she was so kind to me. And now she thinks I'm a troublemaker because of what I did to Mr. Tuttle.

What is she going to do when she finds out I've been cheating on top of everything else?

"You can go," Mrs. Bennett tells me.

I stand up on shaky legs and somehow manage to make it out of her classroom without collapsing. I don't know what is going to happen tomorrow, but it's going to be awful. The principal is going to find out that I copied off Kyle. They're probably going to have to bring in my mother, and then I'm going to see that awful disappointed look on her face.

And maybe worst of all, Mr. Bennett is going to know about it.

I am so furious at Kenzie. She did not have to tell Mrs. Bennett about this. She could have kept her mouth shut. I don't even understand why she hates me so much.

I'm not going to be a doormat anymore. I'm not going to let Kenzie get away with this.

CHAPTER 33

EVE

I'm surprised that when I get home today from the school, Nate is already there waiting for me.

I'm almost always home first. Often, he stays so late that I can't figure out what he's doing there. But today when I get home, he is sitting on the sofa. And when I walk into the living room, he stands up to greet me. He even gives me a kiss.

"How was your day?" he asks.

"Good." I glance over at the kitchen to see if he's got anything cooking in there. "What would you like for dinner tonight?"

"Actually," he says, "I thought we could order something. From anywhere you want."

Nate usually thinks the delivery places are too expensive, and he'd rather have some spaghetti out of the box than get delivery from an Italian restaurant. "That sounds great."

There's a smile playing on his lips. His eyes crawl

down my body, and there's an expression on his face I haven't seen in a long time. "You look nice today, Eve."

Do I? I'm wearing a white blouse with tan slacks. Although I do have on my pair of Manolo Blahniks, which I don't wear all the time, but I needed a boost today. "Thank you."

And then he kisses me again. A long, lingering kiss this time. There is an urgency in his kiss, and a second later, he works the top button free on my blouse.

"Nate," I gasp.

"Let's go upstairs," he breathes in my ear. "Okay?"

I'm not going to say no.

Half an hour later, the two of us are lying breathless in our bed. Nate was so determined to ravage me that I kicked off my Manolos instead of removing them carefully and placing them lovingly back in the closet. The rest of our clothes are strewn about the room. When I look over at Nate, he has a sheen of sweat over his body, and he looks back at me and grins.

"Whew," he says. "That was…"

I nod in agreement. I don't know what changed today, but maybe there is a path back to saving our marriage. Not that I don't care deeply about Jay, but he and I do not have a future together. Nate is the future, for better or for worse.

"Good thing we're ordering in," I say. "I am way too tired to cook."

Nate laughs. "I know."

"We should, you know…" My eyes lock with his. "We should do that more often."

"Absolutely."

I snuggle up next to my husband, and he puts his

arm around me. I rest my head against the muscles in his shoulder, feeling contented with him for the first time in a long time. We do have sex once a month, but it's never like that anymore. It's usually very regimented, like we're brushing our teeth.

This is like back in the old days, when we were first together.

"By the way," Nate murmurs into my hair. "I got this weird note today. It said that you needed to see Addie Severson urgently. Everything okay?"

Addie Severson is the last person I want to talk about when we are relishing in our postcoital bliss, but it feels rude not to answer him. Besides, I want him to know what that girl did. He needs to know what she's capable of.

"Not really," I tell him. "She cheated on her midterm."

He's quiet for a moment. "Cheated how?"

"She was looking at another student's paper. I saw her do it, and then I checked the two papers right after, and the answers were almost identical. That other kid is a stellar student, and there's no way she would have gotten so many right answers on her own."

"Wow. So what are you going to do about it?"

"I'm going to the principal." I'll have to wait till tomorrow morning, but this is the protocol if a student is caught cheating. "I'll let Higgins know what happened, and she can deal with it."

"The principal." Nate shakes his head. "Wow. That's rough. You really have to take it all the way to the principal?"

"I have to. Those are the rules."

"Well," he says thoughtfully as he squeezes my body close to his, "it's not like she did anything nefarious. It's not like she had some cheating scheme that she came up with in advance where she stole a set of answers. She was sitting there during the exam, and she didn't know how to do the math problems, which I can definitely relate to. She panicked."

"She *cheated*, Nate."

"But you don't even have any proof, do you?" He frowns. "You say you saw her copying another paper, but maybe she didn't. Maybe she really studied for it. Did she admit it?"

Technically, Addie did not admit to cheating. But I could *see* her looking at Kyle's paper. After all my years of teaching, it was painfully obvious. Plus, that girl is not capable of getting that kind of grade on her own. And I saw the look on her face when I confronted her. "Not exactly."

"She's struggling." He squeezes me closer to his warm body. "We've all been there, Eve. Didn't you struggle with your English class in high school, and you needed a tutor?"

I don't know what to say to that. It's technically true. "So she could have gotten a tutor. She didn't have to cheat."

"Not every student can afford a tutor. I think we can both agree that Addie has been through a *lot* in the last year."

Under any other circumstances, this conversation would have enraged me. Cheating is wrong, and the fact that my husband would defend a student who copied off another kid is ridiculous. Especially since he seems to have made Addie his little pet project, despite the fact that I warned him about her. But curled up in his arms, I can't work up much anger or even indignation. Nate cares deeply about his students, and I can't fault him for that. It was one of his qualities that made me fall in love with him.

"So what do you suggest?" I say.

"Well," he says, "obviously you can't let her keep the grade, but if you give her a zero and a stern warning, I doubt she'll ever try something like that again. And it will give her a kick in the teeth she needs to pull her act together."

"You think so?" Addie just seems so incredibly hopeless sometimes.

"I definitely do." He kisses the top of my forehead. "I know that deep down, you want her and all your other students to do well. I think this is the best thing for her. You don't want to wreck her life, do you? Even if you are still angry about what happened with Art. You realize that wasn't her fault, right?"

Do I? I suppose he's right. Addie Severson has been through a lot in the last year, and the truth is, I've been hard on her. Maybe because I'm angry that my own mentor lost his job because of her.

"Fine," I agree. "I won't go to the principal. I'll speak to her about it after class and let her know that she's getting a zero, but I won't report her."

"You're doing the right thing, Eve."

He kisses me one more time on the top of the head, and then he rolls out of bed and hits the bathroom. The shower starts running a second later, and my phone buzzes on the nightstand where I left it. I pick it up, and there's a message waiting for me in Snapflash.

Jay: Will I see you tomorrow night?

I look over at the bathroom door, where the shower is still going strong. I've been looking for that kind of passion from Nate for a long time. In so many ways, it was absolutely perfect. Exactly what I wanted, and I'm hopeful there will be more times like it in the future.

And yet something is bothering me about the whole thing.

Maybe I don't love the fact that as soon as it was over, he started talking about Addie. And then jumped right into the shower.

But in the end, it isn't about him at all. It's about the guy on the other end of this conversation. Jay scraped together enough money to buy me a beautiful pair of shoes for my birthday when my own husband got me nothing. I've never had to question if Jay had an ulterior motive. I can see all over his face how much he wants me. So I only have to hesitate a minute before I type a response:

Me: I'll be there.

CHAPTER 34

ADDIE

Kenzie has cheerleading practice until at least five o'clock, maybe later. Her parents with their high-powered jobs won't be home until late as well.

I, on the other hand, have absolutely nothing to do with my time while I wait to find out whether Principal Higgins is going to kick me out of school tomorrow.

I park my bike down the block from Kenzie's house, chaining it to a lamppost. I take my backpack with me as I walk up the street to her large house, the weight of my books causing the straps of my bag to dig into my shoulders. I walk purposefully, like I'm supposed to be here. Like I'm a friend of Kenzie's, coming to visit her.

Even though that couldn't possibly be further from the truth.

I ring the doorbell, waiting for the sound of footsteps. I ring a second time for good measure, but I am met with only silence. Just as I suspected—nobody is home. The house is completely empty.

I glance at the adjacent houses, which look just as dark and silent as the Montgomery house. When I feel confident nobody is watching me, I slip around the side of the house, tromping through the lush green backyard.

When I reach the back door, I dig around in the pouch of my backpack. I pull out the set of keys inside. I ditched the diamond-studded *Kenzie* key ring, but I kept the keys. Of course, it's entirely possible that when Kenzie lost her keys, they decided to change the locks on the door. Then again, she lives in a safe neighborhood. Maybe her parents assumed she dropped her keys somewhere, and it wasn't worth the stress of changing the locks.

Well, either way, we're about to find out.

There are three keys on the ring, but one is larger and looks most like a house key. I take a deep breath and slide the key into the lock. I count to ten in my head, and then I attempt to turn the key.

It turns.

I pause for a moment, listening for the sound of a barking dog. I don't hear anything. So I turn the key the rest of the way in the door, twist the knob, and push inside the kitchen of the Montgomery household.

The first thing I do when I'm inside is look around to see if there is an alarm system. I've seen those before in other people's houses, and what it would mean is that if I don't disarm it, either an alarm will start sounding, or else the police department will be quietly notified. Either way, I don't want that to happen. But I don't see any keypad or signs that the house has an alarm.

Which is stupid on their part, because this house *needs* an alarm. As I step into the Montgomery home, I am taken aback. They have an open floor plan, so from their gleaming new kitchen, I can see the huge expanse of space and expensive furniture in the living room. Our house was built over one hundred years ago, and I doubt the interior has changed much since then. We have had the same refrigerator for my entire life, and I feel like it might outlive me and everybody I care about.

I leave my sneakers by the back door because their carpet is super light in color, and I've already made a few stains on the kitchen floor with my dirty shoes. I creep across the living room, over to the carpeted stairs. And then I start to climb them.

I can't believe I'm doing this. It was bad enough that I cheated on an exam for the first time in my life (and got caught). And now here I am, only a few hours later, breaking into a house, for God's sake. But this whole thing is Kenzie's fault. She didn't have to tell on me to Mrs. Bennett, and she didn't have to do any of the things she's been doing to me all semester. She *deserves* what's coming to her.

When I get to the top floor, the first room I encounter is a bathroom. I step inside, admiring the gleaming white fixtures and the multicolored toothbrushes lined up on the sink counter. Oh my God, is that a seat warmer on the toilet? Would it be weird to try it out?

Yes, it probably would.

For a moment, I stare at myself in the vanity mirror of the sink. This is the same mirror Kenzie uses to look at herself every single day. Except when she looks into this mirror, her reflection shows perfect cheekbones, clear blue eyes, and silky blond hair, rather than my own nondescript features, with mud-colored eyes and hair.

I tap open the medicine cabinet with my index finger. It doesn't surprise me that it's filled with various skin creams and hair products. There are a couple of orange bottles of pills on the top shelf, and I pick up the first one.

Ondansetron. Take one tablet three times a day as needed for nausea.

Before I have a chance to wonder why Kenzie needs to take a pill for nausea, I turn the bottle and see that the prescription is for her older brother. Of course. Kenzie doesn't get nauseous. She's probably never vomited in her whole life.

It doesn't take me long to find Kenzie's bedroom. There are several bedrooms upstairs, but one of them is clearly the master bedroom, the other seems to belong to a teenage boy—her brother, presumably—and Kenzie's is the one with the canopy bed and the large pink jewelry box on the desk. It is for real the nicest kid's bedroom I've ever seen.

I sit down at Kenzie's white desk, sinking into the leather chair. Kenzie sits in this very seat, and she does her homework, and she probably just takes for granted how lucky she is.

I pull open the top drawer of her desk. There's a torn piece of notebook paper stuffed inside with a note scribbled on it: *I can't stop thinking about you. I can't wait to see you tonight.* Ugh, just what I wanted to find—a love note from Hudson. I still can't believe he's dating her.

It was so weird with me and Hudson. When we were younger, I adored him and thought he was cute in a general sort of way with his eager smile and white-blond tousled hair, but I didn't have a crush on him or anything. We played together the way any two kids would, playing Nintendo or doing homework together. When it was summer, we would toss a ball around in his backyard, walk together to the nearest store to get candy, or wriggle under the fence to get into his neighbor's yard to use their swimming pool.

But then when we got to high school, Hudson shot up in height so that he was finally taller than me—a *lot* taller than me—and suddenly, I started thinking about him differently. I started fantasizing what it would be like to kiss him. And I got the feeling he was thinking about me the same way.

Not that it was Kenzie's fault that my best friend stopped speaking to me. That was all because of what happened with my father and what I made Hudson do. But it doesn't make it any less painful to see them together.

I look over at a ceramic figure on her desk. It's a bird, painted light blue and violet. When I pick it up, I can see her initials, KM, etched into the bottom, which means that she made it in ceramics class, even though it looks professional. Kenzie is even amazing at *ceramics*. On a whim, I hurl the bird to the floor, where it shatters into five pieces.

I thought breaking something in her room might make me feel better, but it doesn't. At *all*. And weirdly, I don't feel as upset about her and Hudson as I used to. I still miss Hudson as a friend, but when I fantasize about a guy who I would like to be with, it isn't him anymore.

It's Nathaniel Bennett.

Not that anything could ever happen between me and Mr. Bennett. That is just beyond stupid. But I think about him all the time. At night, when I'm drifting off to sleep, I imagine him smiling at me, his eyes crinkling like they always do. The thought of him finding out about me cheating is so humiliating. There's nothing more important to me than what he thinks of me.

I stand up from the leather chair and walk over to Kenzie's closet. She has a ginormous walk-in closet, because of course she does. I sift through all the sick designer labels she's got stuffed inside. In addition to being pretty and popular, she's also a lot wealthier than most of the kids in the school. It just feels like life isn't fair sometimes, you know?

I pull out a pink top from her closet. The material is soft, and I can tell that it would cling to my chest in all the right places. It's about the right size too. If I took it, she would never even know. I mean, she has about five zillion shirts in this closet. She probably hasn't worn this one in years. Really, I'd be doing her a favor. I'm helping her *declutter*. In fact, I could do even a little bit *more* decluttering here.

And then just as I'm sifting through her shirts, I hear a crash from downstairs.

CHAPTER 35

ADDIE

Someone is home.

Oh my God, this is awful. I thought I was in trouble when I got caught cheating, but this is much worse. The worst thing that could have happened from cheating at school would be to get kicked out of school, and even that was unlikely.

But this is breaking and entering. I could go to jail. Or juvenile detention or whatever. This is a serious crime.

Why did I do this? I had this wild idea about getting revenge on Kenzie, but all I have done is break a stupid ceramic bird and look through her closet. I don't have the guts to get revenge on Kenzie for the things she's done to me.

I freeze, not sure what my next move should be. The noise definitely came from downstairs, so I'm hesitant to go down there and walk right into one of the Montgomerys. But what else can I do?

I could hide. Kenzie's closet is big enough to fit me and half the football team. I can close myself inside and hope that whoever is downstairs goes away, and then I can sneak out. But what if it's Kenzie? Then I'll be trapped in her closet, and it's only a matter of time before I'd be discovered.

Being found in Kenzie's house is bad enough. Being found hiding in her closet would be a nightmare.

No, I've got to get out of here.

I toss the keys into the closet and creep out of Kenzie's bedroom, wondering if I can quickly slip out the back door. If it's Kenzie, I'm screwed. But if it's her parents or her brother, I can pretend she sent me over here. It's not like I look scary in any way.

My heart is jackhammering in my chest as I slowly walk down the stairs. Every few steps, I stop and listen. I don't hear any voices. But there was definitely a crash. And it was loud enough that it couldn't just be the wind or something like that.

Is it possible that at the exact moment I broke into this house, an actual burglar broke in as well?

No, not too likely.

I get to the bottom of the stairs. I still can't see or hear anyone in the house. It feels like the house is empty, even though I did hear that noise. I creep around behind the stairs to the kitchen to return to the back door.

And that's when I see it.

There's a white fluffy cat in the middle of the kitchen, standing beside a pitcher of water that must have been on the counter but is now on the floor. The cat looks up at me and lets out an unapologetic meow.

It was the *cat*.

My whole body sags with relief. I'm not going to get caught for breaking and entering and end up at juvenile hall. Nobody is in this house. Just an entitled cat.

Still, I'm not taking any chances. I grab my sneakers and slip out the back door as quietly as I can, and I close it behind me. I ditched the keys in her closet, so I won't have any temptation to come back.

CHAPTER 36

EVE

Addie comes into my classroom the next day like she's being marched to the electric chair.

I can't help but feel a jab of sympathy for the girl. She has been struggling in my class, and I have known it. Maybe I'm the one at fault for not trying to do more to help her. In the past, when I had other students who struggled the way she has, I offered them tutoring suggestions, which is why I have written down a list of peer tutors who will work with her for a reasonable price.

As soon as the bell rings for class to end, I motion for Addie to come to my desk. She looks like she would rather jump out the window, but she obliges.

"Addie," I say.

She lifts her eyes, which look watery.

"I have decided not to bring this matter to the principal," I tell her.

Her eyes widen. "You…"

"I am giving you a zero on the midterm," I say. That

is a blow that will make it almost impossible for her to pass the class, so if I have any heart, I need to soften it. "And I have made a list of peer tutors. If you bring up your grades significantly by the final, I will drop the midterm grade."

I hold out the list of tutors to Addie, and she takes it with a shaking hand. "Thank you *so* much, Mrs. Bennett. I really appreciate that."

I grunt, knowing that if Nate hadn't been so persuasive last night, I would be marching her to see Higgins now. But he was right. She did what she did because she was desperate, and it wasn't like she planned it in advance. I can let this slide for once. "If it ever happens again..."

"It won't." She looks like she's about five seconds away from getting on her knees and kissing my feet. "I swear. I'm turning over a new leaf."

"Good."

I'm willing to forgive this one lapse in judgment, but I'm not about to become friends with the girl. She's just lucky that Nate sees something in her, because God knows I don't.

CHAPTER 37

ADDIE

I must have swallowed a few too many horseshoe Lucky Charms, because I am having amazing luck.

First I got away with breaking into Kenzie's house.

Then Mrs. Bennett decided she was not going to report what I did to the principal. I didn't even think that was possible, but she was nice to me. She didn't smile, of course—that would be way too much to hope for—but she recommended some cheap tutors that I might be able to afford, and she told me she would drop the zero if I pulled it together by the end of the semester.

And now I am at the meeting of the poetry magazine, and Mr. Bennett thinks the new poem I've been working on for the last two weeks is worthy of being in this issue. I have been so scared Mrs. Bennett would tell him what I did and that he would think less of me, but I guess she didn't tell him, because he is looking at me the same as he always does.

"I love this line," he tells me. "'The blood drains out of my heart with each beat.' What a powerful image."

I look over at Lotus to see if she's listening, but she is looking away. She was so angry about Mr. Bennett entering my poem in that contest rather than hers, she doesn't even speak to me anymore. She doesn't seem interested in being friends, which is saying a lot because Lotus might be the only kid in the school less popular than I am.

The *Reflections* meeting is officially over at 4:30, but the more dedicated members of the magazine usually stick around till five, discussing poems for the magazine and just stuff we read in general that we like. Lotus is the last to leave, slinging her backpack over her shoulder and vacating the room without even saying goodbye. I'm about to follow her when Mr. Bennett says my name.

"Addie," he says. "Hang on."

I freeze, curious to hear what he has to say. I'm even more curious when he walks over and pushes the door to his classroom shut. When we're alone, he raises his eyebrows at me. "So what happened? What did Eve say to you?"

It's strange how he calls her Eve instead of Mrs. Bennett. I mean, obviously he wouldn't call his wife Mrs. Bennett to her face, but it seems like he should call her that around me. But that fact is less significant than the fact that he knows what happened. She must've told him what I did.

God, this is *so* embarrassing.

"Um," I say. "It was...okay."

His voice lowers a notch. "She went easy on you, right? She's not involving the principal?"

I shake my head wordlessly.

He nods in satisfaction. He tugs at his tie, loosening it around his neck until I can see just a little bit of chest hair peeking out. "I told her what a hard time you've had in the last year. I told her to give you another chance to make it up."

It all finally makes sense. I was wondering why Mrs. Bennett suddenly decided to take pity on me. It was because of *him*. He *told* her not to go to the principal.

"You helped me," I blurt out.

"Of course I did, Addie." He smiles at me, his eyes crinkling. "I wasn't about to let my favorite student get kicked out of school. I had to stick up for you."

My head is spinning. Mr. Bennett knows what I did, and he doesn't hate me. Not only that, but I'm his *favorite student*. I almost want to burst into happy tears.

"Thank you," I manage. "Thank you so much."

"Of course," he says. "I only did what was right."

The rush of emotions I feel is almost overwhelming. Before I can stop myself, I throw my arms around Mr. Bennett in a massive hug. My eyes are welling with tears, and I cling to him. I never hugged my dad, not since I was a little girl, and I never even hugged Mr. Tuttle. But I never felt quite this grateful to another person before. He believed in me. He went to bat for me.

Mr. Bennett hugs me back, not pushing me away even as I cling to him. The hug lasts far longer than I intended it to, but I don't want to let go of him, and he doesn't seem to mind either. But then something firm pokes me in the leg. Like a roll of toilet paper.

Oh my God. Is that…?

I leap away from my teacher, horrified. I had hoped

maybe I was mistaken, but when my eyes drop, I can see the telltale bulge in Mr. Bennett's pants. From the look on his face, he realizes exactly what has happened, and he looks completely mortified.

"I am so sorry, Addie!" he cries. He turns away from me, attempting to conceal it, but it's far too late for that. "This is completely... It's unacceptable. I'm so sorry."

"Yes," I say in a small voice.

"It's no excuse," he says in a small voice, "but you have to know that my wife... We have nothing in common anymore. I feel nothing for her. And then I meet you, and it's like... I finally connect with someone for the first time in my life." He hazards a look at me, his face bright red. Even when he is flustered, he is so handsome. "But that's no excuse. *No* excuse. I am just so sorry."

I wish he would shut up and stop apologizing. "Right."

"You should go," he tells me.

I do what he asks of me. I grab my backpack and quietly leave the classroom, although my head is spinning even more than before. As I walk away down the dim hallway, I try to make sense of it all.

Mr. Bennett is the sexiest teacher in the whole school. Everybody knows it. And he's married to a grown woman, who I would assume he has sex with. But for some reason, while I was hugging him, he was getting turned on. By *me*. And then he told me that he's never connected to anyone like he has to me.

The weird part is that I was thinking the exact same thing.

I freeze in the middle of the hallway. I don't know what to do next, but I can't leave right now. I have to figure out what just happened in there. I owe it to both of us.

I turn around and walk back to the classroom. Nobody is around the school anymore. All the clubs have ended, although some of the teams are still meeting outside in the field. Mr. Bennett is sitting at his desk, and when he looks up at me with his soft brown eyes, it feels like the two of us are the only people in the entire school. In the entire *world*.

"Hi," I say.

"Addie." He frowns. "I don't think we should talk about this anymore. Like I said, I am incredibly sorry."

"But I *want* to talk about it."

Mr. Bennett stands up. He can't conceal that he is still turned on. He stares at me across the room. "Close the door," he instructs me.

I do as he says.

I float across the room until I'm standing right in front of him. He's about half a head taller than me, and I have to tilt my head to look up at him. His lips look moist. There were moments with Hudson when I felt a stirring inside me, but never anything like this. This is like that, on steroids.

"I'm trying to resist you," he murmurs. "You have no idea how badly I'm trying."

"You don't have to."

I thought that I would be the one to have to make the first move, so I'm surprised when it is Mr. Bennett who lowers his lips onto mine. It's the first time I have kissed a boy—well, a *man*. At first, it's just his lips on mine. But then a few seconds later, his tongue enters my mouth. I always knew in my head that people kiss with tongue, but I never imagined how it would feel. At first, it feels super weird, like some alien object worming its way inside me, and I'm not sure I like it. I almost want to pull away, but he's holding me tight, close to his body, and also, it would be lame to pull away. He'd be so disappointed.

And then, after a few more seconds, my body starts to tingle. And it's…incredible. My whole body feels like it's on fire, like it's an explosion. I don't want it to ever stop, but then he pulls away.

"This is wrong," he says.

That makes me angry. Yes, he's my teacher, and he's a lot older than me. And married. Okay, that sounds bad. But at the same time, we connect. When two people connect on the same level we do, don't they have a *responsibility* to do something about it, no matter what the circumstances? "I don't think it's wrong," I say.

"It is." His brows bunch together. "But I can't resist you. I'm helpless."

I can't resist you. I'm helpless.

My only fear is that we could get caught. Look at what happened to Mr. Tuttle, and nothing like this even went on with him. But maybe that's the difference. Mr. Tuttle and I weren't doing anything wrong, so we weren't careful. But Mr. Bennett and I will be careful.

Like he's reading my mind, Mr. Bennett looks anxiously at the door. "We shouldn't do this here."

"I know a place."

He looks surprised, but he follows me dutifully out the door to the classroom. There is a place in the school that nobody else knows about where two people could be alone. I took photography last year as an elective, and the class was all digital, but it didn't used to be. There's a darkroom set up next to the classroom that kids used to use to develop photos, but now it's just a small empty room with a large sink and old chemicals. Maybe someday it will be repurposed for something, but now it's a haven of privacy.

I close the door behind us.

"You're really something, Addie," he breathes.

He loosens his tie and undoes the first button on his collar as my heart skips a beat. He's not going to take off his shirt, is he? The thought of it makes me uneasy, but thankfully, he stops after that first button.

"I'm glad you like the room, Mr. Bennett," I say.

He grins at me. "You don't need to call me Mr. Bennett when we're in here."

"Oh." I feel stupid. Obviously, if we are going to be making out in the darkroom, I shouldn't be calling him Mr. Bennett. "Nathaniel then?" It feels so strange saying his first name. Even after kissing him, saying "Mr. Bennett" feels more normal to me.

He grins at me. "Most people call me Nate. But it's your choice."

"I like Nathaniel," I say thoughtfully.

"Okay," he agrees. "And how about you? Do you prefer Adeline?" His smile widens. "Sweet Adeline..."

I have always hated the name Adeline, but I like the way it sounds on his lips. *Sweet Adeline...*

Except it's not really true, is it? There's nothing sweet about what we're doing in this darkroom. "I prefer Addie."

"You got it." He cocks his head at me. "Back in the classroom, was that...was that your first kiss?"

My face burns. I hate for him to think of me as being inexperienced, but I don't want to lie to him. I get the feeling he knows when I'm telling the truth.

"You just seemed uncomfortable at first," he says quickly.

For real? That is *not* what I wanted to hear, even though he's technically right. "Was I bad at it?"

"No. *No.* You were amazing." He shakes his head. "And it doesn't matter if it was your first kiss or not. Forget I asked that. I just… I feel bad. I don't want you to do anything you don't want to do."

I tilt my chin up to him. "I want to do this."

He hesitates for another split second, considering my answer. Then he pushes me against the table used to place developed photos, and he kisses me again.

CHAPTER 38

ADDIE

We spend the next forty minutes in the darkroom, and then Mr. Bennett—I mean, Nathaniel—drives me home after. It's a bit risky, but if he doesn't drive me home, I'm going to be late, and my mom is going to totally freak if she gets home from her shift and I'm not there. So it's a risk we need to take.

As we drive home, I can't stop thinking about what happened in that darkroom. The way Mr. Bennett—I mean, *Nathaniel*—touched me. The feel of his lips on mine set every single nerve in my body on fire. And really, all we did was kiss. He didn't even try to do more than that. He told me he wasn't going to. This is all I dreamed of doing with him.

That's how sweet he is. He doesn't care if all we do is kiss. He just wants to be with me because we have this connection.

When we stop at a red light, he reaches over and takes my hand in his. He flashes me a nervous look. "Is this okay?" he asks.

I squeeze his hand back to show him it is. "Yes."

His shoulders relax. "Sorry, this is… It's new territory for me. Honestly, I feel like a bad person. I'm your teacher…"

"I was the one who made the first move," I point out. "You told me to go away."

He lets out a long sigh, taking his eyes briefly off the road to look over at me. "I married Eve because it was expected of me to settle down. I never met anyone genuinely special before. And now I'm thirty-eight, and I'm meeting my soulmate for the first time, and she's only sixteen." He grimaces. "How cruel is this universe?"

He just called me his soulmate. It's wild because I feel the exact same way, but I would have thought I was imagining it if he hadn't said it. "You can't help who you form a connection with. Right?"

"Believe me, I wish everyone thought about it the way you did. But they're not going to understand."

He's right. If anyone finds out about this, he would get fired. And I'm pretty sure my life would get much worse as well. "I won't tell anyone."

"You have no idea how much your presence in my life has changed me," he says. "Before you came along, I was completely blocked. And now I'm writing poetry again! For the first time in a long time."

That's incredible. Especially because all I want to do is write poems about Nathaniel Bennett. I want to fill a whole notebook with verses about the way the lines crinkle around his eyes. "Will you show me one of your poems?"

"It's all I want to do." He smiles. "Eve…she has no interest in my poetry. She never did. Everything with her has to be practical, and she thinks poetry is such a waste."

I never liked Mrs. Bennett, and now I almost feel like I hate her. Nathaniel loves poetry—what kind of wife wouldn't be supportive of that?

Nathaniel pulls up on the curb a full block away from my house. "I don't think I should get closer than this."

I nod, knowing he's right. I hate that we have to hide, but there's also something exciting about it. "It's fine."

"Addie…" He reaches out to touch my face, and he pulls away at the last second. "You can't tell anyone about this. Not a soul. Not your mom, not your friends—nobody."

"I won't."

"I mean it." He stares at me through the shadows in his car. "My entire career is in your hands. I'm counting on you."

He had pulled his hand away during the drive, and I reach out to take it now. "You can trust me."

I can tell how badly he wants to kiss me, but we both understand the wisdom of not kissing in a car in the middle of the street, even under the cloak of darkness. We can steal moments in the darkroom, but that's it. Anything else would be too big a risk.

But maybe it won't always be that way. Maybe there will be a time in the future when we can be together.

CHAPTER 39

EVE

I am grading test papers on the living room sofa when Nate comes home.

The front door slams, and a second later, he is standing in front of me in the middle of the living room. "Hey," he says.

"Hey." I smile at him briefly, then go back to grading papers. I'm leaving to meet Jay in an hour, and I'm hoping to get through a large chunk of the midterms. "Don't forget I'm going out tonight."

Nate plops down next to me on the sofa. He smiles at me—he looks so dazzlingly handsome when he smiles. "What are you doing?"

"Grading midterms."

He tugs the stack of papers out of my hands. "Feel like taking a break?"

"What?"

I genuinely don't know what he's talking about until I see the look on his face. He tosses my exam papers on the coffee table and grabs me, pushing me down onto the sofa. His lips descend on mine, and he kisses me roughly.

"Whoa!" I struggle to get out from under him. "Nate, I'm in the middle of something!"

"So what?" He silences my protest with another kiss. "You can do that later."

This is so wild. Usually, we have sex, like, a dozen times the entire year, and now suddenly he wants me two days in a row. And his behavior seems strange. It almost feels like he's *hungry* for me, like he's ready to rip my clothing off, which is unusual for him. I haven't seen this kind of passion from him in so many years.

I don't know what's going on. Does he have a brain tumor? Because that's the only thing I can think of to explain this.

I would probably go to the bedroom with him if I didn't have plans for tonight. But the truth is, I'm looking forward to seeing Jay. I don't want to cancel, although I've never had a dilemma like this before.

"Nate." I forcibly push him off me. "Maybe…could we do this another time? I want to get through these papers before I go out…"

"Seriously?"

"Yes!"

Nate looks at me in disbelief as he allows me to disentangle myself from his embrace. "I don't get you, Eve. You are always whining that we don't have sex enough, and now I want to do it, and you're pushing me off you."

"Nate…"

"No, forget it." He climbs off me, a scowl on his lips. "I'll take care of it myself then."

I jump off the couch, calling his name as he storms off. The bedroom door slams upstairs, and now I'm the one staring in disbelief.

What on earth was that all about?

CHAPTER 40

ADDIE

The meetings of *Reflections* used to be the best part of my day, but now all I want is for it to be over so that I can sneak off with Nathaniel to the darkroom.

"This whole poem," Lotus says to me. "It's too... sappy."

"Sappy?" I repeat. The poem she's looking at is one that I wrote while thinking about Nathaniel. It's a love poem, but I didn't think it was sappy.

Your eyes are brown
like freshly fallen
autumn leaves
I crave your embrace
in the misty night
I see you every day
But when I can't be with you
I long to be in your arms
My love for you is like

a black hole
It is so deep
and I can't stop falling

"Yeah." She crinkles her nose. "I mean, look at this. 'My love for you is like a black hole.' Seriously, Addie? It sounds like some lovesick teenage girl wrote it. You don't usually write shit like this."

I snatch the poem away from her, my face on fire. I had been considering showing Nathaniel the poem today, but now I'm not so sure. I didn't think it was sappy. I didn't think it made me sound like a lovesick teenage girl. But then again, Lotus knows her stuff.

"I'm just trying to help," Lotus says. "You need to have thick skin if you want to be a writer. People are going to tell you way worse stuff than that."

"Yeah…" I look across the room, where Nathaniel is talking to another student. He notices me watching him, and he flashes a ghost of a smile. "I guess you're right."

She looks down at her watch, noting that it's 4:30 now. The meeting is just about over. Thank God. "Hey," she says. "You want to go grab some pizza?"

It's the first olive branch Lotus has extended to me in a long time. Except I don't want it. Becoming friends with Lotus would make it harder for me to meet up with Nathaniel. And no friendship is worth jeopardizing that.

"I have to be home for dinner," I tell her.

"Oh. Okay." Lotus looks disappointed, which surprises me. I thought she hated me. "Well, let's go then."

She grabs her bag, swings it over her shoulder, and waits for me. Except I can't leave with Lotus. I'm not missing my opportunity to be with Nathaniel.

"Actually," I say, "I need to talk to Mr. Bennett about something real quick. Maybe I'll catch up with you later."

Lotus gives me a funny look, but she doesn't push me further. She doesn't really have interest in being friends with me.

I let her leave first, but I don't wait for Nathaniel. I leave the classroom and go directly to the darkroom. After all, it would look suspicious if we keep sneaking in there together.

While I wait for him, I smooth out the creases on my shirt and run my fingers through my hair. The last time we were in here, which was our third time, I took off my shirt, but I was kind of embarrassed about my bra. It was this tan-colored utilitarian bra that was basically the opposite of sexy. I wish I could take off my shirt and be wearing something cute and lacy, but I don't own anything like that. And it's not like I can get my mom to buy me a sexy bra. If I even asked for it, she would probably ground me on the spot.

Mostly, we have just kissed and he put his hands on my breasts. Other times, we will just talk, and sometimes he recites poetry for me. He knows so many poems by heart, including his personal favorite, "The Raven." He is super patient with me, and he keeps telling me that we don't have to do anything I don't want to do. He just wants to be with me. He told me it was okay if we never had sex. I think we probably will someday, but I love that he is so patient.

While I'm waiting, my phone buzzes inside my jeans pocket. I pull it out and notice a message waiting for me in Snapflash. A lot of kids use Snapflash so their parents won't invade their privacy and read all their text messages, but I only use it to communicate with one other person: Nathaniel. It was his idea, because the text messages disappear after sixty seconds. It's the safest way to communicate.

I read the message that he sent to me:

Nathaniel: Just finishing up. Will be there in two minutes.

I stare at the message until it disappears from the screen. I love the messages he sends me. Every time I get one, I read it and reread it for the entire sixty seconds.

After the message vanishes, I take out the poem I wrote for Nathaniel and read it one more time. Lotus said it was sappy, but I don't think it is. It really does feel like my love for Nathaniel is this endless black hole. Lotus just doesn't understand because she has never been in love. Really, I feel sorry for her.

The door to the darkroom cracks open, and I get that jolt of excitement like I always do practically anytime I see Nathaniel. But especially in here because I know he's going to touch me. And I love the way his face lights up when he sees me.

"Addie," he breathes. "My sweet Adeline."

"Hi." I always feel weirdly shy when he comes in here. It takes me a few minutes to warm up. "How are you?"

"Really good now that I'm here." He crosses the small space and wastes no time in kissing me. Good thing *he* doesn't get shy. "And there's something I want to show you."

"What is it?"

In the dim light, his cheeks color. "I wrote a poem—for you."

This absolutely takes my breath away. He wrote a poem for me? How could that be? I'm not the kind of person who men write poems for. And yet he means it. Nathaniel Bennett wrote me a poem.

I'm going to faint from happiness.

"Do you want to hear it?" he asks, now shy himself. I nod. "Very much."

He pulls a scrap of notebook paper from his pocket. I recognize his handwriting now, and I can see the scribbles on the page. Words he wrote just for me. I listen in rapt attention as he recites the verses:

Life nearly passed me by
Then she
Young and alive
With smooth hands
And pink cheeks
Showed me myself
Took away my breath
With cherry-red lips
Gave me life once again

When he finishes the last line, I can barely breathe myself. It's such a beautiful poem. Nobody has ever written anything like that for me before. Hudson was my friend, but he was no poet. Even if something had happened between the two of us, he never would have written anything like that for me.

"I love it," I whisper. "So much."

"I mean it," he says softly. "You gave me my life back.

You have no idea how dreary my world was before you came along."

He laces his fingers into mine, and we just stand like that for a moment, staring at each other. I can't even bear to show him what I wrote for him after hearing his beautiful verses. It seems so stupid and immature by comparison. I'll have to keep working on it. Until I write something worthy of him.

"I think about you all the time." He reaches out to tuck a strand of hair behind my ear. "Do you think about me?"

"Every moment of the day," I answer truthfully.

He kisses me again, and he starts tugging my shirt off. He did this last time, so I expected it. But what I don't expect is the way he attempts to unbutton my jeans. I take a step back and smile apologetically, but he doesn't catch my eye—he is wholly focused on getting my jeans open. I take another step back, this time bumping into the table behind me, and now there's nowhere to go. Nathaniel successfully gets the button open and then lowers the zipper as I suck in a breath.

He raises his eyes to look up at me. "You are the most beautiful girl I've ever met, Addie."

I hold in that breath as he tugs down my jeans and then my panties. But I don't tell him not to do it, because…well, how can I? Yes, he told me he didn't care about sex, but I knew on some level it couldn't be true. I'm not totally stupid.

I lose my virginity to Nathaniel in the darkroom that afternoon, and the whole time, I recite his poem in my head, written just for me.

Life nearly passed me by

Then she
Young and alive
With smooth hands
And pink cheeks
Showed me myself
Took away my breath
With cherry-red lips
Gave me life once again

CHAPTER 41

ADDIE

Even though English is my favorite class, it's gotten harder and harder to pay attention.

When I look at Nathaniel—who I have to call *Mr. Bennett* when we are in class together—all I can think about is how it feels when he touches me. I am counting down the seconds until we can be together in the darkroom.

It used to be that when we were in class together, Nathaniel would smile or wink at me. It made me feel like he thought I was special. He's careful not to do that anymore, and even though I understand why, it still drives me wild when he winks or smiles at other girls. We don't communicate at all during school hours anymore, except in the most professional way. If there's something he wants to tell me, he sends me a message through a Snapflash, which vanishes after sixty seconds.

I can't wait until we're alone. It's been over three weeks since we began sneaking off together to the darkroom—nearly every day. On the days he works at the school newspaper, I go to the library and do my homework while I wait for him to be done. I suggested joining the paper myself, but Nathaniel said it was a bad idea. He said the more time we spend together in front of other people, the more likely it is that they will catch on.

Ever since that first time we made love in the darkroom, we have done it every single time. Pretty much the first thing he does when we get inside the room is start kissing me and pull down my pants, sometimes before we've even said two words to each other. It was stupid to think all we would do is kiss. It makes him so happy. I enjoy it too, but it thrills me most how much he likes it. He says that he and Mrs. Bennett don't have sex anymore. That they haven't in a long time.

While I sit in English class, struggling to focus on the lesson, an announcement blasts over the loudspeaker. I recognize Principal Higgins's voice.

"Attention!" she calls out. "I want to offer a big congratulations to the winner of the Massachusetts poetry award, from our very own Caseham High…"

I sit up straight, my heart pounding. That is the poetry contest that Nathaniel entered me in. The one where he chose my poem out of all the others to feature. He was only allowed to choose one, so if the winner is from our school, that means that I won. I actually won a prestigious statewide poetry contest!

The principal continues, "We would like to congratulate Mary Pickering!"

What?

Mary Pickering? That's *Lotus*. But he didn't enter Lotus in the competition—that's why she was so upset.

So I don't understand. How could she have won if he didn't even enter her?

I look over at Nathaniel, but he is looking away. It's like he's refusing to catch my gaze.

If I couldn't concentrate before, it's about a thousand times worse now. I don't understand what happened. He *told* me he entered me in that contest. Was he lying?

No, Nathaniel would never lie to me. We know each other too well for that. Except I can't come up with another explanation.

I try to catch him after the bell rings, but he takes off like a flash, and I'm left behind, my head still spinning. We're supposed to meet after he's done with the school paper, but I can't wait that long. So I grab my phone and sent him a message in Snapflash:

Me: What happened? I thought you entered me in that contest?

Thankfully, his reply comes soon after:

Nathaniel: I promise I'll explain everything when we meet.

I stare at the words on the screen, which don't explain anything. But at least he admits he has explaining to do.

On top of that, he ends up being twenty minutes late for our liaison in the darkroom. I stand there waiting for him, getting more and more irritated, and when the door finally opens, I'm ready to jump out of my skin.

"Addie." He reaches for my hands to try to bring me

close to him. "I am so glad to see you. It's been a long day."

When he touches me, I usually melt into his embrace, but this time, I resist. I am angry at him, damn it. He owes me an explanation. "What happened with that poetry contest, Nathaniel? You told me you entered my poem."

"I know, and I am so incredibly sorry." He hangs his head. "You have to know, you were my first choice. I loved your poem, and I think you would have won easily. But Lotus went to the principal and complained that I had chosen a poem written by a junior, when traditionally seniors are entered in the contest. I wanted to fight for you, but given my feelings for you, I was worried it was a conflict of interest. And you have a chance to be in the contest next year, but this was Lotus's last shot."

I have spent most of the past two hours being furious at Nathaniel, but now I realize that was misguided. Lotus was the one who went to the principal to complain. That is *so* low, especially considering her recent attempts at friendship.

"I'm so sorry." He places his hands on my cheeks, drawing my face to his. "I should have fought for you. I was just scared that the second I said your name to the principal, she would see through me and know how deeply I care for you."

Despite everything, his words warm my heart. He cares for me—*deeply*.

"It's okay," I finally say. "It's not your fault. I understand the position you were in."

"Oh, thank God." His shoulders sag. "I thought you

were angry at me and would never forgive me. I was going out of my mind, thinking that when I got here, you might not be here."

"I wouldn't do that."

He presses his lips against mine, and it makes every part of me spark with electricity. I never knew that kissing another person could be like this. I bet Nathaniel never knew it either. He talks a lot about how hard it is being married to somebody who he never felt any connection to and how being with me is like something he has never experienced before.

"You have become so important to me, Addie," he breathes when his lips separate from mine. "We love with a love that is more than love. With a love that the winged seraphs of heaven coveted."

"Annabel Lee" has been my favorite poem for many years, but I've never felt the words so deeply. After all, I have no other thought than to love and be loved by him. It almost frightens me how head over heels I am for Nathaniel. He's already my first thought when I wake up in the morning and the last thing I think about as I'm falling asleep. When I write poetry these days, it is always about him. I am so in love with this man.

"I only wish I could've met you back when I was sixteen," he murmurs. "How unfair is the universe? I finally meet my other half, and I am two decades older than you."

"At least we've found each other now," I point out. "That's more than a lot of people get."

"Very true."

We don't have a lot of time before both of us have to get home, and there's always the fear of being discovered, so usually we get right to it. It doesn't last long, and Nathaniel says that's normal when you like somebody as much as he likes me. I think of how happy I've been making him and the fact that he is so miserable at home, with his wife. She can't make him happy the way I do. And she's always nagging him to get home, so we can't stick around and talk like we want to.

Not that things would be super easy even if he weren't married. My mother would still get suspicious if I got home too late, and nobody at school could find out, of course. But if he weren't married to Mrs. Bennett, I could go to his house and we could have sex in an actual bed instead of this uncomfortable darkroom. The idea of having sex with Nathaniel in a bed seems so exciting and grown-up.

Plus, eventually I will graduate from high school, and I will get to date whoever I want. But if Nathaniel is still with his wife, he will be trapped.

If only Mrs. Bennett weren't around. It would be so much better.

CHAPTER 42

ADDIE

While I am sitting in the cafeteria, all alone as usual, Kenzie spills my entire lunch on the floor.

To somebody not watching carefully, it looks like an accident. She passes by my table and knocks into my tray, and it falls on the floor. But that's not what happens. As she's walking by, Kenzie grabs my tray, slides it out so it's sticking off the table, then lets it drop to the floor.

And the worst part is that lunch today is chili. French fries and hot dogs would've been bad enough, but now there's a big pile of ground beef and soggy beans all over the floor that I have to clean up, because absolutely nobody will help me.

"Oh my," Kenzie says as her friends giggle. "Sorry about that! But, Addie, you really need to be a little bit more careful about putting your tray so close to the edge of the table."

I glare at her as I jump out of my seat and snatch my

tray off the floor. I have some napkins on the table, but it's obviously not going to be enough.

As I'm crouched on the ground, Kenzie picks up the notebook I had on the table. She is reading a piece of paper on top of the notebook, and my stomach sinks. That piece of paper contains the poem that Nathaniel wrote just for me. I had a hard morning, and I knew I wasn't going to see him later because Mrs. Bennett is making him come home early for some stupid dinner, and it makes me feel good to have a piece of him with me. So I was reading it over and over and over until my eyes felt like they were going to bleed.

"What is *this*?" Kenzie blurts out. She shakes the piece of paper violently enough to crumple it.

"Nothing." I snatch the poem out of her hands before she does any serious damage. "It's just a poem."

"Who wrote it?"

I would love to tell her that Nathaniel Bennett is the author of the poem, and he wrote it for me because I am the first person who has inspired him in many years. But of course, I can't tell her that. So I just say, "I don't know. I copied it out of a book."

She narrows her eyes at me. "You should get that mess cleaned up. And like I said, next time be more careful."

As Kenzie and her friends walk away, laughing to each other, I look down at the piece of notebook paper in my hand. I wince at the smudge of chili in the corner of the page. It would have killed me if she did anything to damage this poem. I read it at least four or five times a day, even though I have memorized it by now.

Life nearly passed me by
Then she
Young and alive
With smooth hands
And pink cheeks
Showed me myself
Took away my breath
With cherry-red lips
Gave me life once again

I imagine him writing these words on the page and thinking about me. I look at it so many times, the paper is getting torn and now has a smudge of chili on it, but if I photocopy it, it won't be the same. It won't be the same paper he wrote on himself when he was thinking about me.

After I use about a gazillion paper towels to clean up the mess on the floor, I get back in line for attempt number two at lunch. I don't have time to deal with another plate of chili, but I could grab a sandwich and eat it in the hallway on my way to math class. I barely got any of that chili in my stomach before Kenzie spilled it, and I skipped breakfast this morning. So I've got to eat something.

At least the lines have cleared out, because there's less than ten minutes left in the lunch period. I grab one of the wrapped turkey sandwiches, which I don't really like, but my options are limited at this point. I bring it to the cash register, and the lunch lady tells me it costs two dollars.

I dig into my jeans pocket and pull out my wallet. I have exactly one dollar bill.

"I only have a dollar," I tell the lunch lady.

She looks utterly unsympathetic. "Sorry, the sandwich is two dollars."

"Can I pay you tomorrow?"

"I'm afraid not."

Great. I have eaten exactly two spoonfuls of chili all day, and now I've got to go and try to learn math. But the worst part is that I won't get to see Nathaniel later. I could deal with anything if I knew I had that to look forward to. He looked as miserable as me when he told me he had to come home early to help his wife with dinner. Apparently, they're having some friends over, although he added, "They're really *her* friends."

I look longingly at the turkey sandwich, my eyes welling with tears. I can't believe I'm about to cry over a turkey sandwich. I feel slightly ridiculous. But I am really, *really* hungry.

"Here's the dollar, Vera."

An arm brushes past me, holding out a dollar bill. I look up, and it's Hudson, his white-blond hair as messy as always. My mouth hangs open.

"Oh," I say. "Um, you don't have to…"

"Yes, I do," he says in that way he does that makes me know I can't argue with him. "You have to eat lunch."

Vera accepts his dollar, and now the sandwich is mine, free and clear. "I'll pay you back," I promise him.

"It's a dollar."

Except a dollar isn't just a dollar to him, probably not even now. Hudson's family was always scrimping for money. If he wanted an allowance, he had to go out and earn it with part-time jobs. Even in grade school, Hudson was always shoveling snow, raking leaves, and mowing lawns for everyone on his block.

Still, there's no point in arguing with him. "Thank you," I say. Although I can't help but add, "You better not tell Kenzie about that."

He doesn't respond. Instead, he says, "Are you okay, Addie?"

"I'm good," I say, and it's closer to being true than it's ever been in the past. Hudson was my best friend, and I'm itching to tell him that I'm in love for the first time ever, but I can't do that. I can't tell anyone this secret. "How about you?"

"Good," he says, and there's a catch in his voice that makes me wonder if it's a lie.

But before I can say another word, the bell rings. Lunch is officially over, so I'm going to be eating this sandwich to go. "See you later, Hudson," I say. "Thanks for the sandwich."

He opens his mouth as if to say something else, but before he can, I dash off in the direction of math class. I'm hoping to arrive with at least a few minutes to eat my sandwich before class starts.

By some miracle, I land in my seat right before the next bell is set to ring. My stomach lets out a little growl, and I put my sandwich down on the desk and unwrap it. I have about two and a half minutes left to devour this.

"Addie!" Mrs. Bennett's sharp voice interrupts me before I can take a bite. "No food in my classroom. Put that away."

"I just need to finish this sandwich," I explain.

There is a smattering of giggles, but Mrs. Bennett does not look amused. Not that I was trying to be amusing. I just want my freaking sandwich. "Put it *away*, Addie."

"But I didn't have lunch!"

"Whose fault is that?" She sighs loudly. "The bell is going to ring any second. Put the sandwich away."

I weigh my options, trying to figure out if it's worth it to gobble down the sandwich even if she's yelling at me not to. If I do it after she scolded me, she'll probably send me to the principal. And I'm already skating on thin ice with Mrs. Bennett. Because of that zero on the midterm, she has every right to fail me, and even though I've been going to tutoring sessions, a miracle isn't going to happen here. If I pass the class, it will be with a D.

Mrs. Bennett is legitimately a terrible person, and I'm not saying that just because of my relationship with Nathaniel, although he has told me a lot of things about her that have made me like her even less.

She's a terrible cook.

She hardly ever smiles at him or says anything kind.

She has this obsession with shoes. He says she's constantly buying expensive shoes, even though they can't afford it. Even if he did divorce her someday, he wouldn't have any money left because she has spent it all on shoes. And the weird part is her shoes aren't even that nice! They're, like, just ordinary shoes.

And now she won't let me eat my lunch.

The bell hasn't even rung yet, and if she had just let me eat, that turkey sandwich would be in my belly right now. Instead, my insides feel completely hollow, and I don't know how I'm going to concentrate. She didn't care about that though. Not that I would expect it.

I asked Nathaniel once if he would consider leaving her. He said it would be difficult. He said it would be very unlikely that she would let him go. He said he thinks he might be stuck with her for the rest of their lives.

I wish it didn't have to be this way, believe me, he told me. *I wish I could be with you all the time instead of her.*

It's not fair. It's not fair that such a terrible woman is married to the greatest guy I've ever met, and she doesn't even appreciate him. Yet she'll never let him go.

Honestly, I hate Mrs. Bennett.

CHAPTER 43

EVE

Dinner with Shelby and her husband seemed like a good idea when we scheduled it, but I had a miserable time.

When I first started working at the high school, Shelby and I were close. But since then, she married a wealthy tech genius husband, and now she's got a three-year-old son who is all that she can talk about. Throughout the meal, Justin couldn't keep his hands off Shelby, which brought more attention to the fact that Nate didn't seem to even want to touch me. The only positive is that at least Nate isn't balding like Justin is, although I actually find bald heads sort of sexy.

So I am incredibly glad when Shelby says she has to get back for the babysitter and declines dessert. Nate looks relieved as well, although he was doing a great job holding up his end of the conversation. One thing the two of us apparently agree on is that we hate socializing.

I walk Shelby and her husband to the door, and the two of us linger on the porch to say our private goodbyes while Justin goes ahead and starts the car. Shelby reaches out to give me a hug, even though I don't feel in a hugging mood right now. I'm just waiting for her to leave.

"That was so fun," Shelby gushes. "Honestly. We should do it again soon."

"Definitely," I lie.

"I better get going." She looks down at her watch. "The babysitter kicks up such a fuss if we're late. You're so lucky you don't have to deal with that. Although I bet you will soon!" She giggles. "How is that going anyway?"

I wish more than anything that I hadn't told Shelby that I was going off my hormonal birth control last year. (Jay and I use a condom, because I don't even want to contemplate *that* situation.) I did think I would probably get pregnant fairly soon, and it's a tribute to how little sex we have had that we are still child free. Or maybe my womb is simply withered and dried up. Who knows?

And it doesn't look like our sex life is improving. I had that glimmer of hope when Nate was up for it two days in a row, but ever since then, we have gone through our worst drought yet. The first Saturday of the month came along, and Nate complained his bad back was acting up. I'm starting to wonder if we will ever have sex again.

"No luck yet," I tell Shelby.

She purses her lips. "Maybe you should see a doctor? They have those infertility specialists, right?"

I don't need a doctor with lots of fancy degrees to tell me that intercourse is required to conceive a child. "Yes, maybe we will."

Shelby hugs me one more time, and then she hurries to her car to take her back to her perfect life. And I am left watching her drive away.

As soon as the headlights of their Mercedes disappear into the distance, all the tension drains out of my body. Thank God she's gone. And despite all her big talk about future dinners, she hates leaving her son at night, so I'm off the hook for at least another six months.

Tomorrow is garbage day, so I go back into the house to empty the refuse from our meal tonight, and I grab the garbage bins and haul them out to the curb. It's a perfect end to my glamorous evening.

Just as I get to the curb, I get this strange feeling. A prickling in the back of my neck, like somebody is watching me. I turn around and look up at the window to our bedroom to see if Nate is up there, but I don't see him.

And then I hear a loud thump.

I take a step back, scanning our front lawn, my heart pounding. I don't see anyone there, but I definitely heard a noise. Could it have been a wild animal? I've seen rabbits hopping around the yard, but that sounded awfully loud for a rabbit.

"Hello?" I call out.

I'm wearing a dress, which means I have no pockets. My phone is back in the house, and there isn't anything that could serve as a weapon in the vicinity. The only thing I could use would be my stiletto heels, although I'd rather a mugger take me down than wreck my pumps. I did take a self-defense class once, although sometimes I worry all it did was give me a false sense of confidence. If someone really did attack me, they could overpower me easily.

I eye the front door to my house. It's probably less than twenty feet from where I'm standing. I could run.

And then I see the rustling in the bushes.

There's something there. It's no animal—I clearly see a shadow of a fully grown person. Someone is lurking in our bushes, and here I am, standing out on the curb in our quiet cul-de-sac in nothing but a scrap of a dress—a sitting duck.

I consider screaming, but it occurs to me that if I do so, it might make the situation worse. Perhaps the intruder will feel a need to attack me to quiet me down. I glance behind me at the nearest house—its lights are out. If I scream, will somebody notice before the attacker descends on me?

I can't take that chance.

I count to five in my head. As soon as I reach five, I take off running in the direction of my front door. The heel of my right stiletto nearly catches on the front steps, but I miraculously manage to right myself. The rustling sound gets louder, and I reach for the doorknob with a trembling hand. And it doesn't turn.

No.

I didn't lock it, did I? I don't even have my keys. Unless Nate locked it when I left the house. But why would he do that?

Why would my own husband lock me out of the house?

I twist harder, and this time, the knob does turn. Thank God—it was just stuck. I push my way into the house, and before I slam my front door closed, I catch a glimpse of a figure darting across my front yard. And for a moment, I can make out her face in a slice of moonlight.

It's Addie Severson.

CHAPTER 44

EVE

I have never been quite this panicked in my entire life. I even removed my stilettos so that I can properly pace across the bedroom. This must be my twentieth lap, and I don't feel any better.

"Are you sure it was her?" Nate asks me.

As soon as I got back into the house, I scurried up to the bedroom and told Nate what I saw outside. He is not upset enough to pace. He is not even concerned enough to climb out of bed. He is not the least bit perturbed that my student was crouched in the bushes outside our house. He thinks it was all in my head.

"I know what I saw, Nate." I stop pacing to turn and glare at him. "Addie was in the bushes. She was watching me. *Stalking* me."

"Why would she do that?"

I clench my fists. I recognize that Nate does not have the same sort of contentious relationship that I have with that girl, but I'm getting awfully sick of him defending her. I should've followed my instinct and dragged her to the principal when I found out she cheated on the midterm. I should have nipped the whole thing in the bud.

"She hates me," I say.

He laughs. "Come on. Why would she hate you?"

"I can see it in her eyes." I saw the flash of anger earlier today when I made Addie put away that sandwich. She was upset, but what am I supposed to do? Allow students to turn my classroom into the cafeteria? I can't compete with the sound of crunching potato chips. "She's a teenage girl and she's got raging hormones. I already caught her cheating, and she's never prepared for my class. Every time I call on her, she scowls at me."

"She *scowls*?" Nate arches one eyebrow. "That's your evidence?"

I plop down on the edge of the bed. "Listen to me, Nate. We already know that girl was skulking around Art Tuttle's house. This is not exactly a far reach. I don't care if you believe me or not—I know what I saw."

The conviction in my voice this time is somehow enough to wipe the teasing smile off his face. He sits up straighter in the bed. "Okay, so say it was her. What are you going to do?"

"I have to go to the principal."

"The principal? That seems extreme."

"Nate," I say through my teeth. "The girl was *in the bushes outside our house*. Art already lost his job because of her. I'm not messing around here."

He's quiet for a moment, mulling this over. I don't understand what he is thinking about though. This is an exceedingly delicate situation, and it has to be handled correctly. Getting the principal involved is the right thing to do.

"I just don't want to cause more trouble for Addie," he says. "You know the other kids have ostracized her because of the situation last year."

"Maybe she needs counseling," I say. It's the kindest thing I can say. I'd hate to say that Addie is simply a bad seed who can never be redeemed.

"Counseling?" He twists his face like he just ate something sour. "Now you're going to get the girl sent to a shrink?"

I don't understand why Nate is fighting me on this. If Addie is troubled, counseling will help her. If he is her advocate, why wouldn't he want her to get the help she needs? There isn't any stigma anymore in receiving counseling.

"I'm going to Higgins," I say. "End of story."

Nate climbs out of bed and settles down beside me at the edge of the bed. I'm not entirely sure what he's going to say, but it turns out he doesn't say anything at all. He just reaches out, places his hands on either of my shoulders, and starts massaging.

"What are you doing?" I say.

"It's been a long night," he says. "You've seemed so tense lately, Eve, and I feel bad. I feel like it's my fault."

"It's not your fault," I say, and it's only partially a lie.

Nate kneads his fingers deeper into my flesh. "Does this help at all?"

I want to tell him that I have no interest in a massage right now, but actually, it does feel quite nice. I hadn't realized how much tension was in my shoulders until he started rubbing them. I forgot how good Nate is at massages.

"Lie down," he instructs me.

Obligingly, I lie down on the bed, on my stomach with my head in the pillow. Nate crawls into the bed next to me, and his fingers work at the muscles in my shoulders and back. All the tension I've been holding on to drains out of me. Against my will, I let out a little happy sigh.

"Also," Nate adds, "hearing all that baby talk tonight, I was thinking that we need to do a little better job trying." He leans closer to me so that I can feel his hot breath on my neck. "You know?"

Nate has seemed so completely disinterested in sex recently, it shocks me to hear that from him. But as he undoes the zipper on the back of my dress, I have no doubt about his intentions.

CHAPTER 45

ADDIE

It was a mistake going to Nathaniel's house last night.

I should never have done it. I have never done anything like that before. Okay, that's a lie. It's not even close to the first time I've gone to a teacher's house without them knowing. That's what got Mr. Tuttle into so much trouble.

Ugh, I still feel awful about that. I don't know what I was doing outside Mr. Tuttle's house that night. I should never have gone. It's just that I was having a bad night, and my mom was crying about my dad, which was ridiculous because he was the worst father in the whole world and an even worse husband to her. I don't know why she still loves him. She's still got all his clothing in the closet, and she won't sell his car, which is sitting inside our garage.

I just wanted to be around an adult who would be kind to me, but then I got to his house, and when I looked in the window, he was having a nice meal with his wife, and I figured he wouldn't want to talk to me. But then I decided maybe I'd wait until after they finished eating, and by the time I made up my mind that I should probably leave, somebody had called the police.

I thought I was in big trouble, but then it turned out that Mr. Tuttle was the one in trouble. Principal Higgins started asking me all these questions about him and our "relationship." I didn't know what she was talking about at first, but then she started asking me if Mr. Tuttle ever touched me. And that was when I knew what she meant. She was asking if he ever touched me in an inappropriate way, which he never did. But he did *touch* me. Like one time when we were studying after school, I got to talking about my father and how hard it was when he came home drunk, and I started to cry, and Mr. Tuttle touched my shoulder. So yes, he did *touch* me. But not like that—not even close.

Still, she saw my hesitation when answering her questions, and she seized on that. And then before I knew it, everyone in the school thought I was having an affair with Mr. Tuttle. Or else they didn't, and they thought I was a liar trying to get attention.

But the worst part of all is what happened to Mr. Tuttle. He was just trying to help me. He felt bad for me because of my dad and because I had no friends and was in danger of failing math. I tried to tell everyone he was only being nice, nothing more, but then the parents started calling on him to resign. He had no choice.

And now I've done it again. Even worse, it's not the first time. I've been to Nathaniel's house twice before without him knowing.

I don't know exactly what I was thinking except that

I missed seeing Nathaniel after school like I usually did. And I started to get curious about what a dinner at his house would look like. It was only a five-minute bike ride from my house, so when my mom went up to her bedroom for the evening, I slipped out the back door and rode over there.

Stupid, stupid, stupid.

It was depressing to watch Nathaniel having a happy couples dinner with his wife and Mrs. Maddox and her husband. The only positive thing I could say was that Mrs. Maddox's husband was very affectionate with her, but Nathaniel barely touched Mrs. Bennett. And believe me, I was watching.

Anyway, I'm super lucky I didn't get caught. There was a moment when Mrs. Bennett was taking out the trash, and I was terrified that she saw me, but then nothing happened. She thought she saw something, but it was too dark out. She didn't know who it was.

Or so I thought. Until I get a message from Nathaniel through Snapflash during second period:

Nathaniel: You were at my house last night. That was a big mistake.

I stare at the words on the screen until they disappear. It wasn't even a question. He knows I was there. Either he saw me out the window or else Mrs. Bennett told him I was there. I write back:

Me: I'm sorry.

Then I get worried my history teacher is going to

catch me on my phone and confiscate it, so I shove it back into my pocket, even though it's killing me not to see what Nathaniel is writing back to me. I'm sure he's angry with me. How angry? He couldn't possibly be so upset with me that he would end things.

Would he?

No, I can't believe that. But the idea of it gives me a sick feeling in the pit of my stomach. Our relationship is risky for so many reasons. He warned me that if anyone catches wind of it, we would have to stop seeing each other immediately. The idea of never being close to him again is physically painful.

I would rather be buried in a tomb in the sea.

As soon as the bell rings, I practically rip my phone out of my pocket. Sure enough, there's a message waiting for me, which I click to open:

Nathaniel: The principal is going to talk to you about it. I did what I could to stop this. Deny everything.

And then a second message:

Nathaniel: My entire life is in your hands.

Sure enough, I've barely made it to third period when an announcement over the loudspeaker instructs me to go to the principal's office. My legs are super wobbly as I walk down to the ground floor, past the main desk where Annie the receptionist sits with her bucket of oranges. Annie's smile is strained when she greets me, and it's no surprise when I get to Principal

Higgins's office to find Mrs. Bennett waiting. I expected Nathaniel would be there too, and I'm not sure what it means that he isn't.

"Adeline." The principal looks at me through her half-moon spectacles and gestures at one of the plastic chairs in front of her desk. "Have a seat, please. And close the door behind you."

Close the door behind you. This is not looking good so far. Especially because I can see Mrs. Bennett has that pissed-off look on her face. Her already thin lips have completely disappeared.

As I sit in the squeaky plastic chair, I try to make my face blank. I remember what Nathaniel told me. *Deny everything.* It must mean Mrs. Bennett isn't entirely sure she saw me.

"Addie." Principal Higgins doesn't look any more pleased with me than Mrs. Bennett does. I remember when she first called me into her office about Mr. Tuttle, she was so sweet and gentle with me—but that changed when she found out I was stalking him (a bit). Now she just looks like she's had it with me. "Mrs. Bennett says that she saw you in the bushes outside her house last night. Is this true?"

Deny everything. "No, of course not. I was home all night last night with my mom."

Mrs. Bennett lets out an angry huff. "I *saw* you, Addie. You were in the bushes, and then you ran across my lawn."

Deny everything. "I... I don't know what to tell you. I was home all night. Like I said, my mom was home with me. You can ask her."

If they do ask my mom, she will confirm that I was home all night. It's so easy to sneak out without her knowing.

220

A twinge of doubt passes over Mrs. Bennett's face. I'm glad Nathaniel texted me to warn me, because if he hadn't, I probably would've confessed everything. But the more I think about it, the more I realize that denying it is the right thing to do. It was dark last night. She doesn't know what she saw.

Principal Higgins continues to look skeptical. "Mrs. Bennett tells me that you have been having some conflicts with her. That you have been struggling in the class, not putting in an effort, and she even caught you trying to look at another student's paper during an exam."

"I... I did take a peek," I admit, hanging my head in shame. "But Mrs. Bennett was nice about it. She even helped me find a tutor."

I chance a look over at Mrs. Bennett and offer her a smile. She does not return it.

"I'm sorry you thought I would go to your house," I say. "I would never do that though." I realize how weak my words must sound, given I was literally picked up by the police outside another teacher's house, so I quickly add, "I learned my lesson after last time."

Principal Higgins flashes Mrs. Bennett a look. Neither of them seems thrilled with me, but it's not like she has any proof.

Deny everything.

"All right, Addie." The principal leans back in her chair. "Whatever happened last night, I expect there will not be any repeat episodes. You can return to class now."

I get up from the plastic chair, astonished that nothing more has come of this. And most importantly, they didn't ask me anything about Nathaniel. I was so sure it was going to be like last time, when Principal Higgins was grilling me about me and Mr. Tuttle. I expected questions about whether Nathaniel has ever touched me, and I was already anxious about trying to answer them because I figured they would see the truth all over my face.

But Mrs. Bennett assumed I was there entirely because of her. Because she knows that I despise her. That I wish more than anything she wasn't in my life.

And in that sense, she is right.

CHAPTER 46

ADDIE

After the meeting with the principal, Nathaniel doesn't answer any of my text messages.

By the time lunch rolls around, I'm almost hysterical worrying that he hates me now. But he did try to protect me. He told me to deny everything, and the strategy worked. Even so, I've worked myself into a big ball of stress.

While I'm sitting in the cafeteria, trying to force down a cheeseburger that tastes like it's three days old, Lotus plops down across from me with her own tray containing a veggie burger. I'm not excited to talk to her after the way she betrayed me, especially today. My poem might have won that contest if she hadn't intervened.

"Hi, Addie," she says.

"Hey," I mumble, not looking up from my burger.

"Are you okay?"

"I'm great." I drag one of my french fries through the little pool of ketchup I made on my tray. "I'm just not interested in being friends with someone who is two-faced."

Lotus's jaw drops open. "Excuse me? How am I two-faced?"

I don't generally speak up for myself, but I'm having a hard day. I want Lotus to know that I know she betrayed me. And it's somewhat gratifying how flustered she looks. "Nath... Mr. Bennett was going to enter me in that poetry contest. And then you went to the principal about it and made him enter you instead."

She stares at me for a moment, an astonished expression on her face. She had no idea I knew what she did.

"Are you serious?" Her lower lip juts out. "That isn't what happened at *all*."

"Yeah, right."

"It isn't!" she insists. "I never said a word. Mr. Bennett took me aside a week after you told me about the contest, and he said he decided to go with my poem instead."

I can't believe she's lying right to my face. I get up out of my seat, grabbing the tray still mostly filled with food. I don't have any appetite even if this burger were edible. And the fries are weirdly uncooked and yet soggy. "Whatever," I say.

"Addie!" She calls out my name, but she doesn't follow me or try to convince me of her lies. I'm glad, because there's no way I would ever believe her. Nathaniel told me exactly what happened.

Nathaniel. I've got to see him.

Nathaniel has a free period now, and in the past, I had suggested sneaking off together since I am free at the same time, but he insisted meeting during school hours was far too risky. But I am losing my mind, and I don't think I can get through the day without seeing him. So I walk through the empty halls until I reach his classroom, hoping I'll find him there instead of in the teachers' lounge.

Sure enough, Nathaniel is sitting at his desk, looking over some papers while noshing on a sandwich. I watch him for a moment, the same way I did last night and every day in class. He's so handsome. I love the curves of his face, his thick dark hair, the way his brown ties match his eyes. And when he smiles at me, it gives me this wonderful warm feeling.

This maiden has no other thought than to love and be loved by him.

But when he looks up now, he's not smiling.

"Addie," he hisses at me. "What are you doing here?"

I slip into the room, closing the door behind me. "I'm sorry. I just… I'm freaking out…"

"Well, coming here isn't going to make that better." He rises from his seat, a frown on his lips. "You should not have come to my house last night. That was a huge mistake."

I chew on my lower lip. "I know…"

"Now you've put yourself on the radar. You've put *us* on the radar." He shakes his head. "I can't believe you would do something so stupid."

The tears that have been pricking at my eyes since I went to the principal's office now threaten to fall. One escapes my right eye, and I quickly brush it away. "I'm sorry. I'm so sorry. I feel so stupid."

Nathaniel notices my tears, and that takes some of the fight out of him. He glances out the small window on the door to his classroom to confirm that the hall-way is still empty, and then he comes around the desk. "Addie, don't cry."

"I just..." I wipe my nose with the back of my hand before I end up with a snot bubble. If he sees a snot bubble come out of me, it is definitely over. No, I shouldn't say that. He wouldn't be so superficial. "I don't want you to hate me. I made a dumb mistake."

"Addie..."

His eyes soften, and after one more look at the door, he reaches for my hands. I was stupid to worry. Nathaniel and I are soulmates. He's not going to throw away what we have because of one stupid mistake I made. We're too important to each other.

"I could never, ever hate you," he says. "You've become my entire world. You're my *soulmate*. But we have to be a little bit more careful now. Just for a little while. I don't want Eve to get suspicious."

"So...we can't meet today?"

I'm hoping he says yes. It's Friday, and my mother lets me stay out later on Friday because I don't have school the next day.

He hesitates, then shakes his head. "Better not. Maybe next week."

Oh God, I'll *die* before then. "Next *week*?"

He flashes me a lopsided grin. "I know. I'm going to go out of my mind."

The idea of not being able to touch him or kiss him for an entire week is enough to make me want to scream. Impulsively, I reach out and grab his brown tie. I tug him closer to me, and even though I can tell he's nervous that we're in his classroom, he lets me do it. If we're not going to be able to go to the darkroom for an entire week, I need something to hold me over.

And he must feel the same way, because he leans the rest of the way over and kisses me more passionately than he ever has before. He laces his fingers into my hair, his lips mashing against mine. The kiss seems to last for an eternity, and it's painful to pull away from him.

I could write a poem about that kiss. And I bet it would win that stupid contest.

"We can't do this again," Nathaniel says in a stern voice. "Not for a little while. I'll let you know when it's safe."

"Can we still text?"

He considers this for a moment. "A little. Once or twice a day. And obviously, only on Snapflash."

I nod, trying to swallow down a lump in my throat. What am I going to do for a week without him? Nathaniel isn't just the best thing in my life—he's the *only* thing.

This is all Eve Bennett's fault.

"You better go," he tells me.

He gives my hand one last squeeze, and that's when the bell rings. I square my shoulders, turn around, and leave the classroom. I'm going to get through this. And someday, the two of us are going to be together. That's what he promised me.

CHAPTER 47

EVE

I feel utterly unsatisfied after the meeting with Higgins.

Addie Severson was outside my house last night, in the bushes. I have never been so sure of anything in my life. I *saw* her, first of all. And she has plenty of reasons to hate me.

When we were in the supermarket that day, Art Tuttle warned me about her. He had a reason to warn me. She destroyed his life, whether she was trying to or not.

And today, that girl lied right to my face.

As soon as Addie left, I looked at Debra Higgins and said, "She's lying."

Debra shook her head. "I agree with you, Eve. But what can we do? It's your word against hers. And she said she was home with her mother."

What a load of crap. When I was a teenager, I did tons of things while my mother thought I was safely tucked away in my room. As far as I'm concerned, that was not an alibi, even if her mother did confirm the story, which she didn't.

As soon as I got out of the principal's office, I texted Nate:

Me: She denied the whole thing.

We were between classes, so his text back to me came quickly:

Nate: Maybe it wasn't her?

His response was so maddening, I wanted to throw the phone.

Soon it will be time for my sixth period math class, when I will come face-to-face with Addie once again, and I am not up for the task. Debra told me that for the second semester, she is planning to switch Addie to a different teacher, but we still have two months left before the term comes to an end. Two months of having to deal with that girl.

"It was definitely her," I rant to Shelby in the teachers' dining area. I brought salad for lunch in a piece of Tupperware, but I've barely touched it. "How could she lie like that?"

Shelby shrugs. "She's a teenager. That's what they do. It's like breathing for them."

"She hates me." I shudder slightly, thinking of the dirty look she was giving me yesterday in class. "She really hates me. And now she's stalking me."

"But why?" Shelby takes a bite of one of her carrot sticks. "I mean, she was following Art around because he was *nice* to her."

"Yes, so?"

"So you're not nice to her. Why would she go to your house?" She sips from her Diet Coke. "I mean, she's not dangerous. Do you really think she would stalk you because you wouldn't let her eat a sandwich in class? That's a little extreme, even for a teenager."

"Maybe…"

"Now if she were stalking Nate—that I could buy." She winks at me. "I mean, all the female students have huge crushes on him. And then you say she joined his little poetry magazine? I can totally see her getting a little too obsessed."

I freeze, a piece of lettuce lying limply in my mouth. I don't know how that thought didn't occur to me before. Maybe because when I was at the curb, I felt like she was watching me specifically. Somehow it didn't hit me that she could have been at the house to see somebody else.

Oh my God. She's stalking *Nate*.

This makes much more sense. I warned him about being too nice to her, and now she is doing the same thing to him that she did to Art Tuttle. And if he's not careful and doesn't handle it right, he's going to end up exactly like Art.

I've got to warn him. He has to deal with this right away.

I excuse myself from the table, and Shelby is likely happy to be able to discuss anything besides Addie Severson. There are still about ten minutes left in the period, and Nate is almost certainly in his classroom. We won't have much time to talk, but I can at least give him a heads-up before he has her in his class.

The halls are mostly empty, since we are in the middle of fifth period, and the heels of my Givenchy leather boots sound like gunshots as they echo through the empty space. I pass a girl with far too much black eye makeup, but that is far from the worst thing these teenage girls do. When I get to Nate's classroom, the door is closed, which strikes me as a little strange. I peer through the window on the door, and sure enough, Nate is inside. But he's not alone.

He's with Addie Severson.

I raise my hand to knock on the door, but before I do, something stops me. I take a step back, ducking slightly out of sight. If Nate was looking hard, he would see me. But not with a quick glance.

Nate and Addie are deep in conversation. I don't know what they're saying to each other, but it looks like she's crying. What is he saying to her that is making her cry? Then again, it doesn't take a huge amount to make a teenage girl sob. Taking away their phone usually does it, in my experience.

And then Nate reaches out and takes her hand.

Okay, this isn't necessarily suspicious. She's crying, and he's comforting her. Granted, it's not the most appropriate way to comfort your student, but it's not the worst thing I've ever seen. Although he's not patting her hand. It seems more like he's holding it. At least sixty seconds have gone by, and his hand is still touching hers. Why is his hand still touching hers? This has reached the upper limit of appropriateness.

But then something happens to make me forget all about the hand-holding. Something happens that makes hand-holding seem like…well, hand-holding. Something that makes me want to throw up the few leaves of my salad that I managed to choke down.

He's kissing her.

No, he's not just kissing her. It looks like he's trying to figure out how her lunch tasted. That kiss… That's not a first kiss. That's a kiss between two people who have kissed many times before and probably done a lot of other things.

And now it all makes sense.

I understand why Addie hates me so much. I understand why she was sneaking around the bushes on the side of my house. I understand why every time I try to tell Nate about something she's done, he defends her. I understand why my husband has zero interest in sex with me except when he wants me to do something to help *her*.

That bastard is cheating on me. With *her*.

CHAPTER 48

EVE

I don't know if I've ever been this angry in my entire life.

Part of me wants to burst into the classroom and bust them on the spot in front of the students and teachers who will soon be filtering out of classrooms. It's what he deserves after all. I imagine the shock on his face, morphing into humiliation as everyone discovers what he has done.

But I don't do it.

I recognize that if I bust Nate here now, I will ruin three lives: his, mine, and Addie's. He deserves to have his life ruined, but I don't. If I make a scene and expose him this way, I will never be able to continue working in the school. It will be too humiliating. And his shame will taint me as well.

As for Addie, the truth is she doesn't deserve it either. Whatever else I can say about her, she is only sixteen years old. She's a *child*. It's not her fault she fell in love with her handsome English teacher. It was Nate's responsibility to keep this from happening.

That's why I don't expose the two of them in front of everyone. But I do one thing: I take a photo.

The age of consent in the state is sixteen. So Nate won't go to jail for this. It's not statutory rape. But his teaching career will be over. My husband will be disgraced, and everyone will find out about it.

My life as I know it is over.

I walk back to my own classroom in a daze. I don't know how I am going to teach a math class in five minutes. I'll have to assign the kids some problems to do and just make them work on it for most of the period. All my lesson plans are out the window.

I reach the door to my classroom just in time to bump right into Addie Severson. She's got a little smile playing on her lips—recently bruised from kissing my husband—but the smile drops right off her face when she sees me. She doesn't want to be in this class any more than I want to have her here. She bows her head and walks quietly to her seat, dropping her bag on the floor.

I have to remind myself again that this isn't her fault. Nate took advantage of her vulnerability. I've been a teacher long enough to know that some girls are more suggestible than others. Some are more likely to succumb to a crush on their favorite teacher.

It's not her fault. It's not.

"I'd like you all to take your textbooks out, and we're going to work on the problems on page one thirty-seven," I tell the class. "Quietly."

I assign far too many problems to do, knowing that they'll be working on them until the bell rings. There are other math teachers who do this with alarming frequency, but I've never resorted to this tactic before—I'm desperate. I drop down behind my desk, and the first thing I do is dig out my phone. After a brief hesitation, I send a message to Jay:

Me: I need to see you tonight.

I sit behind my desk, holding my breath, waiting for his response, not sure if he'll be able to message me in the middle of the day. Thankfully, it comes a few minutes later:

Jay: I'm not closing the store tonight so we can't meet there.
Me: I don't care. We can drive somewhere.
Jay: Are you sure, Eve?
Me: Please.

We arrange an out-of-the-way place to meet. Jay is absolutely the only person I can talk to about this. If I tell anyone else, the secret will be out. But I trust Jay to be discreet. I know too many of his own secrets.

Jay will help me figure out what to do. He may not know anything about school politics, but he has common sense, and he's a good person. But one way or another, I am not going to allow Nate to get away with this.

CHAPTER 49

EVE

After school is over, Jay and I meet in the parking lot of a McDonald's not too far from the shoe store.

We park at opposite ends of the lot, and I walk over to his car and slip inside the passenger seat, and he drives off. Under other circumstances, I might find the secrecy thrilling, but right now, all I can see is my husband's mouth on that little girl's lips.

"Thank you for coming," I tell him as I dig the heels of my boots into the carpet. I'm not entirely sure what he blew off for me, but I appreciate it.

"So what's going on?" Jay asks me.

I open my mouth to tell him the entire story, but before I can get a word out, I burst into tears. Jay glances over at me, a slightly panicked look on his face. He keeps driving until he finds a quiet street without any houses overlooking us. He pulls over and parks the car.

"Eve." He reaches over to envelop me in a hug. "What happened? Talk to me."

I sob into his big, strong arms as he strokes my hair to calm me down. It takes several minutes to get myself under control enough to tell him the entire story. He knows the first part, about the problems I've had with Nate and how distant he has been, but then when I get to the part about finding Nate and Addie kissing in the classroom today, his body stiffens. He pulls away, his eyes wide.

"You're kidding," he says. "You really saw that?"

I nod slowly.

"That piece of shit." He cracks his right knuckles. Jay looks furious, and part of me is scared that he might walk up to Nate and punch him right in the face. And part of me wants him to do it. "That is unbelievable."

"I know." I shut my eyes, but when I do, the image of the two of them kissing doesn't go away. I doubt it ever will. "I don't know what to do."

"Maybe you should kill him."

I look up at Jay's face, and he's not smiling. But he doesn't mean that. Although right now, the idea is tempting. "Really. What do you think I should do? Should I go to the principal?"

He shakes his head. "If you go to the principal, everybody in the world is going to know about this. Is that what you want?"

Speaking with the principal is the proper protocol here, but he's right. There's no way this will be dealt with discreetly, as much as they might try. The situation with Art Tuttle is testimony to that, even though he never did anything wrong. "That's not what I want."

"So then," he says, "you have to lay out an ultimatum for him. You have to do whatever you can to make sure this stops immediately and never happens again. And also…" He reaches for my hand. "You have to get out of this marriage."

He's right about that part. I've got to leave Nate. That is not negotiable. I lift my head, looking into Jay's eyes, wondering for the first time if there's any chance at all of a future with the two of us. I know there isn't, but there are moments when I like to fantasize that it's possible.

But it doesn't matter. Whether I can be with Jay or not, I can't be with Nate anymore.

"You can do this." He squeezes my hand. "Don't be afraid of him. You've *got* this."

He has confidence in me, but the problem is, he doesn't know my husband the way I do.

CHAPTER 50

EVE

By the time Nate gets home, I am more than a bit drunk.

He doesn't arrive until nearly three hours after school ended, which begs the question of what he has been doing all that time. I don't know if he has been with her or doing actual school-related duties. If he's not an idiot, he knows he should be staying away from Addie Severson in the wake of her being found outside our house. Although he must not be thinking entirely clearly if he kissed her right inside his own classroom.

As for me, after Jay brought me back to the McDonald's to retrieve my car, I drove around for a while but eventually ended up back home.

I tried to grade some papers, but that was an exercise in futility. Soon after that, I went for my bottle of wine. Unfortunately, all we had was about a quarter of a bottle left of cabernet. But I did find half a bottle of vodka.

When I hear the front door opening, I've been in

the process of trying on all my shoes. Yes, all of them. I don't know why, but there's something comforting about a fashion show for my feet. Whenever I'm feeling bad about something, I go straight to my shoes. That's something Nate could never understand, but Jay gets it.

Nate doesn't call out my name when he walks inside. He never does. Maybe he's hoping I'm not home so he can jerk off thinking about her. I don't want to know what thoughts are going through his head. I just want him out of my life.

I toss all my shoes back in the closet, except for the Louis Vuitton pumps that I wore on my birthday. I slide them onto my feet, and then I head downstairs.

Nate is in the living room, peeling off his black coat. He plucks the beanie off his hair and runs a hand through his thick locks quickly to smooth them down. As I descend the stairs, I can't help but think back to the first time I laid eyes on my husband and how handsome I thought he was. It was love at first sight—or so I thought. I always believed we would be together forever.

I was so stupid.

"Hello." It's only after the word comes out that I realize my speech is slurring slightly. I should not have had that last shot of vodka. I need to be clearheaded for this. "You're home."

"Uh, yeah." He hangs up his coat in the hall closet. "Did you get dinner started?"

"No." I grab on to the banister to keep from swaying. "I need to talk to you."

"Okay." He loosens his tie around his neck and squints at me. "Have you been drinking?"

This is not exactly how I wanted the conversation

to go, but it doesn't matter. I'm not waiting one more minute to discuss this with him. It needs to end tonight. I step toward him, grabbing on to the sofa this time for balance. I don't know how to begin this conversation, but I plow forward anyway.

"I know about you and Addie Severson," I blurt out.

Nate's hands freeze on the loop of his tie. "Excuse me?"

"I know," I repeat. I have to focus to keep my words from slurring, but he needs to know how serious I am. "I know what you're doing with her. I know that's why she was outside our house the other night."

"That's...that's crazy!" He laughs. "Come on, Eve. You really think I would do something like that? With *Addie*?" He shakes his head. "Where would you get such a silly idea? I think you've had a bit too much to drink. Do you want me to make you a cup of coffee?"

Oh, he is good. My husband is smooth. If it were simply a rumor I heard, I would probably be dismissing it right now. Then again, I always knew he was a liar.

"I *saw* you," I spit at him. "I saw you kissing her. In your classroom during fifth period."

"Oh." The easy smile drops off his face. "I see."

"What do you have to say for yourself?"

Nate tugs at his tie until it comes loose, and then he drops it on the floor. He hangs his head. "I don't know what I can say. I made a massive mistake. Addie had a crush on me, and I thought I could handle it; then today she kissed me. I let it go on a second too long—I know I did. It was stupid, and I'll never let it happen again. I'll make it very clear to her how inappropriate it was."

I clench my fists—I want to pound them against his

chest until he's bruised and bleeding. "No, I saw it. *You* kissed *her*."

"You weren't there. You don't know what happened."

"I saw it!"

A vein pulses in my temple. It feels like there's a very real possibility that it will burst and kill me before we complete this conversation. Before my husband admits to me that he did the thing I watched him do. Part of me wishes it would happen.

But another part of me wants him to suffer.

"Did you tell Higgins?" Nate finally says.

"Not yet."

"Have you told anyone else?"

"No." I did tell Jay, but I'm not going to mention that to my husband.

"I see." He frowns, his entire forehead crumbling. "Will you?"

"I'm not sure yet." I rest back against the arm of the sofa, because my legs feel wobbly. "I haven't decided."

"Is there..." He takes a step toward me, one arm partially outstretched. "Is there anything I can do to convince you not to?"

I look down at his arm like he's offering me poison. "If you touch me ever again, I am going to scratch your eyes out."

"Right, sorry." He steps back again. "Okay, fine. So let's talk about this. What do you want from me?"

"I want a divorce."

He doesn't even hesitate. "Done."

Wow, that was a blow. As much as I want him gone and out of my life, somehow I thought or maybe even hoped he might fight for our marriage a little more.

"Also," I say, "the house is mine."

"But this house—"

"*The house is mine.*"

Nate grits his teeth. "Fine. Take the house."

"Also," I add, "you need to end your relationship with Addie *immediately*. Like, tonight or tomorrow. You need to let her down easy, but make it very clear that you will never see her again. It needs to happen now. Don't wait for school on Monday."

He had to see that one coming. "Fine," he says. "Is that all?"

I have one final demand that I came up with after talking to Jay. This is going to be the hardest one for him, but it's not negotiable.

"You need to resign from Caseham High," I say. "You can't ever work as a teacher for children again."

Nate sucks in a breath. "What? You can't be serious. This is my livelihood, Eve."

"You can still teach. You can teach adult education. But no children. Never again."

"Eve, come on," he chokes out. "I can't possibly agree to that. All the other stuff—fine. But I'm not going to give up teaching high school."

"Fine. Then we can go to the principal and let her decide."

Nate pushes past me and walks over to the sofa, where he sinks into the cushions. He leans forward and presses his fingertips into his temples. "Please don't do this. Be reasonable. You have to be reasonable."

"This is as reasonable as it gets. Really, you ought to be in jail."

"She's sixteen. That's an adult in Massachusetts."

"Yes, I'm sure that's how you think of her. Like an *adult*." I shake my head in disgust. "You need to decide. If you don't resign, I am going to go to the principal about it."

He lifts his face to stare up at me. "And you're sure she would believe you?"

"Why wouldn't she?"

He rises from the sofa and lets out a snort. "Everyone at the school knows you're a complete mess, Eve. You're not exactly trustworthy."

"*Excuse* me? What does *that* mean?"

"For starters, you're drunk at six in the evening." He ticks it off on his fingers. "Also, you hoard shoes. It's really nuts. If anyone got a look at our closet, they would lock you up."

My face burns. He's decided to play dirty, as it turns out. I shouldn't have expected less. "I only have, like, a dozen pairs in my closet. Plenty of women have that many shoes."

"Um, you think I don't know about all the shoes you keep in that giant luggage?"

I did not think he knew about those shoes. But it makes sense he would. I imagine he was in the closet one day, looking for a suitcase for a trip, and he discovered my stash. The thought of him knowing my secret makes me burn with humiliation, but it doesn't change anything.

"Really," he says, "it's your word against mine. Well, mine and Addie's. She'll never admit to anything."

"Right, well…" I lift a shoulder. "Good thing I snapped a photo of the two of you kissing."

What I'd *really* love to have is a photo of Nate's face when I drop that little nugget. All the color drains out of him, and his whole body seems to sag. Yes, I have a photo of him kissing his sixteen-year-old student. He has no power over me.

"Fine," he growls under his breath. "You win, Eve. I'll resign."

With those satisfying words, he turns away from me and stomps up the stairs. I have no idea where he's going, so I follow him, taking the steps two at a time. I find him in our bedroom. He has hauled a duffel bag out of our closet, and he's throwing clothing into it haphazardly.

"What are you doing?" I say.

"Packing." He looks at me like I'm completely stupid. "You're kicking me out, aren't you? Am I allowed to bring some clothes with me, or do I only get to keep the shirt on my back?"

"You can pack."

"Very generous of you." Nate riffles through a dresser drawer and grabs his favorite hooded sweatshirt—the one with a hole in the pocket—and tosses it into his bag. "You know, I was always good to you. I never lost my temper. I never complained when you bought five billion pairs of shoes." He kicks the luggage containing all my hidden shoes. "I came home every single night. What more did you want from me?"

He looks up at me, and I realize this isn't a rhetorical question. He truly believes all those things were enough to make him a good husband. That you can check all the right boxes, and it's okay, even if you don't love your wife. Even if you cheat on her with a little girl.

There's no point in trying to explain to him why what he's done is so wrong. Instead, I go back downstairs and let him pack in peace. After today, he won't be my problem ever again.

CHAPTER 51

ADDIE

I am in the middle of doing my history homework when I get the message on Snapflash.

I'm surprised to see it. Nathaniel is the only one who messages me on there, and he told me earlier today that we were going to cool it for a little while. So I don't understand why there's a new message waiting for me. But of course, it's not like I could resist. Especially if the alternative is learning about the feudal states.

I open the app and find a message waiting for me. It's short and to the point:

Nathaniel: Eve knows.

A cold sensation slides down my spine. *Eve knows.* This is the catastrophe that we both knew had to be avoided at all costs. Mrs. Bennett knows about the two of us. And that means…

Nathaniel: I'm sorry, Addie. I can't see you ever
again.

If somebody took a knife from the kitchen and stabbed me right in the chest, it would be about this painful. I don't understand how it could be over, just like that. Yes, I get that it's bad that his wife knows about us. But Nathaniel and I are soulmates. It doesn't seem possible that she could snap her fingers and it's over just like that.

Nathaniel's words disappear from the screen, and it's almost like I imagined them. But I didn't. With shaking hands, I type in a question:

Me: Did she tell Principal Higgins?
Nathaniel: No. She didn't tell her, but she says she
will if I don't do everything she says.
Me: What does she want you to do?

There's no response for long enough that I wonder if he has abandoned the conversation. But finally, his reply appears on the screen:

Nathaniel: She said that I have to end it with you
immediately and resign from teaching.

The first part is awful enough, but the second part guts me. *Resign*? Nathaniel is an incredible teacher. He has been the only teacher who has truly believed in me and definitely the best poet in the whole school. Maybe the *only* poet in the whole school. How can Mrs. Bennett force him to resign?

She's evil. And not just regular evil. She's *cartoon villain* evil.

Another message from Nathaniel pops up on the screen:

Nathaniel: She also kicked me out of the house. I
hope the ceiling falls on her and kills her.

I write back:

Me: So do I.
Nathaniel: If she were dead, I could still keep my
job, and we could still be together.

I stare at the words on the screen. *If she were dead, I could still keep my job, and we could still be together.* I read them five times before they vanish, and I am left wondering once again what he really meant.

If she were dead, I could still keep my job, and we could still be together.

Well, it's true. If Mrs. Bennett is the only one who knows about the two of us, then if she weren't around…

"Addie?"

My mother's voice rings out from the other side of my closed bedroom door. She knocks once, and when she doesn't get an answer, she barges right in. It's like she can't contemplate that I might be doing something in here that would require privacy. She has no idea that I'm not a virgin anymore.

Although now that I'm no longer allowed to see Nathaniel, I may as well be a virgin again, because there's nobody else I would want to be with. Maybe it'll grow back.

My mother does the things she always does when she enters my room, which is she looks around each of the four corners, like she's worried she might find drugs in one of them. She folds her arms across her chest. I thought she would seem happier after my father was gone, but she doesn't. I don't get how a smart person like my mom could have ever loved someone so awful.

"Addie," she says. "I just wanted to remind you that I'm leaving now."

"Leaving?" I repeat.

Mom always says I sigh too much, but she does it way more than I do. "I have an overnight shift tonight at the hospital. I told you about that."

"Oh. Right."

She frowns. "Are you sure you'll be okay here? Is there some friend that you could spend the night with?"

There isn't. Of course, Nathaniel could spend the night. He's an adult even. But something tells me my mom won't go for that. Although she wouldn't necessarily need to know...

"I'm fine, Mom," I say. "Go be a nurse. Take care of sick people. I'll be fine."

This is only the second time ever that she has left me alone during an overnight shift. Usually in the past, my father was home, although that was worse than being alone.

"Okay..." Mom's fingers linger on the doorknob. "But I'll have my phone, so if you have any concerns..."

As if she could just leave her shift right in the middle because I'm feeling lonely. But if it makes her feel better to offer, then fine.

My mother insists on coming into the bedroom and

planting a kiss on my forehead, which is super annoying. I am basically holding my breath until she leaves the room, and the second she does, I snatch up my phone and send out a message:

Me: My mom just left. Do you want to come over?

I stare down at the phone, waiting for his reply. It comes a minute later:

Nathaniel: I told you, I can't. Eve is not messing
around. She will destroy me if I see you again.
Me: How will she even find out?
Nathaniel: I can't take that chance. Anyway, I'm not
in the mood.
Me: Please? I need to see you.

I stare at my phone, waiting for a reply, but it never comes. He is done with our conversation.

I throw my phone down on the bed in frustration, tears brimming in my eyes. I manage to hold it together just until my mother's car drives away, and then I let loose with loud, ugly sobs that must make the whole foundation of the house shake.

I love Nathaniel. I love him so freaking much, it's almost painful. There are lots of people out there in the world who are dating or married, but I'm fairly sure he and I love each other more than any of those other people. They don't have the connection that we do. Yes, he's a lot older than me, but that doesn't matter. What we have surpasses age.

He never had that connection to his wife. He married

her just because he felt that's what you're supposed to do in life. And now she's the one controlling him. Controlling us.

It's so unfair, I want to scream.

CHAPTER 52

ADDIE

You know things are seriously bad when even ice cream doesn't help.

An hour later, I am sitting in the kitchen with an empty tub of rocky road ice cream, and I don't feel even a little bit better. Actually, I feel worse because my stomach hurts now. I started to feel regret setting in when the tub was three-quarters empty, but I kept going.

The pain of knowing I'll never get to be with Nathaniel again hurts me right in my soul. This hurts worse than anything I have ever experienced. Worse than I felt when my father died, that's for sure.

Well, when I killed him, that is.

That was an *accident* though. An accident that wrecked my friendship with Hudson, which sucked, but at least it started me on the path to Nathaniel. And even though my mother won't admit it, our household is so much better off now that he's gone. My father's death fixed everything.

And if Mrs. Bennett were gone, that would fix everything too.

Despite my churning stomach, I lick the remainder of the ice cream off my spoon. I'm glad for the discomfort, because I want to feel something besides the ache in my chest. But the loss of the love of my life is not the only emotion I'm feeling right now. Almost overwhelming that sadness is another emotion:

Hate.

I hate Mrs. Bennett. I thought I hated her before, but I didn't even know the meaning of the word. She is the worst person I have ever met. She is ruining both of our lives, and it's like she doesn't even care.

If she were dead, I could still have my job, and we could still be together.

I could never do anything to hurt her though. I mean, yes, I was responsible for my father's death, but that was an *accident*. I would never...

I could never...

No. No way. Out of the question.

But one thing I could do is try to reason with her. She probably thinks Nathaniel is taking advantage of me, but that's not true at all. Maybe I could explain it to her. Maybe if she understands how much he and I mean to each other, she'll finally get it. It's not like she even wants him anymore if she kicked him out.

I have to believe that Mrs. Bennett has a decent bone in her body. After all, she did try to help me in math class. She didn't turn me in for cheating, and she helped me to find a tutor.

Maybe she'll listen to reason.

After all, I have to try. It's my only hope.

CHAPTER 53

EVE

This entire day feels surreal.

I caught my husband kissing one of his sixteen-year-old students. He was *having sex* with her. Now I have thrown him out, and as soon as I can, I'm going to file for divorce. I don't need a lawyer. He's going to give me everything I want—everything I deserve.

Or else.

I can't celebrate the end of my marriage though. I skip dinner entirely and end up grabbing some Neapolitan ice cream to soak up the alcohol in my belly. I turn on a movie on Netflix, and three hours later, I am feeling much more sober, for better or worse.

I thought there was a reasonable chance I would spend the entire night awake, but the combination of alcohol and dairy is making me extremely tired. My eyelids feel like they have lead attached to them, and almost against my will, I find myself drifting off on my sofa.

Until I get awakened by a crash.

I scramble off the sofa, tossing aside the container of ice cream. I only finished about half of it, and the rest has turned into ice cream soup. But that's the least of my problems.

What was that noise?

I never quite appreciated how nice it was to have a man in the house when things went bump in the night. And this was more than just a bump. This was definitely a crash. And it sounded like it was coming from the kitchen.

I look over in the direction of the kitchen door. Did I imagine that sound? I was almost asleep and also watching television. The noise might have come from the TV, although it really did seem like it was coming from the kitchen.

But I don't hear anything else.

I collapse back down onto the sofa, my heart still pounding. Okay, first thing on Monday, I am getting a security system in this house. One of those systems where if you don't punch in the code within five seconds of entering, the National Guard will show up at your door. I don't need Nate.

Really, the only person I wish were here is Jay. I would feel *very* safe from intruders if he were in the living room with me. Nobody would mess with Jay. But Jay and me living together is so far from being a possibility, it's almost laughable.

Just as I'm searching for my phone to search for companies to install a security system, I hear a clanging sound.

I didn't imagine it this time. It was definitely coming from the kitchen. And now there's another sound.

Footsteps.

Oh God. There is definitely somebody in this house.

I scan the coffee table, searching for my phone. I don't see it anywhere. There is a fairly good chance that I left it in the kitchen when I was grabbing the ice cream. And we don't have a landline, which means there's no way to call 911 without going into the kitchen.

I should get out of the house. That's what they say in horror movies, right? That the stupid victim is always running toward the intruder rather than out the front door like a normal, rational person. And yet I feel reluctant to leave. This is *my* house, and the last thing I want to do is leave it unguarded while I run off without even my phone.

But I don't want to go anywhere near the kitchen either.

I finally make up my mind. I grab my purse, cursing the fact that I left all my shoes upstairs. All I've got by the doorway is a pair of dirty sneakers, which I really don't want to put on. I only wear them when I do chores out on the lawn. I don't want to leave the house behind with all my beautiful shoes upstairs. What if somebody steals my Christian Louboutin pumps? If I'm going to make a run for it, can I bring my shoes with me?

Oh my God, how could I be obsessing over *shoes* when there's a burglar in the house? Maybe I really do need help.

While I'm contemplating what to do next, I hear another sound from the kitchen. This time, I distinctly hear the sound of a girl swearing.

Addie?

CHAPTER 54

EVE

Addie Severson is in my kitchen.

I'm certain that it's her. There's no other teenage girl who would be sneaking around my kitchen at nine o'clock at night. She's already done it once before. Maybe she thinks that Nate is still here and wants to see him. I have no idea if he informed her that their relationship is over, but I wouldn't be surprised if he hasn't.

At this point, I abandon my attempt to put on my sneakers. I don't want to call the police on Addie. She's already been through it once, and none of this is her fault. This is Nate's fault for misleading her. For not telling her that a thirty-eight-year-old man has no business kissing a sixteen-year-old girl.

I haven't been kind to Addie this semester, and now I feel a flash of guilt. She was struggling all semester in my class, and I could have done more to help her. I *should* have done more to help her. I resented her, because she destroyed the reputation of the man at the school who I looked up to the most, but ultimately, it wasn't her fault.

That girl has been crying for help all year, and I could have helped her. My husband simply took advantage of her.

I'm going to make this right.

I walk in the direction of the kitchen, my footsteps quiet on the wooden floor in my bare feet. I open the door to the kitchen gingerly, not wanting to startle her. Sure enough, there she is, crouched on my kitchen floor. It looks like she knocked over the frying pan I had on the stove, which contained the remainder of last night's dinner. I must not have cleaned it up, with all the excitement of finding Addie hiding in the bushes.

When she hears the door swing closed behind me, she looks up sharply. She scrambles to her feet, blinking furiously. Addie is a couple of inches taller than I am, with a sturdy build. She looks like she could be an athlete, but she hasn't joined any teams. In the time I've known her, I've never seen her in anything besides baggy sweaters and jeans that are a size too large, her face scrubbed clean of makeup. She's pretty, but in an unassuming sort of way. She does not look like the sort of girl who you would think would be having an affair with her teacher.

And yet I saw it with my own eyes.

"Mrs. Bennett," she gasps. She snatches the frying pan off the floor and places it down on the kitchen counter. "I…"

I hold up a hand. "It's okay. I know why you're here."

"You do?"

I nod. "I know about you and Nate."

She squeezes her hands together, her eyes not quite meeting mine. "We're in love, Mrs. Bennett. I'm sorry."

"Addie…" This girl is so far gone. Maybe I should go to Higgins after all. Maybe it's the only way to get this to stop, but I do want to try to spare her that. "You have to understand that Nate is a lot older than you. A *lot* older. And he's your teacher. It's so inappropriate to be in a relationship with him, and honestly…he's taking advantage of you."

She doesn't like hearing this, which is not a surprise. "He's not taking advantage of me. I promise. You just… You don't understand. Maybe you've never experienced anything like what we have, but if you had, you would understand."

Oh, Lord. She is so brainwashed.

"I do understand," I tell her gently. "I know how you must feel, but it's just not healthy. You should have a boyfriend your own age."

"It's not about having a boyfriend." Her round cheeks turn pink. "You don't understand. Nathaniel and I have a *connection*. I know he's older than me, but I understand him in a way that I'm not sure you ever will. I'm sorry, but it's true. And…it's cruel for you to keep us apart."

"You think that, but—"

"It's *true*," she says through her teeth. "I'm sorry you're the kind of person who can't understand the love that the two of us have for each other, but that's not my fault. You don't have to rip us apart. If you care for Nathaniel at all, you'll let us have this."

It's like talking to a person programmed by a cult. I thought I might be able to talk sense into her, but I'm not certain anymore. Maybe it's best to be straight.

"Nate has been lying to you, Addie. He's telling you what you want to hear. A man his age is not capable of having normal adult feelings for a teenage girl, especially not one of his students. He's manipulating you."

"*No, he's not!*" The pink in her cheeks has morphed into a bright red color. "You have no idea what you're talking about!"

"Addie, I've lived a lot longer than you, and I've known Nate a lot longer than you. And I'm telling you, he—"

"No!" she screams at me. "You don't know him at all!"

Oh my.

I take a deep breath. I can't let myself lose my cool, because Addie is getting hysterical. She needs to know that this "relationship" has to end. "Addie," I try again, "I think the best thing to do would be to talk to Principal Higgins on Monday. I wanted to avoid that, but I think it would be for the best."

I didn't want to do it to her, but I can see now it's the only way. Her mother and the principal need to know what has been going on, because she clearly needs help. I wanted to spare her the embarrassment, but there's no other way.

Addie's face is now purple. "You can't do that! You can't tell the principal!"

"I have to," I say quietly.

Addie lets out a heart-wrenching scream. The sound of it chills me to the bone—it almost sounds inhuman. I take a step toward her, reaching out a hand to attempt to comfort her, even though I recognize I'm the last person she wants near her. But just before I can touch her, she snatches the frying pan off the counter.

It all happens so quickly, I couldn't react if I wanted to. Addie brings that frying pan down on my head with all the force in her young teenage body. It connects with my skull with an eardrum-shattering impact. And a split second later, everything goes black.

CHAPTER 55

ADDIE

Eve Bennett goes down the second I hit her with that frying pan.

It's heavy, and I got in a good whack. She crumples and collapses to the floor, her eyes rolling up in her head. But even after I hit her, I still feel the rage coursing through my fingertips. So I hit her again.

And again.

After the third impact, she's very still on the floor. I look down at the back of the frying pan, still caked with the remainder of a meal cooked last night. Now there's blood caked on the back of it too. It's trickling out of Mrs. Bennett's head onto the kitchen floor.

Oh no.

I didn't mean to do that. I didn't come to this house with the intention of bashing my math teacher on the head with a frying pan. I just wanted to *talk* to her. But then she started saying all that awful stuff about how Nathaniel is taking advantage of me and lying to me.

How could she say something like that? She had no idea what she was talking about.

But one thing was clear. She was never going to let me be with Nathaniel. Whether she wanted him or not, she did not want me to have him.

I crouch down beside Mrs. Bennett on the floor. She isn't moving at all. I squint down at her face, trying to figure out if she's breathing. I'm not sure she is.

Oh my God. She's not breathing.

Did I kill her?

I didn't want to kill her. I swear I didn't. I know Nathaniel said that thing about how if she were dead, we could be together and it would solve all our problems. And maybe for a split second, I thought... But not really. For real, I never considered trying to hurt her. But I was having an angry moment. I just needed her to stop talking.

It feels like déjà vu from what happened with my father. Except this is so much worse. Also, back then, I had Hudson with me to help. Now I'm all alone. If they find out what I have done, I'm going to jail. Not kid jail but real *adult* jail, maybe for the rest of my life.

There's only one person who can help me.

I don't have Nathaniel's phone number. He wouldn't give it to me. And even if I had it, it would probably be a bad idea to call from my phone. Then there would be a record of the call, and my mom has access to my phone records. But Mrs. Bennett's phone is right on the kitchen counter. I could use her phone to call him.

I snatch the phone off the counter, but of course, it's locked. It seems to have fingerprint unlocking, so I gently lift Mrs. Bennett's finger to the pad, and miraculously, it unlocks. Now I have access to her entire phone, including her list of contacts. Nathaniel's name is listed as one of the favorites, which gives me a little pang in my chest, but there's no time for that. I click on it without hesitation.

It rings for a long time, and I start to worry he's not going to pick up. After all, she threw him out. He's probably mad at her. But then just when I'm sure it's going to go to voicemail, I hear his angry voice: "What is it, Eve?"

"Nathaniel? It's Addie."

There's a long pause on the other line. "Addie? Why are you calling from Eve's phone?"

"Something happened." I swallow down a ball of fear at the base of my throat. What I have done is so unbelievably awful. I need Nathaniel to help me fix it. "You've got to come home. I…I don't think she's breathing."

"Addie," he gasps. "What are you talking about? What happened?"

"It wasn't my fault," I choke out. "Please, you have to come…"

Again, there's a long silence on the other line. I'm certain he's going to tell me that he's calling the police, and I wouldn't blame him. Or maybe we need to call an ambulance. I can't tell if she's alive or not, but either way, she is badly hurt.

"Okay," he finally says. "I'll be right there."

CHAPTER 56

ADDIE

I'm not entirely sure where he was, but less than twenty minutes later, I hear the lock to the front door turning. I have spent the entire time sitting in the corner of the kitchen, hugging my knees to my chest. Where I am sitting, I can't see Mrs. Bennett's face, but I can see her bare feet. She hasn't moved since I hit her with that frying pan. I am scared that she's dead, and I'm even more scared that if I leave the room, she might come back to life as a zombie.

I can't believe I might have killed Mrs. Bennett. Somehow, this is so much worse than what happened with my father. Because that was a pure accident, but this... I slammed a frying pan into her head three times. That's no accident. No jury would think so.

And while my father was a worthless drunk, it's harder for me to argue that Mrs. Bennett deserved this. I don't think she was a wonderful person, but at the same time, she had good qualities. Even though I struggled to learn the material in class, I could tell she was passionate about teaching.

And now she's dead.

Oh God, she's dead.

"Addie?" Nathaniel's voice calls out.

"In here!" My own voice has a strangled quality. "In the kitchen…"

The kitchen door swings open, and Nathaniel bursts into the room. He looks different than he does at school. His tie is completely off, the first three buttons of his shirt are undone, and his hair is disheveled. Despite everything, I can't help but think how sexy he looks.

"Addie?" He stares at me, curled up in a ball on the floor, rocking slightly. "What…?"

"She's over there."

Nathaniel creeps across the kitchen to where Mrs. Bennett's body is lying. I stand up and follow him, keeping a safe distance behind. I watch his face as he catches sight of her.

"Eve…"he murmurs. Then, "Jesus. What happened?"

"I… I sort of…" There's no point in lying—not to him. "I hit her on the head with a frying pan."

Nathaniel's eyebrows shoot up to his hairline. "You *what?*"

"She was threatening to tell the principal!" I swipe at a tear about to fall from my right eye. "I just… I didn't want to hurt her, but I had to do something."

Nathaniel gets down on his knees beside her body and places a hand on her chest to check if she's breathing. I expected him to look sad or panicked or *something*, but there is no expression whatsoever on his face. "I don't feel her chest moving," he says.

I'm not surprised, but my stomach sinks nonetheless. If she were just hurt, we could take her to the hospital. She might be okay. But if she's not breathing…

"Where's her phone?" he asks.

I've been clutching it the entire time. I hold it out to him, the screen still unlocked. After I got into the phone, I disabled the lock screen.

Nathaniel snatches the phone out of my hand, and right away, he starts scrolling. His eyes are looking intently down at the screen.

"What are you doing?" I ask.

"She said she had photos." His fingers pause, and a tiny smile lights up his face. He jabs at the screen. "But not anymore."

Apparently, Nathaniel has now gotten rid of any incriminating photos of us. But having an affair with my teacher pales in comparison to my much greater crime of killing my other teacher. I look down at Mrs. Bennett, the panic mounting in my chest.

"What are we going to do?" I murmur.

"This is going to be okay," he says firmly. And when he says it, I start to think maybe it's true. "But we've got to cover our trail."

"Cover our trail?"

His brown eyes are still pinned on his wife's body. "I'll buy a train ticket to New York using her phone. Her family lives in New Jersey, and I'll say she planned to visit them. We'll drive her car to the commuter rail station, and we'll leave it there."

"But…" I can't look at Mrs. Bennett. It's too awful. "What about *her*?"

"We bury her in a place no one will find her."

There's a coldness in his voice that surprises me. This is his wife, for God's sake. At one point, he loved her enough to marry her. And now he's talking about burying her body.

"I… I don't know," I stammer.

He looks up at me sharply. "Why not?"

"Because…it's… It's not right…"

"Okay, fine." He scratches at his already messy hair. "Let's call the police and tell them what you did and why. Then I'll see you again in twenty-five years to life."

He's right. The truth is more damning than anything else.

Nathaniel doesn't wait for me to respond. "I need you to go upstairs," he says. "In the linen closet, you'll find some fresh sheets. Grab one of them to wrap her up in."

I don't want to do it. I don't want any part of this. But he's doing this to help me. To keep me out of prison, so that he and I can be together like we have always wanted.

I'll do anything he says.

CHAPTER 57

EVE

I wake up feeling utterly confused.

First of all, I am not in my bed like I usually am when I wake up. I am lying splayed out on a hard surface that I soon recognize to be the floor of my kitchen.

The next thing I become aware of is a throbbing pain on the right side of my head. It feels like somebody clocked me in the head with a brick. Repeatedly. I reach for my scalp, and my hair feels wet and sticky. When I pull my fingers away, I see blood.

Finally, I become aware of the presence of my husband. I am lying on the floor, and he is standing over me. He has my phone in his right hand, and he's scrolling through the screen.

What's he doing? Why am I lying on the floor?

And what is Nate doing with my phone?

I try to sit up but my head spins. For a moment, it seems like I might throw up, but the feeling passes. The floor feels so cold under me. I wish I were in my bed. What's going on?

"Nate?" I croak.

Nate's eyelashes flutter in surprise. He must have come back for something and discovered me lying unconscious on the kitchen floor. "Eve?"

"What...?" My throat feels parched. Again, I get a wave of overwhelming dizziness. "What happened?"

Nate doesn't answer. He doesn't try to help me up. He just stares down at me.

What is going on here? Why would he...?

Wait.

I get a flashback to a conversation with Nate from earlier in the evening. *I want a divorce.* I said those words to him. I told my husband I wanted him to move out. Why would I have said that?

And then, while I lie on the cold kitchen floor, it starts to come back to me. The meeting with Higgins, finding Addie and Nate kissing in his classroom, the ultimatum followed by Nate moving out, and then last of all, Addie breaking into my house. I went to try to talk some sense into her, and then...

She hit me! That girl hit me with a frying pan right on the head!

And now I'm confused. Because I told Nate to move out, and he did. Yet he's standing over me now, holding my phone. How long have I been lying on the kitchen floor? I definitely did not invite him back.

"Give me my phone," I croak.

Again, he doesn't answer me. He just keeps looking at me, a dark expression on his face.

"I... I need you to..." My head throbs with each

word. My God, Addie sure clocked me hard. "Call 911."

He narrows his eyes at me. "Do you remember what happened?"

I attempt to sit up again, and this time, it's a sharp jab of pain in my temple that pins me to the floor. "Addie... she...she knocked me out with a frying pan."

"Are you sure?"

"Yes." My head clears slightly. I make another attempt to sit up, and this time, I'm successful. "Nate, that...that girl is *very* troubled. We need to talk to Higgins about her."

"Easy for you to say." He sneers at me, and for a moment, it's hard to remember why I ever loved him. "It won't destroy *your* life to talk to her."

My head aches too much to have this argument with him. "I'm sorry."

"God, you are heartless." He shakes his head. "What do I have to do, Eve? Do you want me to beg you?" He gets down onto his knees next to where I'm sitting on the floor. "Please, Eve. I'm *begging* you. Don't take this to Higgins."

"Nate," I groan.

"Please. Don't do this."

"I don't have a choice, Nate. It's the right thing to do."

"You don't have a choice." His voice is mocking as his handsome features twist in anger. "You have a choice. You *like* the idea of destroying me. I bet you get a kick out of it."

It feels like an ice pick is jabbing me in my head. I can't have this conversation right now. "Can we talk about this later?" I clutch the side of my head, pressing on my aching scalp. "You need to call an ambulance. She really smacked me hard."

Nate's eyes are glassy. He's looking down at the floor, a dazed expression on his face. "No."

"No? What is that supposed to mean?"

"It means…" He raises his eyes to look up at me. "It means I won't let you wreck my life."

I don't entirely understand what he means by that. At least not until his hands wrap around my neck.

"You're not telling anyone about this, Eve," he growls. "I won't let you."

His grip tightens around my neck, and I can't get a breath in anymore. It feels like my eyes are bulging out of their sockets, and black spots dance in my vision. I desperately claw at his hands, but Nate is much stronger than I am, especially since I just got knocked unconscious.

The next five seconds seem to last an eternity as I realize that my husband has every intention of choking the life out of me. He will do anything to keep me from ruining his reputation—even this.

My vision slowly fades to black. I am dying. This man is killing me, right here and right now. I can't even take a last dying breath because he is crushing my windpipe. And as I die, I wonder who will care that I'm gone. Not my parents, who barely speak to me anymore except on holidays. Jay might care, although on some level, he'll also be relieved.

And certainly not my husband, who is the one squeezing the life out of me and is the last face I see before I die.

CHAPTER 58

ADDIE

I choose a navy-blue sheet to wrap the woman I killed in.

They mostly have white and cream-colored sheets, and I have to search to find a darker color. There's blood all over her hair, and it will go right through the white sheets. Navy blue is a better bet.

As I walk down the steps with the navy-blue sheet draped over my arm, I get a flash of vertigo. I can't believe all this is happening. I can't believe Mrs. Bennett is dead in the kitchen and that it's all my fault. Every time I think of it, my entire body starts to shake.

Thank God Nathaniel is levelheaded enough to know what to do. Obviously he's right that calling the police won't go well for me.

I step into the kitchen, expecting to find everything just as I left it. Except instead of Mrs. Bennett lying on the floor with Nathaniel standing over her, now he is crouched next to her. And his shoulders are shaking.

"Nathaniel?" I say. "Are you okay?"

For a second, it's like he doesn't even hear me. Then he turns around, and I notice his eyes are slightly damp. Was he crying? He looks more rattled than he did when I left the room, but I guess that makes sense. It probably just hit him that his wife is dead. And even after everything she did, he must have cared for her on some level.

After what feels like an endless silence, he gets back to his feet. "I'm okay. Let's do this."

Great.

The next step is wrapping Mrs. Bennett in the sheet. It means I have to get close to her dead body, which makes me almost want to throw up. But I have to do this. If I don't, I'll go to jail for the rest of my life. And it's not like if I come clean, it would bring her back to life.

So I take a giant breath and join Nathaniel next to his wife's body. But the weird thing is she seems to be lying in a slightly different place than she was before. I thought she was closer to the kitchen island.

"Did you move her?" I ask.

He nods. "I thought it would be easier to wrap her over here."

He's thought of everything.

I crouch next to Mrs. Bennett, my heart pounding. Her features are slack, and her lips are tinged with blue. There's blood caked in her brown hair, smeared on the kitchen floor. And I notice one other thing:

Dark red marks on her neck.

I stare at the marks for a moment. I got up close and personal with Mrs. Bennett when I was checking to see if she was alive, and I'm almost certain those marks weren't there before. I would have for sure noticed them.

"What's that on her neck?" I blurt out.

Nathaniel's eyes drop as he studies the red marks. He frowns. "Christ, who knows?"

"They weren't there before, were they?"

He snatches the sheets out of my hands and starts unfolding them. "Yes, they were."

Were they? I chew on my lower lip, unable to tear my eyes away from those angry red marks. They almost look like they're in the shape of...fingers.

That's weird.

"Hey," Nathaniel snaps at me. He's got the sheet unfolded and lined up next to Mrs. Bennett's body. "Are you going to help me with this or not?"

All of a sudden, my head is spinning. Are we really going to do this? Are we really going to dispose of Mrs. Bennett's body and cover the whole thing up? It doesn't sound like the right thing to do.

"I think," I say softly as I get back to my feet, "that we should call the police."

Nathaniel stands up too, following me as I scurry across the kitchen, trying to get as far from the dead body as I possibly can. I almost make it back to the living room before he reaches out and grabs my arm.

"Addie," he says sharply.

I can't even look at him. Why does he even *want* to be with me after what I've done? I need to turn myself in. I've killed two people now. I'm a *hazard*.

"Addie." His voice is softer this time. "Addie, please look at me."

Reluctantly, I turn around. Nathaniel is staring down at me, a deep groove between his eyebrows. "I'm doing this for you," he says.

"You don't have to."

"Addie, you need to know..." His grip on my arm loosens. "Eve was not a well person. She was not a good person. She would have destroyed both of us before she let us be together. And she would have *laughed* about it."

My lower lip trembles. "You don't know that."

"I do," he insists. "I'm sure she provoked you into whatever you did...and now you'll spend the rest of your life in prison for it! I can't let that happen to you."

There's a lump in my throat that's making it difficult to speak.

He reaches out and taps his finger against my chin, drawing my face up to look at him. "I would never let her hurt you. I would never let anyone hurt you, Addie. You know that, right?"

"I know," I finally manage.

He leans in and presses his lips against mine. For the first time, I don't feel any tingling or excitement when he kisses me. I just feel a dark, terrible sensation in the pit of my stomach.

"I won't let them throw you in prison," he says firmly. "We can make this go away, and then we can be together. But we have to handle this exactly right. Do you think you can do it, Addie?"

"Yes," I croak.

"Good girl." He traces the curve of my jaw with his fingertip. "My sweet Adeline. We are going to be so happy together. I'm so lucky to have found you."

I nod wordlessly.

"Remember," he says, "if and when the police come, deny everything."

I will do everything he asks me to. And when it's over, we can finally be together.

PART II

PART II

CHAPTER 59

NATE

I never killed anyone before.

I never thought I would. I'm not a homicidal maniac after all, but writers feel emotions so much more strongly than the general population, so I always imagined under the right circumstances, I might have it in me. More often, writers commit violence against themselves—suicides. Ernest Hemingway shot himself, Virginia Woolf drowned herself, and David Foster Wallace hung himself, to name a few choice examples.

Interestingly, I've never considered suicide. Even in the moment when Eve was threatening my livelihood, the thought never crossed my mind. I have no belief in the afterlife—my feeling is that when you're dead, you're dead. And after death, there is nothing. Nothing but an abyss after which there is no return.

I imagine dying is like standing on the precipice of that abyss, knowing that you will fall in at any second. It is my greatest fear, after snakes.

As I squeezed the life out of my wife, I could see that fear in her eyes. I could see her standing by the abyss, terrified of dropping in.

She has nobody to blame but herself.

And now her body is wrapped up in a sheet in my trunk. Eve purchased those sheets herself, and I recall telling her how much I detested navy blue. Had she any idea that eventually the sheets would enclose her dead body? Doubtful. I take the most satisfaction in the fact that her feet are bare. My wife had an unhealthy obsession with shoes, and it is an apt punishment for her crimes to spend all of eternity in her bare feet.

If I were to get pulled over by the police, the facade of the navy sheet would not last long, but thankfully, I have other plans for her in the near future. We cleaned up her blood on the floor of the kitchen before we vacated the house, and Addie was paranoid about making sure there was nothing left behind. As she scrubbed obsessively, I thought to myself, *Out, damned spot! Out, I say!* But I am doubtful she would have understood the reference. They barely teach the children Shakespeare anymore. I would attempt it, but I'm already gifting them with Poe—I can't be expected to do everything.

Addie is driving the car behind me. Eve's Kia. Addie doesn't even have a driver's license, only a permit, but we have to take this chance. We need to transport Eve's car to the commuter rail station. I used Eve's phone to purchase an Amtrak ticket leaving at close to midnight from South Station, arriving at Penn Station four hours later. I do not expect any of this to hold up to scrutiny, but it will be an adequate story until more information comes to light.

I maintain my speed just below the limit. Addie follows about two car lengths behind. I imagine her gripping the steering wheel with her hands in the nine and three positions, her right foot alternating between the gas and the brake. Even now, even with my wife's body in the trunk of the car, I am aroused thinking about Addie. It is genuinely such a shame.

If we can make it to the commuter rail station, we will be home free.

Or at least I will be.

As expected, the station is nearly empty. Addie gently eases the Kia into one of the outdoor parking spaces. I stay outside the lot completely, in case there are cameras. I wait for her to climb out of the car, and then she darts over to my Accord, hugging her puffy coat to her chest.

For a moment, I consider simply leaving her here. But no. I'll need her for the next part.

Addie's cheeks are bright pink from the cold as she climbs into the passenger seat. Her eyelashes flutter as she looks at me expectantly, and for a moment, I am overcome with a deep sadness that this will be the last time we will ever be together. This is all Eve's fault. Why couldn't she have left well enough alone? I was a completely satisfactory husband. Not a drunk like Addie's father was. I didn't yell at her or beat her or gamble away our life savings. Truly, I deserve a medal for putting up with her neuroses as long as I did.

And then she had the nerve to threaten my livelihood. My *career*. All I felt when my fingers were wrapped around her neck was a deep sense of relief.

"Okay," Addie says in a small voice. "I did it."

She still thinks she was the one who killed Eve. If I

told her the moon was made of green cheese, she would believe me.

"Very good," I say. "But now we must get rid of the body."

Her round face turns green. "Get rid of…"

"We will bury her," I clarify. "Like a funeral of sorts."

"Oh." Addie looks down at her hands. "Okay."

I don't have an exact spot in mind, but I do know the general area. There's a long stretch of deserted road that leads to a pumpkin patch I used to frequent when I was a boy. The pumpkin patch is now overgrown though, and it's already November, so anyone searching for pumpkins will be disappointed. I believe I can locate that road, and it will serve as the resting place for my wife as she falls into the abyss for all eternity.

CHAPTER 60

ADDIE

We are in a pumpkin patch.

Or at least it used to be a pumpkin patch—many years ago, back when Nathaniel was a child. Now the sign proclaiming pumpkins are available for picking is overgrown with weeds and covered with a healthy layer of dirt and grime. I don't know when the last time was that anyone picked a pumpkin here, but it's been many, many years.

Nate parked his Honda about half a mile away, where the road became too difficult to drive on. He popped the trunk, and he handed over two shovels for me to carry; then he heaved his wife's body into his arms. He's been carrying her for the last fifteen minutes, which makes me wonder if dead bodies are heavier or lighter than alive bodies.

I imagine this patch might have once contained lots of plump orange pumpkins, but now any remaining pumpkins are smashed and rotting—partially eaten by animals.

My sneaker squishes right into the innards of one of the pumpkins, and I wince. When I get home, I'm going to have to figure out a way to clean my sneakers, because right now, they are covered in dirt and pumpkin goo and probably some of Mrs. Bennett's blood.

"How about over here?" Nathaniel kicks at a patch of dirt.

Because of the impending winter, the ground has hardened, but it feels slightly softer here. Maybe.

Without waiting for an answer, Nathaniel deposits his wife's body in the dirt. He holds out his hand, and I give him one of the two shovels. He digs the blade of the shovel into the soil and grunts slightly, and then it gives way. After scooping out three shovelfuls of dirt, he looks up at me.

"What are you waiting for?" he asks. "I brought two shovels for a reason."

I look doubtfully at the shovel in my hand. I don't want to do this. I don't want to dig a grave for my math teacher. I just want to go home. Why didn't I just stay home tonight? I could be cozy in my bed, reading a book of poetry.

"I'm cold," I say, because it seems like as good an excuse as any.

"So digging will warm you up." He pulls off his own black beanie to demonstrate how toasty warm he is. "Come on. I don't want to be here all night."

He is staring at me like I don't have a choice. I pick up the shovel and stick the spade into the earth. Not surprisingly, it feels like I'm digging into a rock. The dirt barely crumbles. But Nathaniel is still watching me, so I try again. The second time, I am more successful, and the third even more so. When I scoop out the dirt and throw it on the side, I'm careful to avoid the body wrapped in the navy sheet.

"There you go," he says. "Now let's do this quickly. We don't want to still be digging when the sun comes up."

I don't know when the sun comes up exactly, but it's barely after midnight. The idea that we could be digging for the next six or seven hours is nothing short of horrifying. It's enough to quicken my pace.

We dig mostly in silence for the next ninety minutes or so. Once we get through the first layer of soil, it's a lot easier and we start making good progress. Soon enough, we have a hole in the earth about six feet long by two feet wide and now about two feet deep. We both climbed into the hole when we hit the one-foot mark, and it feels a bit like we're digging our own graves.

Nathaniel pauses and wipes some sweat from his forehead. Despite the freezing temperature, we both took off our coats about an hour ago. "Okay," he says. "Lie down."

I stare at him like he has lost his mind. "What?"

"We need to make sure the hole is the right size," he says impatiently. "So you need to lie down so we can measure. You're about the same size as she is."

"I don't want to do that," I say in a tiny voice.

Nathaniel throws his shovel on the ground. "Do I have to fight with you to get you to do every part of this?"

There's a dark look in his eyes that is unfamiliar to me. I thought I understood him better than anyone in the world. I thought I was his soulmate. But it's beginning to be clear to me that there's a side to Nathaniel that I don't know.

"What were those red marks on her neck?" I ask him for the second time. But now with more urgency.

"What?" he says.

A gust of wind whistles past my ears and I shiver. "Those red marks on her neck. I'm sure they weren't there before. They almost looked like fingers…"

Nathaniel stares at me, his body rigid. "What are you saying?"

"Nothing. I just…"

He blinks at me. "Are you suggesting that I am responsible for the marks on her neck?"

I open my mouth, but the only sound that comes out is a tiny squeak.

"Are you suggesting," he continues, "that she wasn't actually dead when you left the room?" His voice drops several notches. "And that she woke up while you were upstairs and threatened to ruin me?" His voice drops even lower, until it's almost a hiss. "So I had no choice but to strangle her to death…with my bare hands?"

I can't even breathe as he gazes at me, his usually mild brown eyes very dark in the dim moonlight illuminating the inside of the grave. We stare at each other through the haze of the frigid pumpkin patch for what feels like an eternity and a half. The way he said those words sends a horrible chill down my spine. *I had no choice but to strangle her to death with my bare hands.* It sounds so real—like he means it.

And then another terrible thought occurs to me.

If Nathaniel did kill his wife, I am the only other person who knows exactly what happened tonight. He is now counting on a teenage girl not to blab to the police. And we drove out here together in his car, and I texted my mother half an hour ago that I was about to go to sleep and all was well. Nobody knows I'm here with him.

In many ways, killing me right now would be the smart thing for him to do.

"Nate," I whisper. "Please…"

His eyes look like black holes. "Please what?"

I imagine his fingers closing around his wife's neck, cutting off her air. "Please don't…"

My knees wobble, and I'm scared they might give way. I'm scared to *breathe*. Actually, I'm even more scared I might pee in my pants. But then just when I can't stand it another millisecond, Nate shakes his head and steps into a slice of moonlight, which makes his eyes look normal again.

"Stop being ridiculous, Addie," he says. "You know I didn't kill her. *You* did."

I swallow. "Oh."

"Jesus, stop letting your imagination run wild."

"Sorry," I mumble.

As my thudding heart slowly returns to a normal pace, I try to tell myself he's right. I'm definitely imagining things. Nathaniel wouldn't strangle his wife to death. He *wouldn't*.

And if he did—if those finger marks belonged to him—he totally had a good reason. If he did it, it was to protect me. To protect *us*. I trust him.

I think I do at least.

He stares down at the dirt, as if contemplating his next move. I don't want to lie down in this grave—I really, really don't. Finally, he lifts one of his shoulders. "Okay. I'm sure the hole is big enough."

Oh, thank God.

"Hey, listen," he says. "I just remembered that I never grabbed her purse from the trunk. It would probably be better if we threw that in here with her. We can power down her phone."

"Okay."

He glances at his watch. "Let me go grab it. I'll be right back."

"I'll go with you."

Nathaniel gives me a look like I'm stupid. "Addie, you have to keep digging. We've got to get this done. I told you—I'll be right back."

I don't want to be left here alone in this stupid pumpkin graveyard. But it's clear from Nathaniel's expression that he is not going to let me tag along with him. And he does have a point. I need to keep digging.

"Hurry back," I say.

"I promise I will." He gives me a long look. "Remember, whatever else happens: deny everything."

With those words of wisdom, he climbs out of the hole. He retrieves his coat from where he abandoned it in the dirt, and he slides it back on over his shoulders. I watch him walk away until the sound of his boots crunching on the leaves vanishes into the wind.

CHAPTER 61

ADDIE

An hour. It's been an hour.

I have added an extra foot of depth to our make-shift grave, but Nathaniel has not returned. There is no universe in which it would take him an entire hour to walk back to his car and then back to the pumpkin patch again.

So where is he?

"Nathaniel?" I call out. I don't want to start screaming his name, but I need to find him. First of all, he's my ride home. And second of all, where the hell is he? It was no more than a fifteen-minute walk back to the car.

Is it possible that he got back in the car and simply left?

No, it's not possible. Nathaniel wouldn't do that to me. He wouldn't just abandon me.

I climb out of the hole, the knee of my jeans squishing into a rotten pumpkin. The hole might be big enough, but I'm not certain. I assumed Nathaniel would tell me.

"Nathaniel!" I call out again, my voice echoing through the woods.

No answer.

I want to try to look for him, but I'm so turned around, I'm not even sure what direction to go in. If I leave this site, I'm not certain I'll ever find it again.

Eve Bennett's body is still wrapped in that navy-blue sheet. If Nathaniel isn't here, I have to put her in there. After all, that's why we're doing this.

I crouch down beside her body. I don't want to touch her. I know it's stupid. You can't catch *dead*. When I left my father lying at the foot of the stairs, I didn't want to touch him either. It was Hudson who checked to see if he was still breathing.

Come on, Addie. You have to do this.

I take a deep breath and roll her over. Her body is still very limp, like a rag doll. I heard dead bodies eventually get stiff, but it hasn't happened to her yet. I roll her two more times until she's at the edge of the grave we dug. It's the perfect size. So I roll her right in.

The body plummets into the grave with a loud thud. As she falls, something comes out of the sheets. I have to climb back into the grave to see what it is, and I'm horrified when I realize that it's Mrs. Bennett's purse.

We never left it in the trunk after all.

I don't get it. Nathaniel said her purse was left behind in the trunk, but obviously it wasn't. Was he mistaken? Or was he lying to me?

I need to find him. I can't do this by myself anymore.

I drop the purse back into the grave. I don't want to do anything else without finding Nathaniel, but I can't leave the hole like this. I can't leave here with an open grave with a dead body inside, especially if there's a chance I might not be able to find my way back here.

So I climb back out of the grave. I grab the shovel and shift as much dirt as I can back into the hole. I cover the dead body with a healthy layer of dirt—more than enough to keep out animals, but it still seems possible somebody might come across it. I mean, if anybody were wandering around this place where pumpkins come to die.

The leaves have recently fallen off the trees, and there are piles of them everywhere. Instead of bothering with the dirt, I use my shovel to scoop as many leaves as I can back into the hole. I keep going until it's completely full.

There. From a foot away, the grave is now completely invisible.

With that taken care of, I wander back out of the pumpkin patch, following the landmark of the sign for the entrance. I am certain we turned left when we came into the patch, so that means to get back, I should turn right. Right?

Man, I wish I were better at math.

I stumble along the path, which is filled with rocks and slippery leaves. There's a clearing that we walked through, but I'm not certain I'm going the right way. It's entirely possible I'm heading deeper in the woods. After a few minutes, my sneakers are a soggy, muddy mess. "Nathaniel?" I call out again.

No answer. For God's sake, where is he?

I've been walking for about twenty minutes, and there's still no sign of him. I haven't found him wandering around, I haven't found his dead body being feasted on by squirrels—he's nowhere. I'm starting to panic, but then I look down and see something familiar embedded in the dirt:

Tire tracks.

His car was *here*. *He* was here. He made it back to the car; then he took off and left. But why would he do that? He must've had a reason, but I can't even begin to imagine what it was. But at least now I can find my way back.

I follow the tire tracks for another mile. It's now three in the morning, and when I reach the main road again, it's completely deserted. There isn't even another car that I could try to hitch a ride with. Not that I want to do that. When they discover Mrs. Bennett is missing, it won't be good if somebody reports having seen me out here at three in the morning. That would be extremely incriminating.

I pull my phone out of my pocket. At least I have a signal again. Of course, what am I supposed to do about it? I can't exactly Uber home from here. And I definitely can't call my mother and explain to her that I'm out in the middle of nowhere and I need a ride home. I'm supposed to already be home, asleep in bed.

I open up Snapflash and send a message to Nathaniel:

Me: Where are you? I need to get home.

I stare at the screen, waiting for him to reply and explain to me why he left me out in the middle of nowhere. But there's no response. Whatever he did and for whatever reason he did it, he's not answering. And I don't have his cell number.

That means there's literally only one person in the whole world who I can call right now.

Hudson.

We already share one terrible secret. What's one more?

I hesitate, trying to decide if I should wake him up at three in the morning. I hate to do it to him, but it *is* Friday night. He can sleep in tomorrow.

I really, really hope he does not have *do not disturb* on his phone.

I select his name from my contacts. He is still listed as one of my favorites, even though I haven't called him in almost a year. I wonder if I'm still on his list. Maybe he blocked me altogether. Maybe I'm calling him for nothing.

Sure enough, the phone rings and rings and rings, but no answer.

Great.

Well, that's about it. There's nobody else I can call. Hudson was my one lifeline, and he's not answering for whatever reason. Now I have to figure out some way to get home on my own.

Just as I'm about to sit on the road and burst into tears, my phone starts to ring. Nathaniel! I knew he would come through for me. I knew he wouldn't just leave me here.

But then I get a surprise: it's not Nathaniel's name on the screen. It's Hudson.

"Addie?" He sounds tired and confused. "Did you… did you just call me?"

"Yes." I squeeze the phone so tightly, I'm scared ·it might crack. "I… I need your help."

"It's three in the morning," he points out, not helpfully.

"I know."

He lets out an extended yawn. "So what do you need at three in the morning?"

"I need you to pick me up."

"Uh, my parents aren't going to let me take the car at three in the morning. And I only have a limited license, so technically, I'm not even allowed to drive."

"I know."

There is a long silence on the other line. "Where are you?"

I check my GPS. If I didn't have that, I would have absolutely no idea where I am. I recite the address for him. I can tell he's plugging it into his own phone, and then he swears under his breath.

"Addie, it's going to take me close to an hour to get there."

"I know."

I hold my breath, waiting to see what he'll decide. Hudson and I aren't friends anymore. His girlfriend seems to despise me. And if he gets caught sneaking out of the house with the car in the middle of the night, he will be grounded, like, forever. He has about a million reasons to say no. And yet…

"I'm on my way," he says.

CHAPTER 62

ADDIE

He makes it in forty-eight minutes.

He must not have been speeding, because if he got pulled over, they would probably yank his license entirely. But knowing Hudson, he was going as fast as he dared. When his broken-down car pulls up in front of me, I almost cry with relief.

As I slide into the passenger seat next to Hudson, I can see how tired he looks. His white-blond hair is all disheveled, and he's got sleep in his eyes. It's not surprising, considering I pulled him out of bed.

"Thank you so much," I tell him. "I... I owe you one."

He gives me a look.

"One *more*," I quickly add.

His eyes travel down my body, from my dirty and blistered hands to my muddy jeans and finally my sneakers covered in pumpkin guts. But he doesn't comment. He simply gets back on the road and starts driving again.

We drive in silence for the next several minutes. The

radio is on, and because it's so late, there are hardly any commercials. I lean my head against the headrest, letting the music wash over me.

"So," Hudson says, "what was that all about?"

"It's…um…a long story."

"Well, we're going to be driving for the next hour, so we've got time."

I wish more than anything that I could tell Hudson everything that happened tonight. I wish I could tell him and he would understand and then tell me exactly what to do. We used to have that kind of friendship—the kind where he would do absolutely anything for me. But then he did do absolutely anything for me, and now we're not even friends anymore.

"I made some bad decisions," I finally say.

"Okay…"

I can't tell him. I want to, but I can't. In spite of the fact that Nathaniel left me out here, I can't betray him.

So instead of answering his question, I turn away and look out the window. We don't say another word during the entire drive. At one point about fifteen minutes before we reach our destination, his phone buzzes, and I'm scared his parents have realized he's gone and now he's grounded for all eternity. But he doesn't even check his messages. I'm aware of his eyes glancing my way at the red lights, but I try to ignore it. For his own sake, it's better he doesn't know. And if he did, he would definitely never speak to me again. Not for the rest of our lives.

When we arrive back at my house, Hudson turns to me one last time. His pale blue eyes look sad. "You can still talk to me if you need to, Addie," he says.

I bite back a comment about how his girlfriend probably wouldn't like that. "Okay."

He frowns. "I mean it. I'm here for you if you need me. And I'm sorry I've been kind of a jerk to you last year. What happened... It really messed up my head for a while. I couldn't even look at you without seeing... well, you know."

I bow my head. "I know."

"But..." He squeezes the thighs of his jeans with his long fingers. "You're still my best friend, Addie."

Again, I get that urge to tell him everything. I want to so badly. But he's only just forgiven me, and I can't risk it. But there is one other favor I desperately need from him.

"There's one other thing I need you to do for me," I say.

"Anything."

I look him straight in the eyes. "You can't tell anyone at all that you picked me up tonight."

He places a hand on his chest. "I swear I won't tell."

I hope he still feels the same when we get to school on Monday and he discovers that Mrs. Bennett has gone missing.

CHAPTER 63

NATE

When the morning sun dawns on the horizon, I am momentarily surprised to find the space next to me in bed is empty.

Despite my recent lack of affection for my spouse, her companionship is something I had learned to rely on. Every morning, she was beside me in bed—me on the left and her on the right. Her absence is so disconcerting that for a moment, I feel around her side of the bed, searching for her silhouette.

And when my hand touches only the cold sheets beside me, I feel a rush of relief.

Eve is gone.

She set out to destroy my life, and in the course of one night, I managed to solve this problem. Eve is dead—Addie has either buried her in the ground or was caught attempting to bury her after I drove off. And the photographs Eve took on her phone have been deleted from her device, which is buried in the ground with her.

I am a free man.

I rise from the bed, stretching luxuriously. If things had gone differently last night, I would be stumbling out of a motel bedroom, likely clutching my aching back. When Addie called me, I was sitting at a bar, nursing a glass of scotch, contemplating my next move. I didn't realize that phone call would solve all my problems.

Out of curiosity, I reach for my phone, which is charging on the nightstand. I'm not surprised to see several messages from Addie at around three in the morning. Some of them are slightly different, but they all amount to the same thing:

Addie: Where are you?

Poor, wretched Addie. Stuck in the middle of that pumpkin patch in the middle of the night. Truly, I hated to do it to her. I am not a monster. I do hope she made it home in one piece, although it would make my life easier if she came to a bitter end last night while trying to hitchhike with some trucker. I stare down at the phone, wondering if I should risk one last message to her.

No, I can't. I don't know who has her phone right now. I'll simply have to trust that she heeds my final words of wisdom.

Deny everything.

But even if she cracks—and it's hardly unlikely—there's no proof of my connection to Adeline Severson. Eve was the only one who knew the truth, and she didn't tell anyone. The photographs have been deleted. And Addie has proven herself to be unbalanced. She already stalked a teacher, and she got him fired, despite a distinct lack of evidence of wrongdoing on his part. And the girl has no friends whatsoever.

I find myself whistling as I stride in the direction of the bathroom. I have it to myself this morning—Eve isn't here to drain all the hot water, leaving me with a shower that is tepid at best. I should have ended the marriage ages ago, although I did have reasons to keep it going. Eve knows a little bit more about me than I'm comfortable with.

After I relieve my bladder, I rip open the shower curtains to get the water going. But just before my hand descends on the faucet, I freeze.

What the hell?

There's a pair of Eve's shoes in the shower.

I stare down at the pair of red pumps sitting in the bottom of the bathtub. I have discovered Eve's shoes in every nook and cranny of the house, but the bathtub is novel to me. I cannot conceive of why she would have left them there.

Clearly, my wife was even more unbalanced than she let on. All the more reason it's good to finally be rid of her.

The temptation to let the shoes drown nearly overwhelms me, but at the last moment, I rescue them from the tub. Based on our credit card bills, Eve's shoes are worth a small fortune. I can figure out a way to sell them on eBay. I may even turn a profit.

As I am pulling the shoes out of the tub, I hear a sound from behind me. I turn around to look at the closed bathroom door. It almost sounds like somebody is right outside the door. But that's impossible. Eve isn't here, and there's nobody else who has a key.

I am certain I heard something though. It almost sounded like a tapping sound.

I adjust my boxer shorts as I step toward the bathroom door. Gingerly, I pull it open and gaze at the master bedroom. Not surprisingly, it is empty. For a moment, I am reminded of my favorite poem, "The Raven," by the famous Edgar Allan Poe.

Darkness there and nothing more.

I let out a breath and march over to the closet, where I throw Eve's shoes inside. Last night was stressful, and I slept poorly, so it should be no surprise that my ears are playing tricks on me.

I jump into the shower and let the scalding hot water rain down on my bare skin. I have a busy day ahead of me. After breakfast, I have a stack of papers I need to grade. After that, I may go out for a bite of lunch. Perhaps I'll make a stop at the supermarket.

And then after that, I'll be calling the police.

CHAPTER 64

ADDIE

I don't sleep. Not even one minute.

Instead, I lie awake in bed, tossing and turning. Every time I close my eyes, I see Mrs. Bennett's dead body lying at the bottom of that grave in the old pumpkin patch, those angry red marks around her neck.

My mother arrives home in the early hours of the morning. She slips quietly into my room to check on me, and I keep my eyes squeezed shut, pretending to be asleep. I can't deal with her right now. She's going to take one look at my face and know something is wrong.

I lie in bed until it's nearly lunchtime, and then I've got to get up. I've got to face the day and possibly force myself to eat something.

I throw my legs over the side of the bed and reach for my phone. There's a message waiting for me from Hudson:

Hudson: Are you okay?

No, I am not even a little bit okay. But I don't feel like dealing with his questions this morning. I owe him a lot, but I can't face him. Especially since on Monday morning, when he discovers Mrs. Bennett went missing, he's going to put two and two together.

Nathaniel's plan seemed like a reasonable idea last night, but now, in the light of day, I can't imagine how we are ever going to get away with this.

I open my Snapflash app, hoping to see a message from him. After everything that happened last night, he owes me some sort of explanation, right? But there's nothing there.

I tap out a message of my own:

Me: What happened last night? Please tell me
what's going on.

I press Send, but instead of the message going through, an error flashes on the screen:

The account you are sending to no longer exists.

What?

I feel like I'm going to throw up. Nathaniel deleted his account. How could he do that?

But I shouldn't panic. It makes sense that he would want to delete his account. Really, I should do the same. There can't be any sign that the two of us were having an affair, or it would incriminate us both.

Yet I can't bring myself to delete it. Even though his messages are all gone, vanished after sixty seconds. I want to keep the account in case he needs to talk to me again.

I stumble downstairs to the kitchen in my bare feet and throw some bread in the toaster. I'm not even the slightest bit hungry, but my body thinks otherwise—my stomach is growling. I've got the house to myself, because my mother is sound asleep, exhausted from her night shift.

Nathaniel knows what he's doing. He didn't delete his account to torture me. He did it because we need to cover our tracks. Mrs. Bennett is dead—there's nothing we can do about that. But if we get caught, we could both go to prison for the rest of our lives. I have to remember what Nathaniel told me:

Deny everything.

CHAPTER 65

NATE

The unmarked police car pulls up in front of my house at four in the afternoon.

Calling the police was a risky move on my part. Calling the police to report the disappearance of a person who I know that I killed and asking them to locate a body that I buried myself... Well, it takes guts.

Yet at the same time, it is a calculated move. I can't pretend that Eve has simply been home for days when her car is sitting at the commuter rail lot. My best bet is to play the role of the bewildered husband. Fortunately, I have taken several acting courses in my lifetime, and for this role, they will serve me well.

I am wearing a sweater and a worn pair of blue jeans when I answer the door. I don't want to look like I'm trying too hard. It is imperative to show the exact right amount of concern.

When I open the door, I discover my luck has served me well once again. The police officer standing before me is female. My charms invariably perform well on the opposite sex.

"Mr. Bennett?" she asks.

"Yes."

"My name is Detective Sprague." The detective is petite—barely reaching my chin—and she has to tilt her head to look up at me. If she pulled her hair out of that painfully tight bun and put on a little makeup, she might be very attractive—but not at all my type. "I got the report that your wife is missing?"

"That's right," I confirm.

"May I come in?"

A police officer is not allowed to enter your premises without your explicit consent, but I have nothing to hide. I step aside to allow the female detective to enter my home.

"Now, Mr. Bennett," she says. "I just want to be clear about the timeline here. You say you haven't seen your wife since last night?"

I nod in confirmation. "That's right. She was planning a surprise trip to visit her parents, who live in New Jersey. She had a falling-out with them several years ago, and she was determined to make things right, but she didn't want to tell them she was coming because she was afraid they would tell her not to. Anyway, she reserved a seat on a late train, and she was intending to get there first thing in the morning. But I've been calling her all day, and she hasn't been answering—the phone goes straight to voicemail—and I checked with her parents, and they said she never showed up."

I did call Eve's phone several times as well as placing a quick call to Eve's parents, just so my story would check out. They were stunned and a bit skeptical when I told them Eve had been planning a visit. In any case, they got off the phone quickly. They are not exactly enamored of me.

"I see," Sprague says. "And you said she was taking the commuter rail into the city?"

Again, I nod. "Yes. Money has been tight, and she didn't want to take an Uber all the way into the city, so she thought this would be better. That's why I went out to dinner, because she was leaving early to catch the train."

The detective cocks her head thoughtfully. "Okay, well, we did find her car at the commuter rail station, but she wasn't there. And she did buy those Amtrak tickets, but it doesn't look like she was on the train. Her tickets were never scanned."

And this is where the acting skills come into play. I clap a hand over my mouth. "You're kidding."

"I'm afraid not. And it doesn't look like she got on the commuter rail either, from what I can tell."

I stumble backward, finally reaching out to grab on to the banister of our stairwell. "Oh, dear God. Do you think she was attacked at the commuter rail station?"

"It's a possibility, yes."

"I never should have let her go to the station by herself." My voice cracks. "I offered to give her a ride, but she told me it was fine. She never wanted to inconvenience me, you know?"

I look up at the detective's face to see if she is buying any of this. Her expression is unreadable.

"I have to ask you, Mr. Bennett," she says. "Where were you last night?"

"As I said, I went out to dinner at a bar, since my wife wasn't home." I'm sure the pretty female bartender will confirm that I was there for hours. I even flirted with her, although she wasn't my type. "It was late before I came home, and Eve was already gone."

"And what is your relationship like with your wife?" she presses me. "Have you been fighting or…"

I bark out a laugh. "Fighting? God no. Eve and I have the happiest marriage of any couple we know. You could ask any of our friends. In fact…" I swallow so that my Adam's apple bobs visibly. "We've been trying to have a baby."

Sprague's face is still impassive. I may have had the acting classes, but she has the best poker face of anyone I have seen. It's hard to tell if she believes I'm a worried husband or if she's penciling me into her list of suspects. "And is there anyone out there who might have wanted to hurt her?"

I hesitate on purpose.

She raises her eyebrows. "Mr. Bennett?"

"I didn't want to bring this up," I say, "but you're going to find out sooner or later. There is one student of Eve's who seems to have a grudge against her. Her name is Adeline Severson."

"I see." She grabs what looks like a small iPad off her belt and scribbles a few notes. "And what exactly happened between your wife and the student?"

I let out a sigh. "I'm sure this girl couldn't be behind it all, but the truth is it was a bit frightening. Eve caught her cheating on a test, and although she ended up giving her a minimal punishment, it seems that Adeline never forgave her. Two nights ago, we caught her lurking outside our home, although she denied it when we brought our suspicions to the principal."

"Uh-huh…"

"And there's one other thing." I walk over to the desk we keep in the corner of the living room and open the top drawer. I pull out a piece of notebook paper with a handwritten scribble on it. I bring it over to the detective. "She left this for Eve in her mailbox at school."

Sprague's eyes skim over the writing on the page. As she reads, I can hear the sharp inhale of her breath. "This is serious stuff, Mr. Bennett. How come you didn't bring this to the police in the first place?"

"Adeline has had a difficult year," I explain. "About a year ago, her father died. She was stalking another teacher last year, and most of the other students at the school have ostracized her. We didn't want to make her life more difficult, and we tried to deal with it within the school."

Sprague is writing all this down. I even notice her underlining something. When a woman is killed, the husband or boyfriend—*me*—is always the prime suspect. Unless another possible perpetrator is offered.

I am offering Addie.

"All right," she finally says. "Looks like I'll be paying Miss Severson a visit. Before I do, do you mind if I take a quick look around here?"

"Of course. Please go ahead."

I don't know what exactly she is looking for. Perhaps my wife's body sprawled out in the middle of the living room? I suppose there are criminals that stupid.

Sprague makes a quick pass around the living room. She checks the bathroom next, which is utterly

unexciting. Then she points at the room where I strangled my wife to death less than twenty-four hours ago.
"That the kitchen?"

"Yes, that's right."

She opens the door to the kitchen, and when she
gets to the center of the room, her eyes zero in on something lying on the floor. When I realize what she's looking at, my heart drops into my stomach.

CHAPTER 66

NATE

It's another pair of Eve's pumps. Right in the middle of our kitchen.

These shoes are a brilliant blue color. I recognize them as one of her favorite pairs. And the soles are caked with dirt.

I feel utterly nauseated. What are Eve's shoes doing in the middle of the kitchen? The pumps in the shower were odd, but my wife does odd things all the time. But this is different. I was in the kitchen earlier, cooking a continental breakfast. If these shoes had been there, I surely would have seen them.

Wouldn't I?

"These your wife's shoes?" Sprague asks me.

"Yes," I manage.

She crouches down beside the shoes while I try to temper my panic. "These are expensive shoes," she says. "I'm surprised she would take them out and get them so dirty."

"I… I don't know what to say."

I hold my breath, waiting for another question I can't answer, but thankfully, the detective seems to lose interest in the shoes. I take her around the rest of the house, but I can't stop thinking about those shoes in the kitchen. I can barely focus on what's going on in front of me, and every time the detective asks me a question, I'm sure I seem flustered and terribly guilty.

But I can't help it. What the hell are those shoes doing in my kitchen?

When I finally get the detective out the door, I lock it behind her and nearly trip over myself in my haste to get back to the kitchen. When I get there, I realize that the back door has been left slightly ajar, and a bird has flown in through the opening. The bird—small with black and white feathers—is now pecking furiously at the heels of Eve's shoes.

I stare at the scene before me in astonishment. I've left the back door open in the past, and a wayward bird has never before managed to find its way into our kitchen. I fetch a broom from the closet, and I swat at the bird until it obliges and flies out the back door.

Now that the bird is gone, I crouch down beside the shoes, trying to sort out why a bird would have any interest in a pair of suede pumps. After all, birds aren't interested in dirt. They want food.

And that's when I see it:

A piece of smashed pumpkin on the heel of the shoe.

My legs give way under me, my tailbone landing hard on the kitchen floor. My head is spinning, and my vision has tunneled. I could have tried to convince myself that the shoes have been lying here all along and

I simply never noticed them. And the detective made a point—Eve was meticulous about keeping her pumps in perfect condition, and she would never, ever let them get muddy this way. But perhaps she got stuck in the rain and it simply couldn't be helped. I could have tried to convince myself of all that.

But the pumpkin. How did a piece of smashed pumpkin get on the bottom of my wife's shoe?

Even if Eve had been wearing shoes when we buried her, which she wasn't, it's very clear she didn't rise from her grave and walk back home with a piece of pumpkin wedged on her heel. That means that somebody else placed the shoes in the middle of my kitchen, so that I would see them and panic.

And it would have to be someone who knows what we did last night.

Could Addie have done this? It seems unlikely she would be capable of such a thing, and yet I did abandon her in the middle of nowhere last night. Perhaps this is her childish retribution. Although it doesn't seem like her style. Addie is an impulsive teenager, and the idea that she would sneak into my house and plant a pair of Eve's shoes on my kitchen floor seems preposterous to me.

There's another possibility.

I am painfully aware that in the last few years, I have not been able to fulfill my wife's sexual appetites. And of course, the thought occurred to me that she had taken a lover to fill in the gap. The old Eve—the one I fell in love with—would never contemplate such a thing, but I believe the woman I was married to would be capable of it.

So if she was having an affair with another man, is it possible she could have confided in him? And he somehow discovered what we did to her and now hopes to seek vigilante revenge?

Any of these possibilities leaves me incredibly uneasy.

I pick the pumps off the floor and wash the heels under the steaming hot water from the sink. One thing is clear: whoever left these shoes in my kitchen hopes to frighten me, and yet they are reluctant to involve the police. If somebody had incriminating information about me, that detective would have snapped a pair of cuffs on my wrists before the lies left my lips.

No, I am certain I have the upper hand. As long as I am careful, nobody will find out what I have done.

CHAPTER 67

ADDIE

When my mother calls me downstairs, there's a slight tremor in her voice.

I have spent most of the afternoon lying in my bed, staring at the ceiling, too paralyzed to take a stab at any of my homework for the weekend. At some point, I heard my mother emerge from the bedroom and go downstairs, but I kept my own door closed. I can't face her.

I climb down the stairs, vaguely aware of the fact that my T-shirt has a stain over the breast pocket, and my hair feels like a rat's nest. I freeze midway down the stairwell at the sight of the unfamiliar woman in a trench coat standing in the middle of our living room.

"Addie," my mother says. "This is Detective Sprague. She'd like to ask you a few questions."

I knew that I would eventually get questioned by the police, given I was with Mrs. Bennett in the principal's office only yesterday, but I didn't expect it quite so soon. I don't even know how they figured out she was gone so quickly. Since it's the weekend, the only person who could possibly have reported her missing is…

Nathaniel.

"Hello, Addie," the detective says as I slowly walk the rest of the way down the stairs. She is small, but the features of her face look like they're carved from stone, and her hair is pulled back into a super tight bun behind her head. Even though she's tiny, she's frightening. "I need to talk to you for a few minutes, if that's okay with you."

"And I'll be here the whole time," my mother adds.

I look between the two of them. I don't see any possible way to say no, so I nod.

"So, Addie…" Detective Sprague's dark eyes study my face. She is the type of woman who looks like she could see through my lies even better than my fourth grade teacher used to be able to. "The reason I'm here is that your math teacher, Eve Bennett, disappeared sometime between last night and this morning."

My throat feels like the Sahara, which we incidentally learned about last month. "Oh. What happened to her?"

"Well, we don't know," the detective says patiently. "But while doing some research into her disappearance, we discovered that you have had a few run-ins with Mrs. Bennett."

I can feel my mother staring at me, unaware of this turn of events. I'm not entirely sure what to say, especially in front of my mother.

Deny everything.

"Um," I say, "like, I was having some trouble in the class, so it wasn't great, but we weren't enemies or anything."

Sprague's lips twitch ever so slightly. "No, I wasn't suggesting that you're enemies. But she did tell the principal that she caught you snooping around outside her house two nights ago."

Deny everything. "That's not true. I wasn't snooping on her. I was home the whole night."

"That's right, Detective," my mom says. "I was with her on Thursday night. She didn't go out."

"So she wasn't out of your sight the entire night?"

My mother hesitates. "Well, she's sixteen. I don't feel that I need to babysit her all the time. At some point, she was up in her room…"

"So it's possible she could have gone out?"

My mother glances at me, then back at the detective. "I suppose it's *possible*, yes."

"Also…" Sprague reaches into her trench coat pocket and pulls out a folded piece of notebook paper. She hands it over to me. "Did you write this to Mrs. Bennett?"

Mom leans over my shoulder to read the paper she gave me. My knees wobble as I read the angry scribbles. No. Oh no.

It can't be.

I'd like to gouge out your eyes, then fill the sockets with hot coals. I'd like to stab you right in the throat with my pen…

My mother claps a hand over her mouth. "Addie!"

"Did you write this?" the detective presses me.

There's no point in lying. My mother knows my handwriting, so she knows that I wrote this. "Yes," I admit. "But it wasn't… I mean, I wrote it, but I didn't write it to Mrs. Bennett."

Sprague's eyebrows shoot up. "Who did you write it to?"

"I didn't write it to *anyone*," I say. "It was…it was an assignment for English class."

I think back to writing this letter, when I was so mad at Kenzie for stealing my clothes from my gym locker. And then Nathaniel gave me the assignment to write a letter to her, expressing my anger. I didn't mean any of it. I was just being…dramatic. I was trying to impress him.

"An *assignment*?" Mom says in disbelief. Detective Sprague does not say the same, but I can see on her face that she's thinking it.

"Yeah, like…" I scratch at the back of my elbow. "I was supposed to write a letter to somebody I was angry at. But I never gave it to anyone. It wasn't a real letter."

"An assignment." Sprague frowns. "So then…other kids got the same assignment? If I ask them, will they remember it?"

"No, it was just me."

The detective gives me a funny look, but she doesn't question me further on that. I'm not sure if that's a good thing or a bad thing.

"So I need to ask you, Addie," Detective Sprague says, "where were you last night?"

"Home," I say quickly.

She looks at my mother. "And were you here as well?"

My mother's cheeks turned pink. "I'm a nurse, and I had an overnight shift last night."

That crease between my mother's eyebrows that she always gets when she's worried about me has turned into a crevice. She's looked at me like that a lot in the last year.

"So…" Sprague is addressing my mother now. "Did you drive your car to work?"

She frowns in confusion. "Yes."

"And do you have another vehicle?"

"We have..." Mom glances at the door leading to the garage. "My late husband's car is in the garage. But nobody uses that car."

She claims she's been saving my father's car for me, although really, she just doesn't want to get rid of any of his stuff. I bet she wishes she had gotten rid of it now.

"So you had access to a car last night?" Sprague asks me.

Before I can answer, my mother breaks in with "But she doesn't have a driver's license. She only has a learner's permit."

The detective arches an eyebrow. She knows better than anyone that a lack of a driver's license isn't going to keep a teenager from getting behind the wheel. "But the car was in the garage?"

"Yes," Mom says in a small voice.

I don't know why the detective was asking that though. Why would she care if I have access to a car or not? I didn't use my father's car last night. The only reason I would have needed a car last night is if...

If I were working alone.

A horrible, dizzying sensation is coming over me. Detective Sprague acted like she just found that letter, but I'm pretty sure the only way she could have gotten it is if Nathaniel gave it to her. And since the school is closed today, he must have been the one who told her that I was spotted lurking around by their house.

And he abandoned me in the woods.

Is Nathaniel setting me up to take the fall for his wife's murder? Everything the detective is saying seems to point to that, but I know Nathaniel, and he would never do that. Everything he did last night was to protect me—to keep me from going to prison.

Except I can't stop thinking about those angry red marks around Mrs. Bennett's throat.

"Addie," Detective Sprague says in a surprisingly gentle voice, "do you have any idea what happened to Mrs. Bennett last night?"

Both Sprague and my mother are staring at me. I shake my head mutely.

Sprague lets out a long sigh. "All right, Addie. That's all for now. But we might want you to come down to the station later. We're going to have more questions."

"Addie would never hurt anyone," Mom speaks up. "She's not like that."

The detective smiles curtly, but she doesn't say anything. She knows as well as I do that it's not the truth.

CHAPTER 68

ADDIE

After Detective Sprague leaves our house, my mother looks like she's going to have a stroke. Her face drains of all color, and I'm pretty sure her last remaining brown hairs switch over to being white.

"Addie," Mom gasps. "What *was* that? What did you *do*?"

Deny everything.

I drop my eyes, playing with a lock of my messy hair. I wouldn't be entirely surprised if my own hair turned white before the end of this. "I didn't do anything. I was here all night."

"Tell me the truth, Adeline."

My mother can see right through me when I'm lying, so I try a different strategy. "Look, she thinks I took the car somewhere, but I bet that car in the garage won't even start. We haven't used it in so long, I bet the battery is dead."

The last time my mother drove the car was at least

two months ago, when she was considering selling it. Ultimately, she decided to keep it for me, even though the thought of driving that man's car makes me sick.

"Maybe," she says slowly. She swivels her head to look at the garage door again. "Fine. Let me check."

My heart leaps as she grabs the car keys from where she keeps them in the bookcase. I hurry after her as she marches out to the garage. She doesn't say a word as she unlocks the door and slides into the driver's seat. She fumbles with the keys for a moment before fitting them into the lock.

"Mom," I say. I realize I'm holding my breath. She hasn't driven my father's car in such a long time. I bet it won't start. And then I'll be off the hook, right? If I didn't have a car last night, I couldn't have done anything to Mrs. Bennett.

Slowly, she turns the key.

The engine roars to life so loudly that I have to take a step back. The garage quickly starts to fill with exhaust fumes. Really, she should turn it off now, but instead she just sits there, staring glassy eyed at the windshield while the garage fills with toxic fumes.

"I didn't even know it would start," I say pleadingly.

Finally, she reaches out and kills the engine. She pulls the keys out of the ignition and steps out of the car. She looks me straight in the eye.

"What happened last night, Adeline? I want the truth."

"Nothing," I say softly. "I was home."

"Did you do something to Mrs. Bennett?"

"No, I… I would never…"

Anything I say next will be a complete lie. I have

done terrible things in my sixteen years. I pushed my father down the stairs. I was stalking Art Tuttle. I slept with my teacher. I knocked out Mrs. Bennett with a frying pan.

But I'm not sure anymore if I killed her.

"Please tell me the truth, Addie." My mother's voice cracks. "I can't help you if you don't tell me the truth."

I wonder what would happen if I told her everything. If I told her about my affair with Nathaniel. About how I went to the Bennett house last night and I smashed Eve Bennett on the head with a frying pan. What would she do if I told her everything?

The truth is, I'm not sure I want to know.

In the end, I recognize that it will be Nathaniel's word versus mine. And he's going to *deny everything*.

CHAPTER 69

NATE

I receive another phone call a few hours later from Detective Sprague, just before I am about to go to bed.

They have had no luck so far locating Eve, which isn't terribly surprising. They have verified that she definitely never took the commuter rail, which also isn't terribly surprising. All these roads are supposed to lead back to Addie.

"Also," she adds, "I spoke with Adeline Severson."

Addie. I wonder what she must have thought to herself when the police showed up at her door. I'm thankful she has no credibility. "Oh?"

"I definitely think she has something to do with your wife's disappearance," Sprague tells me. "I'm going to talk to her again tomorrow. And I'm trying to get in touch with the principal at your school."

"Good," I say.

Higgins will tell the detective all about what Addie did last year. Between that and the letter I saved, she will appear extremely unstable. When they do eventually exhume Eve's corpse, all the evidence will lead to her. Her fingerprints are even all over Eve's car.

I just have to do my best to distance myself from her. I'm fairly sure she did not tell anyone about the two of us. Eve was the only one who knew. And now I have deleted the Snapflash account that connected us.

I'm sorry, Addie. One of us has to take the fall for this, and it can't be me.

"I'll touch base with you tomorrow," Detective Sprague promises me.

"I appreciate it," I tell her, turning up the charm. I can't outright flirt, since that would be highly inappropriate, but the more she likes me, the less she will suspect me. "Whatever you can do to find my wife…"

"We're going to find out the truth about what happened to your wife," she promises me. "Hang in there, Mr. Bennett."

"Nate," I correct her in a choked voice. I prefer to be called Nate, although I loved the way Addie would say *Nathaniel* in that adoring tone of hers.

When we hang up, I brush my teeth in the bathroom, humming the words to "All Shook Up" as I always do. I splash some water over my face, and then I pull off my undershirt and get into bed. And just as I'm sliding in between the sheets, I hear it.

Someone ringing the doorbell downstairs.

Could it be Detective Sprague? No, unlikely. We hung up not that long ago. It must be somebody else. I glance down at my watch—it's almost eleven o'clock. Who would be at my door at this hour?

I throw my undershirt back on over my head and

then grab my robe for good measure. I pad down the stairs, each step creaking as my bare feet make contact. Our house is so old that practically every tile and floorboard forms a unique sound. Someone walking across our living room could create a symphony.

I hear a sound again. This time, it's knocking at the door. No, more like *tapping*.

'Tis some visitor, tapping on my chamber door.

If there's nobody at the door again, I am going to lose my damn mind.

I check the peephole first. My stomach drops when I don't see anyone standing there. But that doesn't necessarily mean anything. It could have been a package delivery.

At eleven o'clock at night on a Saturday.

I crack open the door, my heart thumping painfully in my chest. But it slows slightly when I see the brown Amazon box sitting on my doorstep. It was just a package delivery. *Only this and nothing more.*

I retrieve the package from my doorstep and carry it over to the coffee table. I have no idea what this is, but I order packages frequently enough. The last item I ordered was a new coffee maker, as the current one has been malfunctioning. It will be nice to be able to drink a decent cup of coffee in my own home again. I rip through the tape on the box and...

It's not a coffee machine. It's a pair of women's shoes.

They are a startling shade of red with long, pointed heels. Eve must have ordered them prior to her death. Of course she did. Eve was always ordering shoes. Unlike the others, though, this pair will be sent right back to Amazon. I start to pull them out of the box, but before I can free them entirely, my blood turns cold. I drop them like they scalded my hand as I realize what I am looking at.

The soles of the shoes are covered in dirt.

Jesus Christ.

I leap off the couch, my whole body shaking. I dart back over to the door and throw it open fast enough that the hinges whine in protest. I stare out at my front yard, narrowing my eyes as I search for any signs of movement. But I see nothing. Not even a squirrel.

Darkness there and nothing more.

"I know you're out there," I call out as loudly as I dare. "I am *not* intimidated by this."

Silence.

"Addie?" I say.

I am greeted with a blast of wind that chills me to the bone. I hug my robe around my chest.

"Eve?" I whisper.

Again, no answer.

I slam the door closed and lean against it with all my weight. My dead wife is *not* haunting me from beyond the grave. That is the only thing I know for sure. I have never believed in life after death. When you are dead, you are dead.

Then who left those dirty shoes at my door?

It occurs to me that there is one other person who could have done this. Someone besides Addie or Eve's mystery lover or the ghost of my dead wife. There is one other person who knows just enough to bury me, and if that person is the one taunting me, I am in deep, deep trouble.

CHAPTER 70

NATE

It should come as no surprise that I sleep horrendously.

I toss and turn, and when I do sleep, I have dreams of a zombielike Eve rising from her grave in the pumpkin patch, wearing a pair of red stiletto heels, which she then proceeds to bludgeon me with. Suffice it to say that every childhood memory I have of that pumpkin patch has been effectively destroyed.

I finally drag myself from my bedsheets and brew myself a cup of instant coffee, as the coffee machine is still on the fritz and the new one has clearly not arrived. I've managed to choke down most of the cup when the doorbell rings.

If there's another package of dirty shoes at my door, I simply cannot cope anymore.

I shuffle to the front door, and when I check the peephole, this time Detective Sprague is standing there. I hope she has good news for me.

The detective seems startled by my appearance when I open the door. I suppose I seemed more put together yesterday. Yesterday, I was playing the role of the disheveled, worried husband. Today, it is genuine. I haven't even managed to shower or put on clothing yet.

"Could I come in, Mr. Bennett?" she asks.

I stifle a yawn. Yesterday, I asked her to call me Nate, but I don't have the energy to correct her a second time. "Yes, please do."

I step back to allow her to enter the living room. I wonder if I should suggest sitting on the couch, but I don't want her to become too comfortable here.

"Any word on Eve?" I ask.

Sprague shakes her head slowly. "I'm afraid not. But I did speak with Debra Higgins this morning."

Good. I'm sure that conversation has solidified Addie as one of her key suspects. "Oh?"

The detective cocks her head to the side, an unreadable expression on her face. "How come you never told me Adeline Severson was in your English class?"

My fingers freeze in the middle of scratching at the stubble on my jaw. "Excuse me?"

"You said Adeline was one of Eve's students," she reminds me. "But you never mentioned that she was one of your students as well."

"Does it matter? Eve is the one she had a grudge against."

"Yes, but you acted like you hardly knew her. Not only was she in your class, but she also wrote for the poetry magazine that you're the staff supervisor for."

I don't like the edge of suspicion that has crept into her voice. I have to nip this in the bud quickly. "I'm sorry if I gave you that impression. I do know Addie. She's always done adequately in my class."

"Just adequate?"

I lift a shoulder. "She was fine. I had no issues with her."

Detective Sprague is studying my face so intently that it takes all my self-restraint not to squirm. "Mr. Bennett," she says, "have you or your wife ever had an extramarital affair?"

"No," I say—too quickly. "Absolutely not. I mean, I certainly haven't."

"But you're not sure about her?"

"I…uh…" I tug at the collar of my robe. "I don't think so, but you never know."

Was Eve having an affair? Did she tell him about my own infidelity, and now he is seeking retribution on her behalf?

"So it's possible," she presses me.

"I… I don't know." I rub my eyes with the balls of my hands. "I'm sorry, Detective. I didn't sleep well last night, worrying about Eve. It's hard to think straight at the moment."

She gives me a sympathetic nod. "All right then. I can give you some space."

I want to fall down on my knees and thank God that this woman is leaving. My temples are starting to throb, and I need a long, hot shower.

"I'll come back later," Sprague adds.

"Oh," I say weakly. "Yes. Okay."

"Or would it be better for you to come down to the station instead?"

The idea of walking into the police station makes me physically ill. "I'll be home all day. You can come by."

Detective Sprague gives me one last look, and I

know that look. She is on to me. Her gut is telling her there is more to this situation than I have let on, but unfortunately, she has no proof. And without that, there is absolutely nothing she can do to me.

CHAPTER 71

ADDIE

I hate the way my mother keeps looking at me.

She's been looking at me that way ever since I got picked up outside Mr. Tuttle's house. Actually, to be fair, she's been looking at me like that ever since my father was found in a crumpled pile at the bottom of our stairs. She didn't understand why I wasn't more sad that he was dead. And then a few days after the funeral, she said to me, *I thought you were planning to study at home that night. Isn't that what you told me?*

It's like she knew. She knew I was the one who pushed him.

And now she knows I have something to do with Eve Bennett's disappearance.

Avoiding her eyes, I grab my coat and take a walk. It's supposed to rain tonight, and now it's just a bit of drizzle. I put up my hood to keep the moisture out of my hair, but the tiny freezing raindrops still smack me in the face. It's uncomfortable, but it also feels good, if that makes any sense.

There are a couple of online news stories about Mrs. Bennett's disappearance, although I've only taken a few peeks. It's hard to read what happened. I got a few text messages from some kids who never had any interest in being my friends before, trying to pump me for information. And one more text message from Hudson:

Hudson: Are you okay?

I don't respond to any of them.

I wonder if Hudson talked to the police about what he knows. He promised he wouldn't say a word to anyone, but that was before he knew he could be an accomplice to a serious crime. I wouldn't blame him, honestly.

As I'm walking a couple of blocks from my house, I notice a black car slowing down beside me. I walk a little faster, ducking down my head, and the car matches my pace. Oh God, what now?

The car pulls up along the sidewalk just ahead of me. The engine cuts out, and for a moment, I wonder if I should make a run for it. And then Detective Sprague climbs out of the car. I'm still thinking maybe I should make a run for it.

"Addie!" she calls out.

I stop, because I think you have to when a police officer tells you to do that. I stand there in the drizzling rain, my hands shoved into my pockets, but I don't say anything.

Sprague darts around the side of her car so that she's standing face-to-face with me. I'm not exactly tall, but she has to tilt her head to look up at me. "Addie," she says. "I'd like to talk to you."

"My mom says I'm not supposed to talk to you if she's not there."

"Right." The detective nods. "That's good advice. But I just want to talk to you off the record. This is important, because I'm trying to find Eve Bennett. I'm worried something bad has happened to her."

I don't know what to say to that, so I keep my mouth shut.

Detective Sprague doesn't have a hood, so the drizzle is getting in her black hair. She doesn't seem to notice or care. Her dark brown eyes are laser focused on my face. "I found out that Nathaniel Bennett was your English teacher."

That seems like a harmless question, so I nod.

"And you were in the poetry magazine he runs too, right?"

Again, I nod.

"So this is off the record, Addie, like I said." She blinks up at me, her eyelashes heavy with water droplets. "Was anything going on between you and Nathaniel Bennett?"

Deny everything. Even if Nathaniel has betrayed me, which I still don't believe he would do, I recognize this information is better kept secret for both our sakes. "No."

"I'm sure if there was," she continues as if I hadn't spoken, "he told you to keep it a secret at all costs. I understand why he would tell you that, but you have to understand that it's not in your best interest. It's in your best interest to be honest with me, and I know it might be uncomfortable to tell me something like that in front of your mother, which is why I wanted to talk to you alone."

"Nothing is going on between me and Mr. Bennett," I say quietly.

"But if it were," she says, "you need to realize that it wouldn't be your fault. He is the adult—your *teacher*—and starting up any kind of sexual relationship would be extremely unprofessional on his part. You would not be at fault, I promise."

She doesn't understand. She could never comprehend the connection Nathaniel and I have. We are soulmates. He wasn't taking advantage of me—I wanted it as bad as he did or maybe even more. He told me no other adult would get it, and he was right.

"Nothing is going on between me and Mr. Bennett," I say through my teeth. "And like I said, you're not supposed to be talking to me without my mother around."

Detective Sprague gives me a look that is both disappointed and sad. I feel bad for a moment, because she seems like she's probably a good detective. She seems dedicated to her job, and she actually seems like maybe she cares about me. But then again, all she really wants is to find out what happened to Mrs. Bennett. Her job isn't to look out for my best interest. She makes it like Nathaniel was manipulating me, but really, she's doing the same thing. Besides, there's no proof anything happened between him and me.

"You need to know, Addie," she says quietly, "that Nathaniel Bennett is painting you to be a stalker who was acting alone. He's trying to make us believe that you followed Eve Bennett to the commuter lot, killed her, and got rid of her body. If you don't speak out for yourself, that is the only story anyone is going to hear."

Is that true? I don't believe that. She must be lying—he would never do that to me..

Right?

Detective Sprague riffles around in the pocket of her trench coat until she comes up with a small rectangular card. She holds it out to me. "This is my card. I wrote my cell phone number on the back. If you want to talk to me, call me anytime. I mean it."

I accept the card, but I don't say anything.

She gives me one last look, and then she gets back into her black car and drives away. After she's gone, I look down at the card she gave me. I turn it around, and her ten-digit cell number is written in black ink. I stare down at the numbers, which blur as the raindrops continue to fall.

CHAPTER 72

ADDIE

I eventually have to return home because the rain soaked my jeans, and also I stepped in a huge puddle and now one of my sneakers is waterlogged.

My mom is sitting on the sofa in the living room, doing something on her phone. As soon as I step back in the house, she looks up at me sharply. "Where did you go?"

"Just for a walk." I step out of my soggy sneakers. "Nowhere in particular."

She raises her eyebrows. "You didn't go anywhere?"

"*No.*"

"Because if you did…"

"I *didn't.*" But I don't tell her Detective Sprague stopped me on the street. Or about the business card wedged in my coat pocket. "It was just a walk. Seriously, Mom."

"I'm just worried." She puts down her phone and stands up to face me. She has started looking so old in the last year. I always thought my mom seemed younger and prettier than most moms, but now she looks like she could be somebody's grandma. "What they are accusing you of is very serious. You have to understand that."

"I know."

Her eyes grow moist. "Addie, please tell me—I won't be mad. Do you know what happened to Mrs. Bennett?"

The urge to tell her everything becomes almost overwhelming. I remember when I was a little kid, I felt like anything that was wrong, my mom could hug me and make it right again. But there is no way for her to make any of this right again. Part of growing up is figuring out that your parents don't have that ability anymore. "No, I don't."

Deny everything.

She swipes at her eyes with the back of her hand. "Because you know I'm on your side, but I can't help you if I don't know what happened."

I open my mouth, but I'm not entirely sure what I'm going to say. But anything I might've said gets interrupted when the doorbell rings.

Oh no. I bet it's Detective Sprague. I bet she's here to arrest me or something.

"I'll get it," I say.

I hurry over to the front door, and I open it up without checking who is outside. But when I see who is standing there, my mouth falls open. Of all the people I would have imagined might be at my door, this is the last person I expected to see there.

It's Kenzie Montgomery.

CHAPTER 73

ADDIE

Kenzie Montgomery.

Great.

It's not enough that the police are investigating me for murder. Now my worst enemy from school has shown up at my front door, presumably to torment me. This day just keeps getting better and better.

Kenzie is wearing a white coat that I've seen her in before, but now it is drenched by what is becoming fairly heavy rain. Her blond hair is plastered to her scalp, and her cheeks are bright pink. It's literally the worst I've ever seen her look.

"What are you doing here?" I say in a voice that is decidedly irritable.

Kenzie reaches out to wipe a few soggy strands of hair from her face. "I need to talk to you. Can I please come in?"

Part of me is tempted to tell her no. She is the last person I want to deal with right now. But there is something in her blue eyes that keeps me from slamming the door in her face. So I nod and step aside to let her in.

Kenzie is dripping wet. A little puddle forms beneath her in our foyer, and I'm hesitant to invite her further inside. My mother quietly goes over to our hall closet and pulls out a towel, which she brings to Kenzie.

"I'm Addie's mom," she says. "How can I help you?"

Kenzie looks between me and my mother. She reaches out and gnaws on her thumbnail, which is a bad habit I'm shocked she would have, but now for the first time, I notice that all her fingernails are chewed to bits.

"Can I talk to you alone, Addie?" she says. "Please?"

I look over at my mother. She seems reluctant to leave, but finally, she nods and heads up the stairs. There's, like, a fifty-fifty chance she's going to be listening at the top of the stairs, but there's not much I can do about that. The walls in this house are thin anyway.

Once my mother is out of sight, Kenzie and I go into the living room and sit down on the couch. I sit at one end, and she sits all the way at the other end. I don't trust Kenzie. She has put me through hell this semester. I can only imagine she's here to mess with me some more, and I am really, really not in the mood.

"What is it?" I say.

"Look." Kenzie flips a few wet strands of her hair behind one shoulder. "I want to apologize for everything I did to you this year. I was a bitch, and I'm sorry."

That's not what I expected her to say at all. Why is she apologizing? And why now?

And yet there's something in her face that looks like she means it. She doesn't have her usual smirk. There are purple circles under her pretty eyes, and one of her nails is bitten so badly, a drop of blood is oozing from the cuticle.

"Okay..." I'm still not sure I trust her, but I'm not going to throw her apology in her face. "Fine."

"Also..." She lowers her voice several notches and glances up the stairs, making sure my mother isn't listening. "I just wanted to tell you that...I know."

My stomach does a little flip. "Know what?"

"I know...about you and Mr. Bennett."

Oh no. Of all the people who could find out, she is *the worst possible person*. If Kenzie knows, soon the whole school will know. And of course, the police. It will be horrible. There's only one thing to do.

Deny everything.

I squirm on the sofa. "There's nothing to know."

"Yes, there is." She levels her blue eyes at me. "You were sleeping with him."

I can see in her eyes that she really does know. She's not asking, she's not digging, she *knows*. She must have seen us sneaking into the darkroom together or... I don't know. Oh my God, this is the worst thing ever. The worst possible person has found out about the worst thing I've ever done—well, the second worst. I wonder how she found out.

"I saw the poem," she says.

That is the last thing I expected her to say. "What?"

"When we were in the cafeteria and you spilled your lunch tray," she reminds me. That's a nice way of describing the day when she threw my lunch on the ground. "There was that poem in your notebook. He wrote that and gave it to you. You know... 'Life nearly passed me by, then she, young and alive—'"

341

"Stop it!"

I hold up my hand to get her to stop talking before she ruins my favorite poem forever. I will never forget the verses that Nathaniel wrote just for me. I have every word memorized.

Life nearly passed me by
Then she
Young and alive
With smooth hands
And pink cheeks
Showed me myself
Took away my breath
With cherry-red lips
Gave me life once again

I narrow my eyes at Kenzie. "How do you know he wrote me that poem?"

She starts chewing on her fingernail again. "Because he didn't write it for you."

"Yes, he did. Trust me."

"No." She shakes her head. "He wrote it for me."

CHAPTER 74

ADDIE

My whole world feels like it has just turned upside down. What? What is going on? What is Kenzie talking about?

"He wrote it for me two years ago," she says. "I... I have it memorized."

Thankfully, she doesn't try to recite the poem again, because I would have had to run out of the room, holding my ears and screaming.

"I don't understand," I say. "Why did he write you a poem?"

"Because Nate and I have been sleeping together since my freshman year."

No. *No.* That's not possible. She's making this up just to torture me.

I refuse to believe it.

"I was on the school newspaper," she explains. "We were both staying late one day while he was helping me with an article I was writing, and...we got to talking."

She takes a shaky breath. "My brother had cancer at the time. Well, he still has it but he's in remission. Leukemia. He was getting chemo and he was sick all the time, and it felt like nobody in my family even knew I existed anymore. I know that sounds selfish but…"

I remember that bottle of pills I found in Kenzie's medicine cabinet, prescribed for her brother. *For nausea.* I had no idea he had leukemia—they must have kept it quiet.

"Nate was so kind to me," she murmurs. "He paid so much attention to me in a way that my parents never did anymore. And he's so… I mean, I couldn't stop thinking about him. So when he kissed me…"

This doesn't make sense. Nathaniel told me he had never been unfaithful to his wife before. Also, if he was with Kenzie since she was a freshman, she was only fourteen years old then. Nathaniel would never…

"He told me I was his soulmate." She lets out a barking laugh. "I completely believed it. I was so stupidly in love with him. I would've done absolutely anything for him. And then when all that stuff happened with you and Mr. Tuttle, he said we had to cool it. He couldn't see me anymore because there was too much scrutiny." She chews on her nail again. "That's why I was so mad at you this year. Nate barely spoke to me, and I felt like it was all your fault. Even though I realize now how dumb that was. And…I'm sorry for how I treated you."

"But what about Hudson?" I blurt out. "I thought he was your boyfriend?"

She shakes her head. "No, Hudson and I are just friends, that's all. He's a nice guy who has been really kind to me while I've been struggling this year, but nothing happened between us—I was too hung up on Nate."

It's true that I never saw Hudson and Kenzie kissing. They seemed to be together a lot, but I never saw them making out in the hall like some other couples.

"And then I saw that poem in your notebook." She rubs her slightly pink nose. "And I realized he must have given it to you too. And I just felt... I felt so *stupid*. I realized that the whole time, he was playing me. I bet he said all the same things to you that he said to me."

I don't know what to say. I thought Nathaniel was the most amazing man I had ever met or would ever meet. And now I'm beginning to wonder if I might have had it all wrong.

"I don't know what happened with Mrs. Bennett," she says, "but I'm going to go to the police and tell them everything that happened between me and Nate. And I'm hoping you'll come with me so we can do it together."

I shake my head. Kenzie has a lot of evidence, and yeah, it sounds bad. But Kenzie is my *enemy*. She's been tormenting me all year. How can I believe her?

"I was only *fourteen*, Addie." Her lower lip trembles. "I feel so stupid for believing everything he told me and letting him do all that stuff to me. It messed me up so bad. I just want to keep him from doing it to anyone else." She sniffles loudly. "Please come with me."

Her shaky voice is breaking my resolve—I've never seen her be anything but perfectly poised. I wring my hands together. "They're probably not even going to believe us. I don't have any proof at all. We only talked on Snapflash, and all those messages are gone."

"Nate and I talked on Snapflash too," she says. "But I took screenshots."

"You did?"

She bobs her head. "At the time, I did it because I wanted to remember what he was saying to me. But they're all there. All the lies he told me."

She digs into the bag hanging off her shoulder and pulls out her phone. She brings up a photo on the screen, and that's when I see it.

You're my soulmate.

The same words he had written for me. But for Kenzie.

I'm too sick to keep reading. I shove the phone back in her direction and turn away, blinking back tears. Is it all real? Could Nathaniel really have said the same exact words to Kenzie that he said to me? This must be some kind of prank.

Except when I look at Kenzie's face, I know it's not.

She reaches out and takes my hand in hers. "Please, Addie. Please come with me. I don't want to be the only one."

With my free hand, I reach into my jeans pocket, where I moved the card that Detective Sprague gave me earlier today. I pull it out to look at the number scrawled on the back. The ink is slightly blurred by the rain, but I can still read every single digit.

"Okay," I say. "I'll go."

CHAPTER 75

ADDIE

I am absolutely terrified.

When we came to the police station, they put us in a tiny room that gave me a creepy-crawly claustrophobic feeling in the back of my neck. The lighting is scary dark, and the two plastic chairs look uncomfortable. And when we sit on them, they feel uncomfortable. If I were here alone, I would be terrified.

But I'm not alone. I'm with Kenzie.

I didn't tell my mother what I was doing. She would have insisted on hiring a lawyer and making it into a whole *thing*, and then I would've lost my nerve. So I told my mother I was going to take a walk with Kenzie, but instead we came here.

But now I think I might have made a mistake. I should have waited for a lawyer. Or maybe just said nothing at all. Kenzie sounded so sure of herself, but it's not like she's my best friend. She's been tormenting me all year! And now somehow I trust her?

Kenzie is obsessively playing with a lock of her blond hair. She's tugging at it hard enough that I can't help but wince, and she frowns at the silky blond strands as if angry at them. "My hair is like straw," she complains.

I look at her in disbelief. Kenzie has the most perfectly silky hair I've ever seen. And why is she worrying about her freaking hair when we're at a *police station*? "You have beautiful hair."

She rolls her eyes at me and goes back to making faces at her hair.

I am going out of my mind waiting for Detective Sprague to talk to us. Maybe she was nice to me on the street, but that could've all been a fake-out. And what I am going to tell her is bad stuff. Kenzie had an affair with Nathaniel, but what I did is much worse. I helped him bury a dead body. And I'm not even entirely sure which of us was the one who killed her.

It feels like an eternity, but it's really more like twenty minutes before Detective Sprague comes into the room. She's still got her hair in that bun, but it has loosened over the course of the day, and that makes her face look softer. I hope she really is on my side. I hope I don't spend the rest of my life in prison.

I look over at Kenzie, who is still playing with her hair. Very reluctantly, she tucks the strands behind her ear and raises her eyes to look at the detective.

"Hello, Addie," Sprague says. Then she turns to Kenzie and gives her a curious look. "Kenzie Montgomery?"

Kenzie nods. "I... Addie and I need to talk to you about Nathaniel Bennett."

Sprague doesn't look particularly surprised. She sits

in one of the plastic chairs across from us and folds her fingers together. "I'm listening," she says.

Kenzie and I exchange looks. We hadn't agreed beforehand who would go first. I don't want to go first, and I guess I assumed Kenzie would since it was *her* idea to come here.

"Kenzie?" Sprague prompts her.

Kenzie glances at me, panic in her eyes, then looks back at the detective. "Oh. Well, we...we just..."

"Is this about Mr. Bennett?"

Kenzie nods wordlessly.

Sprague's voice softens. "About your relationship with Mr. Bennett?"

Kenzie bows her head, nodding slowly. The detective is quiet, waiting for Kenzie to say something more, but she seems too choked up to say another word. Even though it was her idea to come here, she doesn't look like she can go on. She squeezes her knees with her chewed-up fingernails as her eyes fill with tears.

I always thought Kenzie seemed so mature, but right now, she looks so *young*. Like a little girl. She was only fourteen when Nathaniel slept with her. *Fourteen*. And Nathaniel...he's almost forty! He's an *adult*. Our *teacher*. I was hurt when I realized that Nathaniel lied to me, but this is the first time that it all hits home.

What he did to us was truly horrible. *Unthinkable*.

He needs to pay. And Kenzie and I are the only ones who can make sure he gets what he deserves.

"Detective Sprague," I blurt out, "the truth is Mr. Bennett and I have been sleeping together the entire year. He...he told me not to tell anyone."

Detective Sprague shakes her head, her eyes on fire.

She looks like she wants to take that gun off her holster and empty a few rounds into Nathaniel Bennett. She hasn't been lying about wanting to help me. You can't fake the look in her eyes. "That bastard."

I reach out for Kenzie's hand, and she gives it to me. We are going to do this together. We are going to tell the truth. I don't care what kind of trouble I get into. I am tired of lying for that man. He deserves everything that is about to happen to him.

"Now, Addie," the detective says, "tell me what happened to Eve Bennett."

And I do. I tell her everything.

CHAPTER 76

NATE

I've spent the last two hours driving around in the rain.

I was losing my mind at home, worrying about Detective Sprague returning to question me and what she might say, so I had to get out of the house. I drove around town, listening to classical music and letting my mind wander. At one point, I drove by Simon's Shoes, which used to be Eve's favorite shoe store, and for a moment, a wave of sorrow came over me.

I used to love her. I truly did.

It's dark by the time I return home. I pull into the garage, since it's raining, and enter the house through there. Just as I'm stepping into the living room, my phone rings in my pocket. When I pull it out, the same number Sprague was calling from this morning is flashing on the screen.

I don't want to answer it. I don't want to receive any more updates from a woman who I am increasingly certain believes I murdered my wife. But if I don't answer the phone, she will surely come here. So I take the call.

"Hello?" I say.

"Mr. Bennett?" Her voice echoes slightly, like she is on speakerphone. "Where are you, Mr. Bennett?"

"I'm home."

"You are? Because we were just there, and you didn't answer your door."

They were here? I'm glad I missed them. "Yes, sorry. I went out for a drive. It's been hard sitting around the house, waiting for news."

"Mr. Bennett, we need to speak to you as soon as possible," she says. "I'm going to send that patrol car back around to pick you up."

"A patrol car?" My mouth goes dry. "Why are you sending a patrol car? Am I under arrest?"

"No, not at this time."

Not at this time.

That doesn't sound positive. And there's a hard edge to her voice that wasn't present yesterday. She's received new information. I wonder if Addie broke and told her about the two of us. Even worse, what if Kenzie went to the police?

That would be cataclysmic. Kenzie was only fourteen when our relationship commenced. If she goes to the police, I'm in deep trouble. The kind of trouble where I'll be wearing an orange jumpsuit, and when I get out, I won't be able to live a certain radius from a playground. That kind of trouble.

To be fair, Kenzie didn't look fourteen. She was exquisitely beautiful. More beautiful than 99 percent of all grown women out there. Most people don't understand what it's like, to have all these beautiful young girls throwing themselves at you year in and year out. I'm not made of stone.

"Mr. Bennett?" Sprague is saying. "Are you there?"

"I...yes," I choke out. "I'm here."

"Great. Stay put. I'll have a patrol car there in a few minutes."

The line goes dead, and I am left staring at my phone, a growing sensation of dread in my chest. I almost feel like I'm choking. I need some water. I need some water before I suffocate.

I hurry into the kitchen to grab a glass of water. I race over to the sink, snatch a cup from one of the cupboards, and fill it with lukewarm water. I down the entire glass, and then I stand there, still gasping for air. And that's when I see it. Right in the middle of my kitchen, in the exact spot where I found Eve's shoes yesterday.

It's a pumpkin. A jack-o'-lantern, to be specific.

Of course, Halloween has already passed. And for that reason, the pumpkin has started to rot. The rotting flesh of the pumpkin has caused its features to become distorted. What used to be a toothy grin has morphed into an evil grimace.

And then, as I take a step closer, the jack-o'-lantern moves.

What the hell?

Now it shifts even more violently, and a second later, a black bird shoots out of the top of the pumpkin. Is it...a raven? I startle, backing up against the kitchen counter as the bird flaps its wings, trying to escape from my kitchen. After a few failed attempts, it rests on top of the jack-o'-lantern for a moment, staring at me.

Nevermore.

I grasp at strands of my hair with the tips of my

fingers. Who is doing this to me? Who is talking to the detective about me? Why is this all happening?

It's not Addie. I don't believe she would do this to me. I don't think Kenzie would do it either. The truth is there's only one person I believe to be capable of this.

I've got to get out of here.

CHAPTER 77

NATE

I'm driving far too fast.

If I get pulled over by the police, it will all be for nothing, and I'll be in trouble with Sprague for leaving the house when she instructed me to stay put. But then again, I am already in trouble with Sprague. If I go to that police station, I will likely never leave.

It's still raining, and my Honda only has front-wheel drive, so I need to slow the hell down and be more careful. Eve always told me to get a car with four-wheel drive, but I was stubborn. In spite of everything—in spite of what might happen to me if the police catch up with me—I do not want to be killed in a fiery car wreck tonight. Death is worse than prison.

Before, I was driving aimlessly, roaming the streets and willing to go anywhere but home. But now, I know exactly where I'm going. I'm going back to that pumpkin patch.

It's risky, but I need to do this. I need to prove to

myself that my wife is truly dead and buried among the rotting pumpkins. If I get to that patch and find her grave intact and her body rotting in the earth, that can only mean her soul has returned to haunt me.

Because there is nobody but Eve who would plant a raven in my kitchen.

It takes me over an hour because it's raining and because—unlike during the wee hours of Saturday morning—there is some amount of traffic. While I am making the drive, my phone rings several times. I am certain it is Detective Sprague, but I allow each call to go to voicemail.

At long last, I reach the narrow road leading to the pumpkin patch. Unlike on Saturday morning, when the road was dry and crumbling, the rain has turned the soil moist, and my tires slip on the fresh mud. But even so, I drive until I can go no farther.

And now I have to go the rest of the way on foot.

At least I thought to bring my boots, and I'm wearing a waterproof coat. I tug on my beanie and put up my hood as I climb out of the car. Immediately, my feet slip out from under me, but I manage to catch myself before I fall.

My fingers are tingling with anticipation. I should never have left Addie here alone. I should have helped her finish burying Eve's body. I thought she could handle it alone, but now I realize I made a terrible mistake.

But Eve was dead. I saw the life drain out of her with my own eyes. I couldn't feel a pulse in her neck. She wasn't breathing.

At least I don't think she was. I'm hardly a doctor.

I squint through the rain until I can see the sign for

the pumpkin patch, overgrown with weeds and now covered in mud and rain. My boots sink into the mud with every step, and it feels like it takes half an hour to traverse the small distance to the patch, and when I finally make it there, I'm breathing hard. But I can't stop. I'm too close.

I know exactly where we buried her. I walk across the pumpkin patch, stepping over rotting pumpkins that look much like what's in my kitchen. I chose the space right by the old chicken coop. I step closer, expecting to see an irregular mound of dirt. But that's not what I see.

I see a gaping hole in the ground, roughly two feet by six feet.

My heart is pounding. Christ, I don't want to drop dead of a heart attack in this pumpkin patch in the middle of nowhere. I step over to the grave we dug two nights ago, and I lean forward, squinting into the darkness. I expect to see the navy sheet that had covered my wife's body. Or perhaps animals have chewed through it, and instead her partially decomposed corpse is lying at the bottom of this hole. But none of that is there.

The grave is empty.

I fall to my knees, sinking into the mud, as tears prick my eyes. Aside from the sound of the pouring rain, the pumpkin graveyard is silent. The silence is unbroken, and the only word spoken is my own whisper:

Eve…

And as I wait for an echo to murmur back the word, something slams into the back of my head and everything goes black.

PART III

PART III

CHAPTER 78

EVE

If you've never been buried alive, I don't recommend it.

Taphephobia is the fear of being buried alive. In biblical times, people were wrapped in shrouds and their bodies were placed in caves so somebody could check on them days later to be certain they were actually dead. Even George Washington requested that he not be buried until two days after his death. In the past, during epidemics, safety coffins were developed, which included a device (such as a cord attached to a bell) for the allegedly deceased to signal to the outside world that they were still among the living.

Such a device would not have been useful to me, since the people who attempted to murder me were the ones who buried me and left me in the middle of nowhere in hopes that I would never be found. Finding myself buried under the dirt was one of the worst experiences I have ever had in my entire life.

But it's not worse than what's about to happen to my husband.

TWO NIGHTS EARLIER

Where am I?

Everything is dark. The last thing I remember is Nate's fingers wrapped around my neck, squeezing. First he was choking me, and then I blacked out.

I can hardly move. My body feels like it's wrapped in something—a sheet or blanket—which is keeping me still. And then there's a layer of something else on top of that. Something cold and heavy.

And then I hear the sound of a shovel digging into the earth.

My head is throbbing, and it feels like there are knives in my throat when I try to swallow. I am lying on something cold, irregular, and very uncomfortable. It makes it hard to focus on what is happening around me. The shovel scrapes against the ground again, and this time it is accompanied by something hitting me in the leg. I close my eyes against the blackness, trying to get my thoughts in order.

I think...

Oh God, they're trying to bury me.

If that's true, then I don't know what to do next. I could scream or try to break free from this sheet I'm wrapped in, but considering my husband has already tried to strangle me to death once and Addie clocked me with a frying pan, I don't want to give them a third shot at me. I doubt I will survive a third time.

But I can't let them bury me alive.

While I am weighing out my options, a young female voice above me calls out, "Nathaniel?"

There's a long silence in which there is no digging or dirt falling on me. She calls out his name once again, but I don't hear my husband's voice.

There's a rustling sound and a shadow of something darker above me. It feels like it's about to land on me, and I brace myself for a heavy impact. But instead, it feels light. Leaves?

What little moonlight I could see becomes obscured as more leaves are shuffled on top of me. But I remain still. I don't move. I don't scream.

"Nathaniel!" she calls out one last time. Her voice sounds farther away. So do her footsteps.

I take a shallow breath, just to reassure myself that I still can. Although I have been buried in the dirt, I am not in a coffin six feet under. I am wrapped in some sort of sheet, and it feels like there's only a thin layer of dirt on top of me, and then perhaps some leaves. The sheet is preventing me from inhaling any dirt. I'm not going to suffocate down here.

The only thing that will kill me is if they find out I am still alive.

So as painful as it is, I wait. Shivering in the dirt, with a bunch of soggy leaves as my blanket. I wait until the sound of footsteps has completely disappeared, and then I wait another hour after that. I think it's an hour anyway. It's hard to know what time it is when you're buried in your own grave.

Once enough time has passed, I decide to attempt to get out of here.

That is not incredibly easy. Despite the fact that I am

not buried under six feet of dirt, the shallow layer of dirt and the leaves do have some amount of weight, and on top of that, I'm wrapped in the sheet like a mummy—all of which means I'm completely pinned down. On top of that, my head is throbbing. It would be accurate to say that every part of my body hurts.

My first attempts don't get me very far. I struggle to sit up, to get the sheet loose, but it just gets me frustrated. And then I start to panic. What if I can't get out?

I'm hyperventilating now. There isn't much fresh air down here, and I can't take the deep breaths I want. My fingertips start to tingle. I'm trapped. I'm never going to get out of here. What if I really die down here?

No. *No*. That's impossible. My hands aren't tied down. I can get free. I *will* get free.

After all, it's the only way to make sure my husband pays for what he tried to do to me.

The second time, I do better. I find a corner of the sheet, and I start working my way free. When my hands first feel the dirt, I know I have gotten loose. But I need to be careful. I don't want to inhale a lungful of dirt and suffocate.

It takes me the better part of another hour, but I finally claw my way free from my own grave.

The second my head breaks through the surface, I take a big gasp of fresh air. I thought I was going to die down there. It's freezing, but I don't even care. I don't care about anything except the fact that I'm no longer buried alive. That was the most terrifying thing I have ever experienced.

As I struggle to get to my feet, I look at my surroundings. What is this place? It looks like some sort of graveyard, except for pumpkins instead of humans. How the hell am I going to get back to civilization?

And then I see something lying in the sheet that I just escaped from.

Oh my God, it's my *purse*.

They buried it here with me. I snatch it off the ground and dig around inside. I gasp with joy when I find my phone inside. It's powered down, but when I press the button on the side, the screen lights up. Unfortunately, there's no service. But if I keep walking, I'm sure to reach a place where I can get a bar or two.

I'm going to get home. And then I'm going to make Nate pay for this.

CHAPTER 79

EVE

They buried me without any shoes on.

If only I had taken those few seconds to put on my sneakers before I confronted Addie in the kitchen, this journey back to the road would be much easier. Instead, I am carefully picking my way along the uneven dirt, branches stabbing the soles of my feet. On top of that, I'm freezing. I took the sheet with me, and I fashioned it into a makeshift shawl to try to keep me warm. It's got to be below freezing though.

After I've been walking for about half an hour, I come to what looks like a small road. I dig my phone back out from inside my purse—hallelujah, I've got cell service. One bar. It's a miracle.

I start to dial 911, but then I stop myself.

I could call the police and get my husband thrown in jail for what he did to me. But he'll get a lawyer and be out on bail a few days later. Get a few women on the jury and—let's face it—he would probably end up with a slap on the wrist. If it even went to trial at all. Nate has a way of weaseling out of things.

No, I have to make sure that he pays for all the things he has done.

So instead, I send a message to the only person I can think of who might be willing to come get me in the middle of the night.

Jay takes twenty minutes to respond to my Snapflash message. Twenty minutes of me shivering on the side of the road, wondering if the alert sound will be enough to wake him—I have his number but it's too risky to call him. Just when I'm considering giving up and calling the police, his name flashes on the screen of my phone. He almost never calls me, and I imagine him hiding in the bathroom of his house so that *she* doesn't hear him and he doesn't wake the baby.

"Eve?" he says. "What's going on?"

"I need you to pick me up," I tell him. "I...I'm sorry. I know it's early." My watch reads almost five in the morning.

"Where are you?"

He's coming for me. Thank God.

I wait for him on the side of the road, shivering underneath my sheet. I hope I don't get pneumonia. When I finally spot his car pulling up along the side of the road, I burst into tears. Salt water is running down my cheeks when I climb into the car beside him. He looks startled by my appearance.

"Eve," he says. "Where are your shoes?"

That only makes me cry harder.

Jay doesn't make me explain though. He just starts driving, and we sit together in silence while I cry quietly.

When we get back to Caseham, I start to tell him not to go to my house, but then I notice he's going in a different direction. A few minutes later, he pulls into the parking lot for Simon's Shoes.

"Come on," he says. "Let's get you some shoes."

I follow him out of the car, the parking lot pavement cold against the soles of my feet. He peels off the sheet on top of me, still wrapped around me like a shawl, and he gives me his own coat, even though it's not far to the entrance of the store. Then he takes my hand and we walk together to the door to the shoe store. He grabs the key from his pocket and unlocks the door.

"Take whatever you want," he tells me.

I select a pair of hideous black snow boots, different from anything else I have in my closet, but they're on sale. I start digging around in my purse, searching for my wallet. Of course, I need to pay cash…

"Don't worry about it," Jay says.

"But—"

"I said don't worry about it. Really."

I don't argue with him further. I put on the black snow boots, and even though they're ugly, they immediately warm up my feet. I keep Jay's coat on, and I drop down onto one of the benches. He sits beside me, not saying a word. He's being very patient, even though soon the sun will come up.

"Nate…he…" I choose my words carefully. I don't want him to know Addie was involved too. No good can come of that. Anyway, this is between me and my husband. "He tried to kill me."

Jay looks up at me, his expression frozen in horror.

"He tried to bury me in the dirt," I say. "But I wasn't

dead. I waited for him to leave, and then I got back to the road."

"Eve," he breathes.

I shiver under his coat. "I want him to pay for this."

"We'll call the police right now."

"No," I say firmly. "I want to do this my way. I want to make sure that he pays for everything he has done."

His brows knit together, below that jagged scar on his hairline. "Okay…"

"Is…is there anywhere you know that I can stay for a few days?"

"We have a tool shed," he says thoughtfully. "It's out in the back. Nobody ever uses it. I could stick a sleeping bag out there. It won't be comfortable, but it's warm enough with the door closed."

"Perfect," I say. "And there are a few other things I need your help with."

He looks at me with absolute devotion in his eyes. "I will do whatever you want."

And he does.

CHAPTER 80

EVE

It was Jay who hit Nate on the head with a rock and knocked him out.

I wanted to do it, but logically, it made more sense for Jay to do it. He is taller than Nate and likely stronger. If I did it, I might not have knocked him out. I couldn't risk that. Not after the things I did to ensure he would end up in this very spot.

Jay and I have spent the last two days tormenting my husband. It was risky but worth it. I knew after he saw that raven in the kitchen, he would be convinced I was still alive and end up right here. Nobody else but me would torment him that way.

"The Raven"—his favorite poem of all time. I know it all too well.

Nate is unconscious on the ground, his handsome features slack. I want to take the rock from Jay and hit him again, but I need him to be able to wake up because we are far from done. He'll regain consciousness soon, so we have to act quickly. Jay reaches into the pocket of his coat and pulls out a roll of duct tape. He holds it out to me.

"Want to do the honors?" he asks.

I certainly do. I bind my husband's wrists together in front of him, and then I bind his ankles as well. As I finish tying his ankles together, he groans on the muddy ground. His eyes slowly crack open.

"He's waking up," I tell Jay. "Throw him in the hole."

If Nate wasn't awake before, dropping him into that shallow pool of freezing cold water does the trick. His eyelids flutter open, and he stares up at me, blinking against the droplets of rain. Jay stays carefully out of sight.

"Eve?" Nate croaks.

I don't say anything. I allow him a moment to take stock of his situation. The fact that he is lying in a shallow grave, in a pool of muddy water, and his wrists and ankles are bound together. I watch the panic dawning on his face.

"Eve," he gasps. "What are you doing? What's going on?"

I stare down at my husband. When I stood before him in front of a judge on our wedding day—the happiest day of my life—I never imagined that I could hate him as much as I do at this moment. "You tried to kill me. You buried me in this hole."

"I..." Nate shifts, struggling to keep his face above the muddy water in the grave. "I'm so sorry I did that, Eve. I made a terrible mistake. That's why I came back."

"That's not why you came back. You came back to make sure I was really dead."

His Adam's apple bobs. "Okay, fine. You're right.

I did a terrible thing. I'm a terrible person." He blinks water out of his eyes again. "But you're not. This isn't you. I *know* you."

"You don't know me." I bark out a laugh. "You haven't known me in years. And you definitely don't love me."

"I admit, we've had our problems…"

I laugh again. "Have we now?"

Nate is struggling to sit up, trying to keep his head above the shallow pool that has formed at the bottom of the grave. "Please, Eve. This isn't you. You don't want to do this. It won't solve your problems."

"Yes, you know all about my problems, don't you? Considering you are the cause of all of them."

"Fine, that's fair." When he speaks, some of the muddy water gets into his mouth, and he grimaces and spits it out. "Just get me out of here, and we can talk about this. I'll do whatever you want me to do."

"No," I say quietly. "That's not going to happen."

"Eve!" The panic in his face has intensified. He starts struggling against his restraints. "You realize I'm going to drown in here, right? Please stop messing around! Whatever you want, I'll give it to you. I'll quit teaching, leave town. Whatever you want, okay?"

"Don't worry," I tell him. "I'm not going to let you drown."

For a moment, his shoulders relax and he stops his struggle with the duct tape. "Good. Thank you. I know you wouldn't."

I pick up the shovel lying on the ground beside me. "I'm going to bury you first."

With those words, I scoop up a shovelful of dirt, and I throw it on top of him.

"Eve!" he screams. "Jesus Christ, what is wrong with you? Have you lost your mind?"

I scoop up more dirt and throw it into the hole.

"Eve!" His face is bright red. "Eve, sweetheart, I'm so sorry for everything! I love you! You have to know that! You can't do this to me!"

And another scoop of dirt goes into the hole.

"Eve!" he gasps. "Don't do this to me! Eve! *Eve!*"

Nate is thrashing now in the grave, trying to get free. But he isn't going to. I tied him up much too tightly. I'm about to scoop in more dirt when Jay grabs my arm. He tugs me away, out of the earshot of my husband.

"Eve," he says. "You're going to kill him."

I lift my chin. "I know."

Jay glances over at the grave, where my husband is screaming his lungs out, even though nobody can hear him but us. "He's right. It won't solve your problems to kill him."

"You'd be surprised."

His brows bunch together. "Are you sure you want to do this?"

"I've never been so sure of anything in my life."

Jay stares at me for a moment, and then he picks up his own shovel. He walks back with me to the grave. And when I scoop up some dirt and throw it in the hole, he does the same.

"Eve!" Nate screams. "For the love of God, Eve, don't do this! You can't do this!"

I can and I will. Two more scoops of dirt go into the hole.

"You'll go to jail. You know that, right? You're

going to spend the rest of your life rotting in jail, you crazy bitch!"

Two more scoops of dirt. One of them hits him in the face, and he starts to sob.

"Please, Eve." His left eye is obscured by mud as he stares up at me. "Please don't do this, Evie. I'm begging you. Please..."

Nate once said to me that he thinks death is like being on the precipice of an abyss, or some pretentious garbage like that. He was terrified of death, more than anything else in the world. I don't know if I believe in an afterlife, but if I do, I am certain that my husband will spend the rest of it burning in hell.

He alternates between begging us to stop and screaming threats until the mud completely covers his face. Shortly after that, he goes blessedly silent. We keep shoveling in dirt until the hole is completely filled. And as I put the finishing touches on my husband's grave in the woods, I recite to myself the poem he once wrote for me many years ago, back when I was fifteen years old and he was my English teacher fresh out of college who swore to me I was his soulmate:

Life nearly passed me by
Then she
Young and alive
With smooth hands
And pink cheeks
Showed me myself
Took away my breath
With cherry-red lips
Gave me life once again

EPILOGUE

SIX MONTHS LATER

ADDIE

When I get to the school parking lot, Hudson is leaning against his car, talking to some of his football buddies, even though the season is over. I watched every single game, and Hudson killed it. He deserves the title of star quarterback. He's going to get a scholarship to a great college—they're all going to be fighting over him.

When Hudson sees me, he raises a hand in greeting. "Addie!" he calls out, as if I could possibly miss him.

I jog the rest of the way over, a dopey smile plastered on my face. I'm smiling a lot more lately. Ever since I got my best friend back, the world seems a lot brighter. I'm still not Miss Popularity, but I don't care. Hudson is all I ever needed.

And this year has definitely been wild.

After Kenzie and I talked to Detective Sprague, she attempted to get an officer to bring in Nathaniel, but then he took off. I guess he knew he was in deep trouble and decided it was better to disappear than to be labeled as a sex offender.

They might have searched harder for him, except Mrs. Bennett suddenly materialized. She had some story about deciding to take a bus somewhere to get away for a few days. She paid in cash, she said, and she had no idea everyone was searching for her. Sprague had my story on record about what Nathaniel and I did to her, but she refused to confirm it—and she was not, in fact, dead and buried—so there was nothing the police could do.

Of course, Mrs. Bennett and I both know the truth. And we both know that if I had buried her with dirt instead of leaves, everything could have gone very differently.

In any case, she never returned to Caseham High. She resigned when the scandal came out with her husband, and then she left town. We ended up with a substitute teacher for the rest of the term. I wished it could have been Mr. Tuttle, but I heard through the grapevine he got another job at a high school two towns over. They're lucky to have him.

As for Mr. Bennett, it turned out that Kenzie and I weren't the only "soulmates" he had among his students. It makes me sick when I think about it sometimes. I feel so stupid.

One thing I'm grateful for is that I have Kenzie to talk about it with. She and I have for real become close friends this year. We have spent hours talking about Nathaniel. It makes me feel better that somebody as smart and beautiful and popular as Kenzie Montgomery could be taken in exactly like I was. And she says talking to me makes her feel better about the whole thing too.

Plus we're both getting professional talk therapy. It all helps.

"Took you long enough," Hudson teases me when I reach his car. "What were you doing in there?"

I was late because Lotus and I were putting the finishing touches on the poetry magazine, which we have been doing entirely ourselves since Nathaniel took off. But I don't want to tell him that, because I want it to be a surprise when he sees the magazine. "Sorry! I'm here now at least."

One of Hudson's football buddies laughs. "Your girl really got you whipped. How long does she have you waiting for her anyway?"

Hudson laughs too, and he doesn't correct his friend who called me his "girl." It makes me wonder. Especially since when we walk from his car to the school every morning, he sometimes reaches out and takes my hand in his. He's not dating Kenzie at least. I'm pretty sure he was seeing some girl at the beginning of the year, but not anymore.

"You taking off then?" one of the guys says to Hudson as he opens the door for me. It's unnecessary that he does that, but it's sweet.

"Uh-huh," Hudson says. "Addie and I are going to get some milkshakes before I have to get to work. See you later, Walsh?"

"Later, Jay," the other kid says to Hudson.

As Hudson climbs into the driver seat next to me, I say to him, "Okay, I've got to ask. How come all your football buddies call you Jay?"

"Well, you know, we all call each other by our last names," he says. "But *Jankowski*? That's a mouthful. So they just call me J for short. I kind of like it."

That's fine, but he'll always be Hudson to me.

"All right," he says, "we better go. My shift at the shoe store starts at five, so we've only got one hour for milkshakes."

Hudson really does work harder than anyone else. Aside from school, he works at Simon's Shoes several days a week, and he also babysits his one-year-old brother all the time. But even with all that going on, he always makes time for me.

We pull up into the lot near the diner that has the best milkshakes in the entire town. I wonder if we'll share a single milkshake, and if we do, what will that mean? I like Hudson. A lot. Is he my soulmate? I don't know. I kind of think that's a stupid question.

Just after he parks, Hudson's phone buzzes, and he pulls it out of his pocket. He reads a text message, and a smile touches his lips.

"What?" I say.

He shoves the phone back in his pocket. "Nothing. Just this old friend of mine."

"Girlfriend?"

His smile becomes sheepish as he rubs the scar he got on his forehead back when we were stupid kids worming under the fence surrounding his house. "You could say that. She…uh…she really liked shoes and used to come to the shoe store all the time, and, um, yeah."

Hudson's pale skin turns bright pink, which makes me think this customer at the shoe store was a whole lot more than just a customer, but for whatever reason, he doesn't want to admit it. Of course, that makes me wonder even more who she was. And if he had fallen for her the way I'm starting to fall for him.

"Anyway," he says, "she…uh…she was having a hard time for a while and was pretty messed up, but she's doing a lot better now. I've known her for a while, and she seems happy for the first time ever, so that's nice, you know? I want her to be happy. She deserves it."

Definitely a girlfriend—I can see it all over his face. I wonder if this is the same girlfriend he had at the beginning of the year, but I'm afraid to ask. Anyway, it's none of my business. He's not with her anymore.

We both get out of the car, and Hudson reaches for my hand. He laces his fingers into mine, and when he smiles at me, I smile back. As we walk to the diner together, I decide that I am going to get a vanilla milkshake with a lot of whipped cream and a cherry on top, because I deserve a treat.

Keep reading for a look at another
Freida McFadden thriller, *The Inmate*!

CHAPTER 1

PRESENT DAY

As the prison doors slam shut behind me, I question every decision I've ever made in my life.

This is not where I want to be right now. At *all*. Who wants to be in a maximum-security penitentiary? I'm going to wager nobody wants that. If you are within these walls, you may have made some poor life choices along the way.

I sure have.

"Name?"

A woman in a blue correctional officer's uniform is looking up at me from behind the glass partition just inside the entrance to the prison. Her eyes are dull and glassy, and she looks like she doesn't want to be here any more than I do.

"Brooke Sullivan." I clear my throat. "I'm supposed to meet with Dorothy Kuntz?"

The woman looks down at a clipboard of papers in front of her. She scans the list, not acknowledging that she heard me or that she knows anything about why I'm here. I glance behind me into the small waiting area, which is empty except for a wrinkled old man sitting in one of the plastic chairs, reading a newspaper like he's sitting on the bus. Like there isn't a barbed wire fence surrounding us, dotted with hulking guard towers.

After what feels like several minutes, a buzzing sound echoes through the room—loud enough that I jump and take a step back. A door to my right with red vertical bars slowly slides open, revealing a long, dimly lit hallway.

I stare down the hallway, my feet frozen to the floor. "Should…should I go in?"

The woman looks up at me with her dull eyes. "Yes, go. You pass through the security check down the hall."

She nods in the direction of the dark hallway, and a chill goes through me as I walk tentatively through the barred door, which slides closed again and locks with a resounding thud. I've never been here before. My job interview was over the phone, and the warden was so desperate to hire me, he didn't even feel compelled to meet me first—my résumé and letters of recommendation were enough. I signed a one-year contract and faxed it over last week.

And now I'm here. For the next year of my life.

This is a mistake. I never should have come here.

I look behind me at the red metal bars that have already slammed shut. It's not too late. Even though I signed a contract, I'm sure I could get out of it. I could still turn around and leave this place. Unlike the residents of this prison, I don't have to be here.

I didn't want this job. I wanted any other job but this one. But I applied to every single job within a sixty-minute commute of the town of Raker in upstate New York, and this prison was the only place that called me back for an interview. It was my last choice, and I felt lucky to get it.

So I keep walking.

There's a man at the security check-in all the way down the hall, guarding a second barred door. He's in his forties with a short, military-style haircut and wearing the same crisp blue uniform as the dead-eyed woman at the front desk. I looked down at the ID badge clipped to his breast pocket: Correctional Officer Steven Benton.

"Hi!" I say, in a voice that I realize is a little too chirpy, but I can't help myself. "My name is Brooke Sullivan, and it's my first day working here."

Benton's expression doesn't shift as his dark eyes rake over me. I squirm as I rethink all the fashion choices I made this morning. Working in a men's maximum-security prison, I figured it was better not to dress in a way that might be construed as suggestive. So I'm wearing a pair of boot-cut black dress pants, paired with a black button-up long-sleeved shirt. It's almost eighty degrees out, one of the last hot days of the summer, and I'm regretting all the black, but it seemed like the way to call the least attention to myself. My dark hair is pinned back in a simple pony-tail. The only makeup I have on is some concealer to hide the dark circles under my eyes and a scrap of lipstick that's almost the same color as my lips.

"Next time," he says, "no high heels."

"Oh!" I look down at my black pumps. Nobody gave me any guidance whatsoever on the dress code, much less the *shoe* code. "Well, they're not very high. And they're *chunky*—not sharp or anything. I really don't think…"

My protests die on my lips as Benton stares at me. No high heels. Got it.

Benton runs my purse through a metal detector, and then I walk through a much larger one myself. I make a nervous joke about how it feels like I'm at the airport, but I'm getting the sense that this guy doesn't like jokes too much. Next time, no high heels, no jokes.

"I'm supposed to meet Dorothy Kuntz," I tell him. "She's a nurse here."

Benton grunts. "You a nurse too?"

"Nurse practitioner," I correct him. "I'm going to be working at the clinic here."

He raises an eyebrow at me. "Good luck with that."

I'm not sure what that means exactly.

Benton presses a button, and again, that ear-shattering buzzing sound goes off, just before the second set of barred doors slides open. He directs me down a hallway to the medical ward of the prison. There's a strange chemical smell in the hallway, and the fluorescent lights overhead keep flickering. With every step I take, I'm terrified that some prisoner will appear out of nowhere and bludgeon me to death with one of my high-heeled shoes.

When I turn left at the end of the hallway, a woman is waiting for me. She is roughly in her sixties, with close-cropped gray hair and a sturdy build. There's something vaguely familiar about her, but I can't put my finger on what it is. Unlike the guards, she's dressed in a pair of navy-blue scrubs. Like everyone else I've met so far at this prison, she isn't smiling. I wonder if it's against the rules here. I should check my contract. *Employees may be terminated for smiling.*

"Brooke Sullivan?" she asks in a clipped voice that's deeper than I would have expected.

"That's right. You're Dorothy?"

Much like the guard at the front, she looks me up and down. And much like him, she looks utterly disappointed by what she sees. "No high heels," she tells me.

"I know. I—"

"If you know, why did you wear them?"

"I mean…" My face burns. "I know *now*."

She reluctantly accepts this answer and decides not to force me to spend my orientation barefoot. She waves a hand, and I obediently trot after her down the hallway. The whole outside of the medical ward has the same chemical smell as the rest of the prison and the same flickering fluorescent lights. There's a set of plastic chairs lined up against the wall, but they're empty. She wrenches open the door of one of the rooms.

"This will be your exam room," she tells me.

I peer inside. The room is about half the size of the ones at the urgent care clinic where I used to work in Queens. But other than that, it looks the same. An examining table in the center of the room, a stool for me to sit on, and a small desk.

"Will I have an office?" I ask.

Dorothy shakes her head. "No, but you've got a perfectly good desk in there. Don't you see it?"

So I'm supposed to document with the patients looking over my shoulder? "What about a computer?"

"Medical records are all on paper."

I am stunned to hear that. I've never worked in a place with paper medical records. I didn't even know it was allowed anymore. But I suppose the rules are a little different in prison.

She points to a room next to the examining room. "That's the records room. Your ID badge will open it up. We'll get you one of those before you leave."

She holds her ID badge up to the scanner on the wall, and there's a loud click. She throws open the door to reveal a small dusty room filled with file cabinets. Tons and tons of file cabinets. This is going to be agony.

"Is there a doctor here supervising?" I ask.

She hesitates. "Dr. Wittenburg covers about half a dozen prisons. You won't see him much, but he's available by phone."

That makes me uneasy. At the urgent care, I was never alone. But I suppose the issues there were more acute than what I'll see here. At least that's what I'm hoping.

Our next stop on the tour is the supply room. It's about the same as the room at the urgent care clinic, but of course smaller—also with ID badge access. There are bandages, suture materials, and various bins and tubes and chemicals.

"Only I can dispense medications," Dorothy tells me. "You write the order, and I'll dispense the medication to the patient. If there's something we don't have, we can put it on order."

I rub my sweaty hands against my black dress pants. "Right, okay."

Dorothy gives me a long look. "I know you're anxious working in a maximum-security prison, but you have to know that a lot of these men will be grateful for your care. As long as you're professional, you won't have any problems."

"Right."

"Do *not* share any personal information." Her lips set into a straight line. "Do *not* tell them where you live. Don't tell them *anything* about your life. Don't put up any photos. Do you have children?"

"I have a son."

Dorothy regards me in surprise. She expected me to say no. Most people are surprised when I tell them I have a child. Even though I'm twenty-eight, I look much younger. Although I feel a lot older.

I look like I'm in college, and I feel like I'm fifty. Story of my life.

"Well," Dorothy says, "don't talk about your kid. Keep it professional. Always. I don't know what you're used to in your old job, but these men are not your friends. These are criminals who have committed extremely serious offenses, and a lot of them are here for life."

"I know." Boy, do I know.

"And most of all…" Dorothy's icy-blue eyes bore into me. "You need to remember that while most of these men will see you for legitimate reasons, some of them are here to get drugs. We have a small quantity of narcotics in the pharmacy, but those are reserved for rare occasions. Do not let these men trick you into prescribing narcotics for them to abuse or sell."

"Of course."

"Also," she adds, "never accept any sort of payment in exchange for narcotics. If anyone makes an offer like that to you, you come straight to me."

I suck in a breath. "I would *never* do that."

Dorothy gives me a pointed look. "Yes, well, that's what the last one said. Now she's gonna end up in a place like this herself."

For a moment, I am speechless. When the warden interviewed me, I asked about the last person working here, and he said that she left for "personal reasons." He didn't happen to mention that she was arrested for selling narcotics to prisoners.

It's sobering to think that the last person who had this job before me is now incarcerated. I've heard that once you're in the prison system, it's hard to get out of it. Maybe the same is true for people who work here.

Dorothy notices the look on my face, and her expression softens just the tiniest bit. "Don't worry," she says. "It's not as scary as you think. Really, it's just like any other medical job. You see patients, you make them better, then you send them back to their lives."

"Yes…" I rub the back of my neck. "I was just wondering…am I going to be responsible for seeing *all* the prisoners in the penitentiary? Like, do I just cover a segment or…?"

Her lips curl. "No, you're it, girlie. You're seeing everyone. Any problem with that?"

"No, not at all," I say.

But that's a lie.

The real reason I was reluctant to take this job isn't that I'm scared a prisoner will murder me with my own shoe. It's because of one of the inmates in this prison. Someone I knew a long time ago, who I am not eager to see ever again.

But I can't tell that to Dorothy. I can't reveal to her that the man who was my very first boyfriend is an inmate at Raker Maximum Security Penitentiary, currently serving life without the possibility of parole.

And I'm the one who put him here.

READING GROUP GUIDE

1. How does the prologue set up the mystery of the novel? As you were reading, who did you think was burying the body? Were you right?

2. How does Eve portray her and her husband's relationship? Are they happy with each other?

3. What do people think happened between Addie and Mr. Tuttle, and how does this ruin Addie's reputation? What actually happened between the two of them?

4. Eve and Addie might be considered unreliable narrators. Why? Provide some examples of when they may have not been telling the full story.

5. This novel is, for the most part, set at a high school. How is the school environment portrayed? Compare your experiences of school with Addie's experiences.

6. Throughout the story, we see Eve's way of coping with her marriage through shoe shopping. Why does she use shoes as her form of escape? Then, discuss how shoes play a major role at the end of the novel.

7. What did Addie and Hudson do to Addie's father, and how did that affect their friendship? Did you see this twist coming? Why or why not?

8. What happens between Addie and Mr. Bennett? How did you feel about this? How would you have reacted if you were Eve?

9. What do Addie and Nate do to Eve, and why? Did you see this coming?

10. The story is told from the perspective of multiple characters. What does this add to the suspense? Was there a perspective you enjoyed reading the most?

11. The story ends with a shocking twist. Did you see this coming? If not, what did you think was going to happen?

ACKNOWLEDGMENTS

When I was writing *The Teacher*, I said to my teenager, "Do you think you could write me a poem that a teenager would think is really deep, but it's actually painfully bad?"

In response, she sat down beside me, snatched the laptop from my lap, and said, "Give me two minutes." I then watched her create *the greatest bad poem I had ever seen*. I was blown away. "It's so perfect," I told her before I obviously changed a bunch of things.

With the publication of *The Teacher* on the horizon, I reminded her of that poem she wrote for me. I told her how much I loved it and that I was going to give her credit for the poem in the acknowledgments. And she said, "Ugh, *please* don't."

Hmm. Maybe I shouldn't have told that story.

Well, she's not going to read this book anyway because she *would rather die*. Someday when she's all grown up, she'll have this to look back on and feel mildly embarrassed and/or nostalgic.

Thank you also to Jenna Jankowski (who Hudson absolutely was not named after, but it just proves some things are truly kismet) for your amazing feedback and help with shaping this book into the story it became, as well as to the entire Sourcebooks team for an incredible job. Thank you to my mother, who always is the first one to read my books and never, ever understands the twist at the ending. Thank you to my beta readers, Pam, Kate, and Emily. Thank you to Daniel and Val for help with proofreading! And a huge thank you to my agent, Christina Hogrebe, and the JRA team for your support!

Last but definitely not least, thank you, thank you, thank you to all my readers! I am genuinely just so grateful to all the readers out there who have supported me on my journey. I hope my books have brought you even a tiny bit as much joy as it has given me to see so many people reading them!

ABOUT THE AUTHOR

New York Times, Amazon Charts, *USA Today*, and *Publishers Weekly* bestselling author Freida McFadden is a practicing physician specializing in brain injury. Freida's work has been selected as one of Amazon Editor's Best Books of the Year, and she has been a Goodreads Choice Award nominee. Her novels have been translated into more than thirty languages. Freida lives with her family and black cat in a centuries-old three-story home overlooking the ocean. To learn more about Freida and sign up for her mailing list, please visit freidamcfadden.com.